Adventures *of an* Ice Princess

Adventures *of an* Ice Princess

Liz Maverick

NEW AMERICAN LIBRARY

New American Library
Published by New American Library, a division of
Penguin Group (USA) Inc., 375 Hudson Street,
New York, New York 10014, USA
Penguin Group (Canada), 10 Alcorn Avenue, Toronto,
Ontario M4V 3B2, Canada (a division of Pearson Penguin Canada Inc.)
Penguin Books Ltd., 80 Strand, London WC2R 0RL, England
Penguin Ireland, 25 St. Stephen's Green, Dublin 2,
Ireland (a division of Penguin Books Ltd.)
Penguin Group (Australia), 250 Camberwell Road, Camberwell, Victoria 3124,
Australia (a division of Pearson Australia Group Pty. Ltd.)
Penguin Books India Pvt. Ltd., 11 Community Centre, Panchsheel Park,
New Delhi - 110 017, India
Penguin Group (NZ), Cnr Airborne and Rosedale Roads, Albany,
Auckland 1310, New Zealand (a division of Pearson New Zealand Ltd.)
Penguin Books (South Africa) (Pty.) Ltd., 24 Sturdee Avenue,
Rosebank, Johannesburg 2196, South Africa

Penguin Books Ltd, Registered Offices:
80 Strand, London WC2R 0RL, England

First published by New American Library,
a division of Penguin Group (USA) Inc.

First Printing, October 2004
10 9 8 7 6 5 4 3 2 1

⬤ REGISTERED TRADEMARK–MARCA REGISTRADA

LIBRARY OF CONGRESS CATALOGING-IN-PUBLICATION DATA:

Maverick, Liz.
Adventures of an ice princess / Liz Maverick.
p. cm.
ISBN 0-451-21300-9 (trade pbk.)
1. Young women—Fiction.   2. Unemployed women workers—Fiction.
3. Americans—Antarctica—Fiction.   4. Rejection (Psychology)—Fiction.
5. Female friendship—Fiction.   6. Antarctica—Fiction.   I. Title.
PS3613.A885A6   2004
813'.6—dc22   2004013335

Set in Century Light
Designed by Ginger Legato

Printed in the United States of America

PUBLISHER'S NOTE
This is a work of fiction. Names, characters, places, and incidents either are the product of
the author's imagination or are used fictitiously, and any resemblance to actual persons, living or dead, business establishments, events, or locales is entirely coincidental.

To my fellow 2002–2003 and 2003–2004 summer season residents at McMurdo Station, Antarctica. The good, the bad, the ugly, the total nutcases, and all. I'm included somewhere in that description.

With extra hugs to:

Tony Buchanan
Michael Davis
Samantha McQuiston
and most especially, Brian Connell.

Acknowledgment

Special acknowledgment goes to my editor, Kara Cesare.
Thank you so much, for everything.

Chapter One

There are few things more humiliating in a woman's life than having an engagement party thrown in her honor when the man in question hasn't proposed.

As she stood blushing violently in the doorway of the office conference room, Clarissa Schneckberg tried to look on the bright side of the situation. Although it was much, much worse than the typical fast-resolving, base-model public humiliation (say, walking around all day with something stuck to your ass), it was considerably better than the sort of life-changing disaster which might involve an unwitting female in some combination of excessive nudity, a police chase, and a national television broadcast.

It didn't take long to assess what she faced. Kate had clearly told everyone that the engagement was a done deal. In her friend's defense, of course, Clarissa had clearly told Kate yesterday that she really, really expected to be engaged by morning. Of course, she'd been saying that every night for the last three months (okay, probably longer), so she didn't think it would be out of line to wish that a little more discretion had been used in the choice of party themes. Of course, Clarissa managed to delude herself every day about this particular subject, so why she should expect more of someone who wasn't even going to be involved in the marriage was a good question.

Equally clear was that Kate had not passed the word amongst the party subcommittees in time to prevent the wedding theme from taking irreversible root in what could have been just a standard going-away gathering.

An unsightly divot marred the center of a sheet cake rimmed with gigantic pink plastic roses where someone obviously had removed one of those hideous bride-and-groom cake toppers and then tried to disguise it (unsuccessfully) with adjacent frosting. Next to it sat wedding bell–themed paper plates and napkins, a chipped company logo mug filled with white candied almonds, and a meat cleaver standing in as a cake knife. A small pile of presents wrapped in silver and white paper perched on one of the vacant chairs. And just about every visible surface was littered with iridescent wedding ring and champagne glass confetti.

The biggest giveaway, however, was a lopsided banner stretching from one end of the room to the other. It started out just fine, with fat, bubble-style silver letters:

CONGRATULATIONS ON YOUR

But then things got a little . . . awkward.

Stapled to the R hung a piece of computer paper (undoubtedly covering the word "engagement"), upon which was hastily scrawled the following amendment:

. . . quitting.

Witness to the scene from her peripheral vision was a rumpled and abandoned Bridal Betty doll lying with legs inappropriately splayed up against the backrest of a chair in the corner.

Clarissa took all this in with a growing sense of horror as twelve pairs of eyes blinked nervously back at her. The hideous silence now stretching out toward the realm of the unbearable ended only when one girl finally blurted out, "Surprise!" A burst of chatter exploded through the room and everyone jumped up for a hug, the bustle of it all managing to camouflage Clarissa's gobsmacked emotional state.

She took a deep breath, put on her happy face, and started hugging. "Oh, you guys, you shouldn't have!" Really.

The incredibly slow girl from customer service frowned in confusion. "So, you're not . . ."

"Nope," Clarissa chirped. "Not yet." She punched the air playfully in that giving-it-the-old-college-try sort of way and added, "Almost, though!"

A thirty-something woman with too much jangling gold jewelry whom Clarissa knew obliquely from accounts flipped her Jaclyn Smith hair and said in a world-weary tone, "What an *ass*. Just as well, though, if you ask me."

"Oh, no. It's not like that. Kieran's wonderful. We've already agreed we're going to get married. We just haven't . . . or rather, he hasn't . . . um, well, he hasn't quite come around to a proposal, is the thing." She forced a laugh. "But getting married was originally his idea."

There was another difficult pause. "Let's eat cake!" the college intern shouted out, and started passing out forks.

"If you ask me, you need to be more aggressive." Human Resources Lonnie tucked her salt-and-pepper pageboy hairdo behind her ears. Clarissa had had a bit of an uncomfortable run-in with her just that morning when she'd panicked unexpectedly and tried to rescind her resignation. She'd already had quite enough of Lonnie's go-get-'em style for one day. In her enthusiasm to get her to sign the severance package and avoid another layoff statistic, the woman had practically shoved the pen up Clarissa's nose. That aside, frankly, Clarissa wasn't about to take advice from a woman whose wardrobe consisted solely of sensible skirts that hit just at the spot guaranteed to make one's legs look as fat as humanly possible.

"I agree. Today's men have too many choices," another woman said. "You've got to reel them in these days. There's always someone younger, prettier, and more fertile just around the corner. Waiting around passively doesn't get you anywhere."

Clarissa shifted uneasily, inwardly praying for a quick end to a rather depressing conversation that seemed to be hitting hot buttons she didn't even realize she had.

"I'll agree with you there," Jaclyn Smith said, as she went over to the table, grabbed the meat cleaver and hacked out a large piece of cake. "What's the quickest way to a man's heart?" She turned around suddenly and made a stabbing motion with the cleaver. "Through his chest with a sharp knife." And then she burst into hysterical laughter.

"Well, you know what they say," said one of the girls from the finance department with a sympathetic smile. "The minute you get married your sex life goes down the drain."

The college intern nodded as sagely as it was possible for an eighteen-year-old to nod. "You've got to keep it fresh and sexy."

"Fresh and sexy?" Clarissa asked.

"That's what Puff Daddy said to J.Lo."

"I guess he wasn't fresh enough in the end. Passed his use-by date," Lonnie joked.

Jaclyn snorted so loudly Clarissa jumped in her seat. "Fresh and sexy. What the hell does that mean? Are we back to wrapping ourselves in saran? This is how far we've come?"

Clarissa realized with mixed feelings that she wasn't necessarily going to miss some of the people she'd worked with.

"Oh, hell," Jaclyn Smith continued. "Married men don't care about fresh and sexy. They care about blow jobs. Blow jobs never get stale . . . what? What did I say? Okay, tell me one thing men prefer to a stark naked woman and a blow job." She looked from one side of the room to the other.

"Two stark naked women and a blow job?" the college youngster offered helpfully.

The pretty blond administrative assistant who made certain to reassure everyone periodically that she was still a virgin turned white and pushed her cake away.

Mary, a sushi pal from marketing, stumbled into the conference room balancing a wholesale-sized package of toilet paper. "I've got extra toilet paper for games if there's time after the skit!" Two male network administrators wearing toilet paper wedding dresses trailed behind her.

They looked like grotesque little troll brides with hairy legs and the sort of garish makeup you end up with if you accidentally get snared by one of those department store cosmeticians who've majored in Prostitute Chic. Clarissa sighed and tried not to look directly into the train wreck. She'd have nightmares for months.

Being somewhat shorter than the toilet paper tower, the unfortunate Mary was apparently unable to see from the hastily made adjustments that things had not transpired—so far—as Clarissa had planned.

The geeks noticed. One said, "Dude. The wedding's off? Does this mean we don't get cake?" He fingered his woolly black beard and adjusted his flopping toilet paper veil. The second geek elbowed his friend hard, then poked his enormous rectangular amber-lensed truck driver glasses back up the bridge of his nose, accidentally smearing his lipstick on his hand.

Kate Washington suddenly appeared behind them, and Clarissa breathed a sigh of relief. Finally, a little support. She, Kate, and the third member of their best-friend triumvirate, Delilah, had met at the beginning of the high-tech boom at one of those flashy networking events for the young and unreasonably

wealthy. They'd hit it off in the sort of way one does with people who understand how you got where you are, exactly what it
is you do and how much you make doing it, and Clarissa always
felt a little better when one of them was around to handle this
sort of unpleasantness—even if they were responsible for creating the unpleasantness in question.

"Oh, shit, I'm WAY too late, aren't I? What a HUGE mistake.
This is, without a doubt, the BIGGEST party disaster I've
EVER had." She panted, exaggerating the severity of any
shortness of breath that could possibly have resulted from a
couple of laps around the office. As usual, Kate had a way of
making . . . everything . . . seem larger or more extreme than in
actuality. She was a study in the contrasts of large and small.
On the top of her petite little stick-figure body balanced a plus-
sized brain with matching ego that dreamed up enormous sce-
narios and plans. Unfortunately (or was it fortunately?), her
tiny attention span had a way of distracting her from following
through with most of them.

"We must have somehow passed each other," Kate said as
she grabbed plates of cake off the table and shoved them at the
bridal trolls. "I was out there trying to ward you off. Thanks
anyway. Please leave."

"All men are jerks," Jaclyn said, watching them go with ill-
concealed distaste. "If you really think about it, somewhere in
the world, every nanosecond, a guy is being a jerk. This is an
epidemic right up there with, say, Ebola."

Kate nodded ruefully as she scraped the frosting off her
cake and piled it on the side of her plate. "You'd think that, it
being a disease specific to men, there would already be billions
of dollars allocated for the study and treatment, but there you
are. There's no money allocated at all."

"That's because women would be the main beneficiaries of a
cure."

"How long have you been going out with this guy?" the college intern asked.

"Eight years."

"Eight years is a long time," Jaclyn said. "So, he's already had his midlife crisis, then?"

Clarissa smiled confidently. "Oh, I don't think Kieran's the type. He's very stable."

Jaclyn Smith's high-pitched squeal of laughter arrested the entire room. She swirled the contents of her cup, and Clarissa was beginning to wonder if there was more than just Coke in there. "They are *all* the type. It's a generational thing, all right, but it's no generation you're familiar with. X, Y, these have nothing to do with the male species. All men belong to the same generation—Generation Why. As in 'why me,' a close relative of 'poor me.' As in 'Why am I here and how did my life get to this point?'" She paused and studied the contents of her cup very carefully, then wrinkled her forehead. "Or maybe I'm getting it all wrong. Maybe it's Generation Whine . . . oh, that's good."

Lonnie broke through the latest awkward silence. "She has a point. Anyway, when you think about it, Kieran would only end up being your first husband. Not your last. If he never proposes, you can just skip the whole unpleasant starter marriage step and save yourself a lot of trouble. Go straight to spouse number two, your keeper spouse."

"Yeah, don't waste your time on a guy who hasn't had his crisis yet. You want to get 'em postcrisis. You want to be the solution, not the problem," Mary said.

"I'm not Kieran's problem. I'm his . . ." Clarissa said in a very small voice.

"His *what?*" Jaclyn drained half the contents of her cup, dribbling a little down the corners of her mouth. "I think we all know what's going to happen in this scenario. He's been with you for eight years with no marriage proposal ever materializing in spite of his confessions of love and yadda yadda and then he'll break up with you and marry the next girl he dates within two months. I can tell ya from experience. They'll already have three kids and a golden retriever before you even meet a new guy worth your time. Clarissa, are you listening to me?"

Clarissa smiled a polite frozen smile and saw Kate mobilizing a couple of girls from the back of the room by using hand signals.

Jaclyn kept going. "This is life, people, this is reali—"

"Okay, upsy-daisy!" The girls literally scooped Jaclyn up under the arms and proceeded to drag her to the door. "Let's go back and test out that brand-new ten-key, shall we?"

"Sweet Jesus," the virgin muttered, crossing herself as she watched Jaclyn being bodily removed.

The cake felt like craft paste in Clarissa's mouth. If it had been possible to inch lower in her chair, she would have. She watched Jaclyn, dissipated and cynical at thirty, slosh her drink all over the beige hall carpet as a couple of office mates led her out of the room.

Kate put her arm around Clarissa's shoulder. "She's just a bitter, bitter, BITTER woman, Clary. Don't think twice about it." She looked around and made a large sweeping gesture with her plastic cup to the remaining party participants. "Well, ladies, thank you so much for coming to Clarissa's little send-off and making it so special."

With something akin to mass relief, the remaining partygoers cut themselves extra pieces of cake, bid Clarissa a hasty congratulations regarding whatever form her new life might take, and got themselves out of there.

Having finished all her cake, Kate forked a large dollop of frosting into her mouth and looked at Clarissa. "Are you okay? I'm SO sorry about that. SO, SO sorry. HUGE mistake. My bad."

Clarissa smiled weakly. "Don't worry about it. It's the thought that counts."

"So, what happened last night? I thought yesterday was P-Day, Proposal Ground Zero."

"Well, I just assumed he wouldn't wait until the absolute last day. But perhaps he's building anticipation or something . . . Kate, it was horrifying. No woman on earth wants to appear desperate, and let's just say I came perilously close to the classification. In fact . . . I may have crossed the line."

"How so? You didn't propose to *him*, so how bad could it be?"

"I wore that robin's-egg blue halter dress, a white satin ribbon in my hair, and black sandals."

"So? Oh! Ohhhh." Kate reared back. "You *didn't.*"

"I *did.*" Clarissa nodded shamefully.

"You dressed like a gift box from Tiffany?" Kate stared with huge eyes and bit her lip to prevent herself from laughing.

"It was Delilah's idea."

"That's brilliant. Sublimina Fashionista—"

"—Patheticum."

"Nah. That's just out-of-the-, er, 'box' thinking, my friend."

"Hah," Clarissa said glumly. "A polite euphemism. I mean, dear god, if one is going to humiliate oneself with that kind of hideous display, at the very least it ought to have the desired effect." Clarissa blinked her eyes to ward off the weepies. "Unfortunately, it did not. At least not last night."

"I think you're still okay."

Clarissa bit her lip. "It shouldn't have to be this way." Okay, now she was definitely going to cry. She didn't want to be one of those girls who had to nag their boyfriends to marry them. Somehow it tainted the whole notion of commitment itself. She wanted to be one of those girls who would run in to the office one morning all googly-eyes and surprises, muffled screams of delight coming from a cubicle crowded with work girlfriends flashing competitively large gemstones under the harsh fluorescent lights.

"I had no idea it was coming," they'd always say, all aglow. Clarissa wanted that. And while they'd discussed getting married a while back, she'd been under the assumption that one day, before the last possible moment, Kieran would give her that.

And now it *was* the last possible moment, and she was beginning to wonder if he was going to give her anything at all.

"I'm really trying to stay positive, but why doesn't he just ask me already? I mean, I've been carrying a disposable camera in my purse for three months now. Just in case."

"Have you come right out and asked him about it?"

"No, that would sort of poison the moment. It's just that . . . well, you already know. Kieran and I have discussed this. Ages ago. He brought it up! He said, 'When we get married . . . etc., etc. . . .' And we planned the whole timeline out. We would save a certain amount of money. Which we did. I would quit my job. Which I did. And then we'd get married and start a family and then it's just happy ever after. But he hasn't proposed, and I'm not haaaaapy." The waterworks started in earnest. She barely managed to get out the words, "What did I do wrong?"

"Nothing! You've done nothing wrong. And nothing's 'gone wrong' yet! The deadline's tomorrow. You have to think positive."

Clarissa shrugged hopelessly and blew her nose into a party napkin.

"He's just building the anticipation. It's going to be really special." But Kate looked worried, like she was working really hard to believe her own words.

"I'd believe it more if tonight wasn't the S-VEG charity auction. It's just not a proposal sort of event."

"Nah. Think about it. You're putting on a fancy dress. He's wearing a tux. It's perfect. He'll just whisk you away at some point and propose on a . . . on a . . . moonlit balcony at the hotel or something . . . it'll be a night to remember."

She had a point there. Kieran was very frugal and it sort of made sense to take advantage of a romantic situation they'd already paid for. Clarissa considered that for a moment, and really did feel better. It was a plausible explanation. The most plausible explanation she'd thought of in weeks. "Thanks, Kate. I feel better." She made a silent promise not to cry again or else she'd be puffy in the photos later that night.

Kate nudged her shoulder playfully. "Of course, you could increase your chances. You could tattoo 'De Beers' on your eyelids. That might work. Or get that Brazilian woman at Silicon Strip Salon to trim your pubic hair into the shape of a heart, just like the call girls get."

Clarissa laughed.

"That's better. Now, why don't you get yourself together, and I'll meet you back at your cube so we can get your stuff to the car." Kate got up, tossed her plate into the trash, and headed out the door. "I'll take care of this mess later."

Clarissa took a deep breath, surveyed the ruins of her party, then propped the meat cleaver against the cake and squinted at her reflection.

What if he doesn't ask me?

He wouldn't do that, Clarissa. He wouldn't do that after all the time you've invested in the relationship.

She wiped at the makeup smears under her eyes, tightened her ponytail so the blond streaks lined up straight, then hitched her black-rimmed "sexy secretary" glasses back up the bridge of her nose and confirmed that nothing, indeed, was stuck to her ass. Then she psyched herself up and headed to her cube for the last time.

More traffic than usual crowded the pathway leading to her workspace, and at first Clarissa thought she'd turned down the wrong lane. But she'd carefully decorated her cube in late neo-classical Martha Stewart meets postmodern Kate Spade, and she could see the decoupage lampshade she'd made poking up from the corner.

Clarissa tried to elbow her way through the crowd and had her toe run over by a couple of guys from the art department wheeling out her office chair (with her lumbar support still strapped on it) upon which sat her seventeen-inch Trinitron computer monitor.

They stopped short, almost toppling the monitor off the chair, and stared at her with guilty smiles. "We thought you'd gone already."

"Not yet," she chirped pleasantly, although she was starting to feel not so pleasant.

"Oh. Well. You don't need this anymore anyway." And off they went down the hall.

"Get back! Get. Back!" Kate heaved herself through the growing crowd. "You people are animals!"

Clarissa was jostled aside and backed up a few steps. "I think a mob is beginning to develop. Let's get this stuff out to the car."

With tensions this high and layoffs in the air, it didn't take much to trigger mass hysteria. Fair enough. The company wasn't spending any more money on supplies and you had to do what you had to do. Within the last two months, every time the stock market had dipped, it triggered a labeling frenzy. People were putting their names on everything. Borrowing a hole punch wasn't just borrowing a hole punch anymore. It was an issue of trust. Friendships built on anything less than a solid foundation were collapsing, watercooler alliances shifting.

Clarissa flattened herself against one side of the cubicle to avoid the flying elbows of a couple of graphic designers ripping down her wallpaper. "Um, hey, guys . . . guys? Hey, guys . . . guys?"

But it wasn't until Suki Lurman pulled open a desk drawer in full view and stole the staple gun that Clarissa had legitimately stolen from a supply closet only three months ago that she lost it. The Schneckberg label was clearly visible on that thing.

"Um, please don't take that just yet," she said politely.

Suki ignored her.

"You need to be more aggressive, Clarissa," Jaclyn hissed, as she tucked Clarissa's fern under one arm, loose soil spilling onto the floor. "You tell Suki where she can stick that stapler." She put her hand on Clarissa's back and shoved her forward. Clarissa reached out to maintain her balance and latched on to the staple gun in Suki's outstretched hand.

Suki, holding the gun by the muzzle, apparently interpreted this as an act of war and instigated a tug-of-war which ended with Suki losing her grip and flying backward out the cubicle entrance to the hallway floor with Clarissa catapulting on top of her.

The bridal trolls and other assorted geeks became irrationally excited over the sight of two women grappling on the floor and began to cheer.

"You pastel-wearing freak!" Suki screamed, as her bright green-and-white Pucci-inspired wrap dress gaped dangerously.

A pale yellow twinset and a charcoal gray pencil skirt in stretch jersey did not a "pastel-wearing freak" make, as far as Clarissa was concerned, but she decided to be the better person. Unfortunately, while she did her best to scramble off Suki, the girl must have misinterpreted her actions. She just kept struggling and the two got tangled up even more.

The geeks cheered even louder as one of Clarissa's

adorable little Sabrina heels went flying. Between the noise and the confusion and Suki pulling on the staple gun like it was the Holy Grail, one refrain began to pound into Clarissa's head:

What if he doesn't ask me?

And the realization dawned on her that without her job and without a commitment from Kieran, she'd be cut loose from everything that had kept her anchored for so long. At least it explained why she'd stormed into Lonnie's office that morning and tried to get the woman to conspire in the retraction of Clarissa's resignation.

Some people might see this notion of being anchored as being weighed down or trapped. Clarissa saw it as having a purpose, a source of comfort, and so the harder Suki pulled, the harder Clarissa held on.

Kate pushed her way through the crowd to the girls. "What on earth are you doing?"

Suki stopped struggling and they froze in place with Clarissa straddling her, the staple gun pointing at her forehead.

"Layoff roadkill," someone muttered, peering at Suki like she was a dead squirrel. "Just when you thought Silicon Valley had already hit rock bottom. Now we're offing our own."

Clarissa was only faintly aware of Kate taking her by the shoulders. "Clary, are you okay? It's me. Kate. Give me the gun. Nothing's going to happen to you. Just put down the gun and move away from the girl."

Clarissa climbed off Suki, who got off the floor and fixed her dress, glaring at Clarissa all the while. The crowd dispersed, at least temporarily.

Clarissa swallowed hard.

"Clary! The gun. Now!"

Clarissa felt sick. How was she supposed to explain that suddenly it seemed like letting go of the staple gun represented something much larger than just . . . letting go of the staple gun? "What if he doesn't ask me?"

"What are you talking about? What is the matter with you? Give me the gun."

"If Kieran doesn't ask me, what do I have? This job is all I have. I'll be adrift, afloat. You know I'm a lousy swimmer."

"Nonsense," Kate said, looking her square in the eyes. "Let go. Now," she barked. "Besides, it's too late. You've signed the papers."

Clarissa surrendered the gun.

"Absolute nonsense. Honestly. What's the matter with you? Wrestling Suki Lurman over a staple gun? Is it the party? You're not still upset about the party, are you?"

"No." Clarissa picked up a stack of boxes she'd packed earlier. "Could you grab that for me?"

Using her left hand as a balancing mechanism, Kate picked up the lamp in her right hand and staggered to the exit toward the car in high-heeled boots and a miniskirt with enormous black-and-white horizontal stripes that would have looked much worse on a lesser woman. "The boss wants to see me in five minutes. No long good-byes. We'll be talking very soon about you know what, anyway."

At the car, Clarissa balanced the boxes on the bumper while she opened the trunk. "It was my fault, really. I should have called you last night and told you it didn't happen." She put her hands to her face and moaned. "I think I'm becoming delusional."

"Clarissa, what's this all about? You've been talking about this day for months on end, and now that it's finally here, anyone with a modicum of intelligence could see that you're suddenly, inexplicably uncomfortable with your decision to quit your job."

"I'm not uncomfortable with my decision. So what if I went to Lonnie this morning and tried to rescind my resignation."

"Are you kidding? What did she say?"

"She said that since there was a hiring freeze, she couldn't hire me any time soon. Not unless the position was mission critical."

"Oh. That's a problem."

"Yeah, I know. My job isn't mission critical. In fact, it became completely pointless long ago."

"It's not that bad."

"It is. I'm the human equivalent of vapor," Clarissa said sadly. She was a "relationship manager," responsible for liaising with partners who were contributing content to her company's entertainment software projects. This usually entailed making phone calls to the powerless assistants for powerful people at Hollywood and New York City entertainment companies.

Unfortunately, it was a lot less glamorous than it sounded to most people, and it didn't really surprise Clarissa, nor seem particularly unfair, really, that someone whose sole job it was to facilitate the flow of information would be seen as dispensable during an economic downturn.

"I just talk to people. I de-escalate problems and propose compromises. I don't make things, and I don't sell things. I don't increase market share or profit, and I don't improve product performance. I don't enhance operating efficiency, and I don't expand or extend consumer relations. I'm . . . I'm . . ."

"Useless in today's economy?" Kate offered helpfully.

Clarissa blanched, and Kate hastened to clarify her statement. "What I meant is that I see the problem. But the point is, you were ready to move on. Truth be told, you did the right thing, and you know what? I'm thinking about taking that severance package, myself."

"I guess I should be glad she didn't let me stay," Clarissa admitted. "Sometimes I think it takes a force of nature to get me to do anything off the beaten track."

Kate nodded. "You're following your instincts. And frankly, I think this is all just cold feet."

"Cold feet. Don't talk to me about cold feet," she said grimly. "I'm not the one with cold feet."

"Tonight. Tonight's the night. Everything's going to be fine."

Clarissa opened the trunk, dumped the stuff in, and slammed it closed. She looked at Kate, thought about the words, and a slow grin came over her face. "Yeah. Tonight's the night."

Chapter Two

"Kier, I'm home!"

Silence.

"Kier? Sweetie?" She could hear the faint hum of the television set coming from the second bedroom they'd converted into an entertainment room. "Are you ready to go?"

No answer. Clarissa rolled her eyes for her own edification and glanced at her watch.

A belated "Yes" piped up suddenly, the voice a bit strained.

She put her hand on the doorknob, but then it occurred to her that Kieran might be trying to get things organized in there. She hadn't said exactly when she'd be home. And maybe he had the ring out. Maybe he was arranging flowers or candles. That would have a very nice effect on the apartment, actually.

The two-bedroom was a comfortable enough sort of place, not overly sterile, with lots of dark woods, plump pillows, and colors like "silver sage" and "wounded eggplant." The darkish colors were more Kieran's look than Clarissa's, but she liked it very much, even if there was nothing in it that was . . . well, *specific*.

It was the sort of apartment that at first glance seemed full of unique and attractive objects the occupants had picked up while traveling. At second glance, you realized that just about everyone in a certain income bracket had the same unique and attractive objects, all made in the same overseas factory, all available at the local mall.

Clarissa went into the bedroom, instead, and kicked off her shoes. "Okay, I'm going in to shower now!"

He didn't answer. Maybe he just didn't hear.

Clarissa took a fast shower, slipped on the gown and shoes she'd set out that morning, fixed her hair in a quick updo, and carefully reapplied her makeup. Holding her purse and the ballgown skirt of her extremely well-executed pink Vera Wang knockoff (it was only coincidence that it looked a bit like a pink bridal gown), she headed back to the entertainment room and knocked.

"Kier, did you have a nice day?" She knocked again and the door swung open.

It was obvious Kieran had not had a nice day. In fact, it wasn't clear that he'd ever gone out and had a day of any sort.

What's more, there were no candles, no flowers, and as far as she could tell, no ring. Just Kieran, slumped on the eggplant-colored velvet plush couch in a rumpled tuxedo. On one side of his head, the baby-fine blond hair stood straight up, waving gently in an invisible breeze. His arm hovered in midair, fully extended, knuckles gripping white around the giant master remote he'd programmed to control an entire wall of electronics.

On the coffee table, a near-empty bottle of Niebaum-Coppola and a full wineglass perched off the edge of a *Consumer Reports* car-buying guide. A faint pinot noir mustache dusted his upper lip and his blue puppy-dog eyes looked almost as blurry as the wine stain seeping into the cover photo of a silver minivan.

All things considered, he looked, well . . . sort of unappealing, for a loved one.

Kieran gave no sign he'd heard her, apparently fixated on a decision-making process involving a Dukes of Hazzard rerun versus the PGA Tour on thirty-six-inch picture-in-picture.

"Kieran? I asked how—"

"My day was fine," he said with a touch of false bravado, the kind people use when things are distinctly not fine but they are going to make you pull whatever really isn't fine out of them.

Clarissa chewed her lower lip. "Something's wrong."

"Nothing's wrong." His voice went froggy for a moment, as if he hadn't used it in a while even though he'd just spoken. He had to clear out his throat between the two words.

"Something's wrong," Clarissa insisted.

"Nothing's wrong," he repeated, his tone vaguely irritated.

"What's wrong? Just tell me."

"I'm fine. I'm just . . . tired." He turned the television off and tossed the remote on the sofa.

Clarissa sighed. It was a half-day Friday at Conspro, if he'd even gone to work at all. "Oh. Okay." She nervously checked her watch. "Do you want to stay home?" she asked, likewise unable to conceal the irritation in her voice.

"Don't worry," he said. "I'll rise to the occasion." And by the time they'd made it to the auction, he had; Kieran was officially "on." After all, he enjoyed these sorts of affairs, and S-VEG put on a good party even if it wasn't really "his crowd."

Of course "her crowd" was becoming a whole lot smaller these days. S-VEG was a Silicon Valley philanthropic society for young and wealthy dot-commers, and tonight was the Fifth Annual Silicon Valley Extreme Generosity Charity Auction. Clarissa had been to the charity auction every year since the club's inauguration, and when she and Kieran stepped through the door, it was clear that things just weren't what they used to be.

There was a sheen of decay, a ominous air about the proceedings, although the events committee had done well with the new, modified budget. It was still quite the fancy affair, and the unpracticed eye probably wouldn't even notice the difference. It was just that certain people who'd attended for years were missing, the decorating committee had actually reused last year's décor (gasp!), the band had been downgraded to nine pieces from twelve, and some of the women were wearing formal gowns Clarissa recognized from *three years ago*.

Most telling, the infamous S-VEG dessert table was a mere shadow of its former self. It featured a very large bowl of strawberry trifle that was clearly designed to take up so much space it would camouflage the deficiencies of the other desserts.

Gone was the lavender-infused crème brûlée, the burnt-sugar bird's nests with egg-shaped fondant, the marzipan Star Wars action figures.

This year it was the obligatory chocolate mousse, those mundane little trays of éclairs, cream puffs, and custard tarts, and a very old-school fruit and cheese platter.

Yes, if the dessert table barometer was accurate, Silicon Valley as they'd known it for a few brief high-flying, big-spending, dreamy years, had gone Code Blue.

Determined to have a good time, Clarissa blocked the unpleasant warning signs from her mind and concentrated on scanning the crowd for her S-VEG gal pals. Since she and Kieran had been spending most of their social time with other couples from his workgroup, she hadn't seen them in ages. And while discussing the product extension possibilities of salad dressing had its interesting moments, really the only person she had anything in common with from Conspro was Kieran's platonic friend, Luna Fong, who'd provided Clarissa with a recommendation for an absolutely brilliant hairstylist.

An awkward lull fell over the crowd. Everyone simultaneously took a drink, and the clank of ice and faint slurping sound
of liquid trying to move through a cocktail straw conveniently
filled the void.

Clarissa craned her neck to see if she could find anyone she
recognized. She couldn't, and was forced to lead Kieran to a
table with only two couples and a slew of empty seats just as the
events chairperson tapped on the microphone and triggered a
high-pitched squeal. "At this time, if we could all find our
seats . . . yes, thank you . . . that's right, everyone, please go
ahead and return to your tables . . ."

The chairperson paused and waited for mass movement,
which was not forthcoming. "Dim sum appetizers will be
served at each table throughout the evening so it's not necessary to get up. You can, er, just *go back to your seats* . . . thank
you . . ." She cleared her throat. "At this time, I would like to
introduce our auctioneer, our celebrity guest. Ladies and gentlemen, please give a warm welcome to the Fifth Annual S-VEG
Charity Auctioneer . . ."

". . . Mr. William Shatner!"

Everyone froze. Then, as if collective panic struck, the audience burst into over-the-top, hysterical applause. William
Shatner bounded to the stage, and . . . and . . .

It wasn't William Shatner. It wasn't even William Shatner,
for god's sake. It was clearly and undeniably a man impersonat-
ing William Shatner. Clarissa shifted uncomfortably in her seat.

Kieran leaned over. "Last year the auctioneer was Sharon
Stone."

"I know," Clarissa said, unwilling to let the evening de-
press her.

"No, it was *really* Sharon Stone."

"I *know.*"

"This is an imposter."

"I *kn*—"

"Nothing's what it used to be."

Clarissa's stomach did a peculiar little flip. "What?"

Kieran just cracked a little smile. A tentative sort of thing. An almost desperate sort of thing. "Nothing."

"What's the matter with you?"

"Nothing. I'm fine. Everything's fine. I'm just . . . just . . . wow, you know, I'm really hungry." He stood up from the table and looked around him restlessly. "So, um . . . if the pot stickers come by, go ahead and . . . just put a couple on my plate, or something. I'm going to the restroom."

Nonplussed, Clarissa watched him weave his way to the back of the room through the crowd. *It's just a phase . . . oh, god. What if he doesn't ask me?*

Don't be ridiculous! Of course he's going to ask you. Not asking is not an option. She turned her attention to the fake William Shatner now previewing the items up for auction.

Last year, the items included a tour of the Galapagos Islands, a Lexus SUV, and a week at an overseas cooking school. Now it was a hypnosis session, golf shoes, and two rusting cans of curried tongue presumably from the same shipment used by Shackleton during his famous expedition to the South Pole.

Clarissa raised an eyebrow at that one and turned to the woman closest to her. "Only someone completely out of their head would drop more than three dollars and sixty cents for canned anything at a charity auction."

The auctioneer was finished with the preview by the time Kieran reclaimed his seat. Clarissa leaned over. "There's an interesting little weekend being auctioned off. Sort of a . . . honeymoon kind of arrangement." She said the word "honeymoon" as quickly as possible to kind of blend it in with the rest of the sentence. "Are you up for a vacation? I think you deserve one. It's been forever. What do you think?"

"I think we should see other people."

Clarissa blinked. "I'm sorry?"

"Me too."

William Shatner asked for a drumroll from the band. "Let's begin the bidding. Two cans of curried tongue in pristine condition, unopened, uneaten, label intact, held in the hands of and then rejected prior to voyage by Shackleton, the world-famous explorer, himself. A matched set, folks. Possible bookends? Do I have one hundred, that's one hundred dollars . . ."

Clarissa went catatonic for a second and then snapped out of it. "Wait, *what? What* did you say?"

"I said I thought we should see other people."

"One hundred dollars, that's the gray-haired gentleman in the back . . . can we go to three? That's straight to three hundred dollars. Authentic curried tongue . . ."

"Oh, you're so funny, Kier!" Her voice sounded oddly robotic. "Did you get enough to eat? I could get us some spring rolls if you don't like the pot stickers."

"I don't want any Chinese." He put his hands on his stomach.

"Kier, what's wrong? Do you need a doctor?"

"You know when there's something you need to say and it never seems to be the right time? And then suddenly it's the right time and you just have to say it or you know you're going to explode?"

"No." But then again, Kieran did seem to have difficulty expressing himself.

"I want . . . I want . . ."

You to be my wife?

"It's just that . . . okay, here's the thing." He cleared his throat again. "Will you be . . ."

My wife?

"No." He sighed and scuffed his toe against the ground under the table. "I'm just going to say it. I think you are the most . . . er, wonderful woman in the world."

Clarissa's heart was beating so fast. This was the happiest moment of her life. "I love you, too, Kieran."

He frowned. "Of course, I love you, it's just that . . ."

"It's just that?" That was not a phrase she could work with. She stared at him, a sick feeling beginning to come over her.

"I'm breaking up with you, Clarissa."

"What just happened in the bathroom?"

"I beg your pardon?"

"You went to the bathroom, you came back from the bathroom, and you said you wanted to break up. What just happened in the bathroom? Did you meet someone? Did you find Jesus?"

"Don't be sarcastic, Clarissa. Nothing *happened*," he said impatiently. "I peed, okay? Look, I don't think this is going to work out."

"You don't think this is going to work *out*?" Clarissa took a deep breath and wiped at the sweat beading on her upper lip.

"Don't try and come up with one of those convoluted debates. I know you're trying to form an argument that's going to get me all mixed up, and I don't want to be harsh with you, but frankly, you'd be wasting your time."

Clearly he was already mixed up. "I don't know what you're talking about."

"You see? We can't even communicate."

Clarissa started compulsively eating Kieran's pot stickers. With her mouth full, she tried to right things as best she could. "I'm really glad you've brought this up. I think you're right about our lack of communication. Now that we've recognized that we have a problem, I think we can look at this as a turning point in our relationship, an opportunity of a lifetime, if you will."

"It *is* an opportunity of a lifetime—I don't want to spend any more of my life with you."

"And we do have four hundred dollars! Thank you very much, the lady in the lovely gold satin in the back . . ."

She gritted her teeth and forced a smile, vaguely aware that when she'd tested the expression in the mirror once, it made her look toothily insane. "Usually, you're so repressed. This new expression of feelings . . . I see this as a real positive. A chance to change things up."

At this point Clarissa realized she was running on at the mouth, a hairsbreadth away from becoming totally hysterical. Yet on she ran: "Like this whole business of me quitting my job, but on a much bigger scale. This could be wonderful, Kier. I don't know what took you so long to bring it up. We could reinvent ourselves. We could adopt a better way of life—"

"There's nothing wrong with my life," he said. "It's our life I have a problem with."

Good god. "I see." Clarissa swallowed the last of the pot sticker, clasped her hands very tightly in her lap, and forced herself not to scream.

"And I'm really sorry, Clarissa, but to be honest . . . I don't consider you quitting your job to become a housewife a positive or constructive way of reinventing yourself. Frankly, it's embarrassing."

"Embarrassing. Embarrassing? Who's the housewife? Not me. Because, apparently, *I'm not getting married!*"

At this point, the two other couples at the table got up and left.

Meanwhile, William Shatner was having trouble moving beyond four hundred dollars. He hefted the cans above his head to show them off to the crowd. "Anyone? Anyone?"

"I thought you liked the idea of me not working."

"Not really."

"I thought we decided all this together."

He shifted uncomfortably. "I don't really remember exactly what was said."

"Why haven't you said anything before this? Why didn't you say something when we could still work on a solution?"

"I didn't want to hurt your feelings."

"I see. As opposed to, say, suggesting we break up."

"It's not a suggestion."

"I think you completely missed the point just then."

"I think you're missing the point right now," he said gently.

Clarissa narrowed her eyes at him. Kieran rarely did anything upsetting. They so rarely argued. His sonar never pinged, his radar never blipped. That was the whole point of him. The whole point of calm, stable, predictable Kieran. And now this. Blindsided by evil rogue personality traits that had lain dormant for nigh, oh, a decade.

Kieran suddenly speared a pot sticker with his chopsticks and popped it in his mouth, more, it seemed, to give him something to do than anything else.

But with that one act, it all suddenly became clear. Excruciatingly clear.

"Oh."

He looked puzzled. "What?"

"Oh!" Clarissa pushed her chair back, staring down at the pot sticker scraps on his plate. "You *do* want Chinese. You *do* want Chinese!"

"What's the matter with you? Have you gone insane?" he hissed.

"It's Luna Fong, isn't it?" Luna Fong, queen of perfect hair, Kieran's so-called platonic friend.

Kieran sighed heavily. "Come on, Clarissa. You had to know something was wrong. I'd lost all that weight."

"You were on *Weight Watchers*. You were *trying* to lose

weight . . . oh good god. You were losing weight for *her.* The svelte new you was all for Luna Fong."

"Don't be ridiculous. Luna is just an, er, *platonic* friend."

Clarissa suddenly became filled with the urge to do something really out of character. Like impale her boyfriend with chopsticks. But since that was out of the question, she decided to spend.

"What a joke." She grabbed an auction paddle from the center of the table.

"I'm really sorry, but this is not a joke."

"Yes, it is." Clarissa heard her voice crack. "It's as funny as this auction. See, watch me bid on this lot."

"Stop it, Clarissa."

William Shatner pointed at Clarissa's outstretched paddle. "Five hundred dollars. We have five hundred dollars. I call that *stellar!*"

"See how funny this is? I'm buying rancid polar expedition food supplies."

"It's not funny. This is serious. I'm leaving you. You take the car, and I'll get a cab." And with that, he handed her the valet slip, pulled two dollars from his wallet for a tip, and put it on the table in front of her. "I'm sorry, Clarissa, but it's for the best."

And then he was gone.

"Sold! Sold to the lovely blonde sitting completely alone, by herself, in the back."

Clarissa put her paddle back down on the table. It was serious. *He* was serious. Odd thoughts passed through her mind. This couldn't be real. What a relief. What a nightmare. Wasn't *West Wing* on tonight? She wanted her mommy. She wanted a drink.

The rest of the evening passed in a haze. There was no need for explanation since she still hadn't come across anyone she recognized. In fact, just about everyone left early after shoving leftovers into plastic Ziploc bags and tucking them into fraying Louis Vuitton novelty clutches. Clarissa only had room in hers for the curried tongue, and even then she couldn't close her purse.

As the mad dash for cabs began, she stepped out into the cold city air, punched autodial on her cell phone, and uttered the four most depressing words in a twenty-five-year-old's vocabulary: "Mom, I'm moving home."

And then Clarissa burst into tears.

Chapter Three

"*C*larissa, open the door."

Clarissa lay curled in the fetal position on her childhood canopy bed in a room that looked as though Laura Ashley had come in and been violently ill.

Her plain gray sweats clashed with the celebration of English sprigs and blossoms all around her, but the vast number of empty pleated chocolate truffle cups and towering stacks of romance novels seemed to fit right in.

She sighed, reached over from the bed, and unlocked the door.

Mom came in with Kate right on her heels. "Clarissa, I want you to go outside today. Kate's here, and I'd like you to please get out of bed."

"Oh, thanks, but I'm not planning to leave the house today."

Mom and Kate looked at each other. "Clarissa, please sit up and greet your friend properly." Mom sounded very stern. In fact, she looked very stern. She had on a black pantsuit with a white blouse that couldn't have looked any crisper, plus a couple of gold pins on the lapel. She looked insanely competent, as usual, which always had the immediate effect of making Clarissa feel less so. "I'd like you to go *outside* today."

Clarissa sighed. Woe to the daughters of insanely competent mothers. "Maybe tomorrow," she offered tentatively.

Mom folded her arms across her chest and tapped one Ferragamo on the floor. "You need some air. You need some sun."

"It's not like I'm trying to photosynthesize."

"Well, you're going to have to eat, and your father and I are booked for dinner for the rest of the week. Since I've instructed Kate and Delilah not to bring you any more takeout, you're going to have to start fending for yourself. It's time you stopped wallowing over that . . . that . . ." The exact words used to describe Kieran were lost in the grinding and gnashing of her mother's teeth. "Now get out of bed and make something of your life."

If the Delilah and Kate takeout solution to Clarissa's continued survival was being cut off at the source, this really was a problem. Clarissa swung one leg over the side of the bed and made a big show of feeling for the ground with her toe. It was too much. She grunted and heaved the leg back on the bed.

Mom shook her head and glanced at her watch. Then she leaned down and brushed the hair out of Clarissa's eyes. "Kate, do something with her. I'm starting to worry."

Do something with her? It hadn't been that long, had it? Had the statute of limitations on wallowing really expired? It couldn't have been more than two weeks . . . could it? Granted, she'd been busy, distracted, having spent the better part of her time weeping profusely, shaking her fist in anguish at the two cans of Shackleton's curried tongue perched on the bureau, rolling around on the bed clutching herself around the shoulders in her most dramatic tortured state, and beseeching her

parents, various gods, and an assortment of television person-
alities to deliver her from the unmitigated agony of it all.

"Take my hand," Kate said.

Clarissa, not thinking clearly, did so, and Kate yanked her up.

Clarissa smiled pleasantly and fell back on the bed. "Is it absolutely necessary that we all do something with me *right now?*"

"Your mom is right. Why wallow? It's counterproductive."

"Why wallow? Why wallow? That's the only good thing
about a relationship ending. You have free license to wallow.
You have an excuse to whinge and moan and exhibit your absolute worst personality traits in all their dubious glory, and
everyone has to let you get away with it."

Kate produced an uninterpretable snort while Mom cleared
her throat and said, "I think we're done with that stage now,
aren't we?"

Clarissa trumped Kate's snort with an even louder unintelli-
gible noise.

Kate reached into her computer bag and pulled out a disk
which she placed on the desk. "I brought over this new career
planning software to help Clary figure out her next move, since
that which was previously known as her life has been torn horribly asunder," she said, flinging her arms out dramatically.

Clarissa cringed, but Mom seemed more than satisfied with
the idea. "Excellent. I'm off to a meeting, and then your father
and I are scheduled for the museum tonight. You're welcome to
join us. Have a productive day." And she was out the door.

Have a productive day. The standard Schneckberg farewell.
Clarissa nestled productively back into the bedsheets.

Kate came up to her. "So, Clary, seriously. How are you feeling today?" She sat down on the bed and gave Clarissa's head a
sympathetic pat since that was the only body part available
above the covers.

"Okay. It hasn't been that long." She sniffed and rested her head against Kate's arm.

"As your mom would say, you must not overindulge," Kate said.

"You said he would ask me. He didn't ask me."

"Well, what do I know? I'm still single. Why are you taking *my* advice? Say, did Delilah come by last night?"

"Yeah." Clarissa perked right up. "She brought spaghetti. And I'm thinking falafel would be good tonight. Make sure they include enough pita with the order."

"Um . . . right. So, anyway, did she mention she's invited us to come to the office tomorrow at lunch and try out some new products?"

"She said something about that."

"Good." Kate moved to Clarissa's desk where she turned on her laptop and leaned against the desk while waiting for it to boot. "This would be the ideal opportunity to have a talk with her about what's been bothering her. We'll just keep it casual, ease into the discussion."

"Delilah's smarter than that," Clarissa said unenthusiastically. "I'm sure she already knows we're up to something."

Kate shrugged. "I'll be smooth."

Clarissa shrugged back. "Whatever. I'll follow your lead. I don't think she's in as bad a way as you do anyway."

Kate shot her a glance. "So, uh, don't you think it's excellent timing, this business of the three of us being single at the same time? I think it's really great. I think it . . . I think it . . . could be a good thing."

Clarissa just stared at Kate in misery, hardly hearing her. Her eyes filled with tears. *Oh, god. He didn't ask me.*

"Clary, are you sure you're okay?"

"I'm not okay, actually. I lied. I think I'm going to puke. My heart hurts. I want Kieran. I wanted to marry Kieran." She started to cry in earnest. "And I really thought he wanted to marry me. I gave him the best, most . . . most fertile years of my life, and he trampled on me."

"I hope you don't mind me asking this, but did you ever sense what was coming? Do you think you might have been in denial at all?"

"There were times where he acted a little strange, but I thought he was just going through some sort of phase men go through," Clarissa said, wiping her face on the sheets.

"What sort of phase?" Kate asked. "The sort of phase where they sleep with other women?"

Clarissa covered her face with her hands. "I'm so embarrassed about all of this. Frankly, I can't even tell if I'm more upset because of the heartbreak or the humiliation."

"Yes, yes," Kate said. "That's so healthy! You're horribly hurt and humiliated. But not broken." She raised her fist in the air. "Never broken. Right? Right?"

"Right. I guess."

"So that should be a comfort, a relief, even. A better, more fabulous post-Kieran Clarissa is easily within your reach. Agreed?"

"I guess."

"Which brings us conveniently around to my point."

"You had a point?"

"Since you can no longer rely on Kieran, you're just going to have to get out of bed and do this test so you can move on with your life. So out. Out of bed."

Clarissa sighed, and had a go at it, for real this time.

Kate watched with a pained expression. "I feel like I'm watching that scene where Grandpa Joe gets out of bed after something like twenty years so he can go with Charlie to the chocolate factory. This is really sad."

Clarissa stood up and winced from the head rush. "Whoa."

"Okay." Kate rubbed her hands together and punched something into the computer. "This thing is brand-new, and they say it's the most accurate test out there. It crosses the Minnesota Multiphasic Personality Inventory with the Rorschach inkblot test and the Meyers-Briggs. It will generate the most applicable career options for your personality type."

Clarissa wasn't wholly opposed to the idea of choosing a new path, it was just that it seemed awfully soon. But she saw the value in Kate's exercise. Really, there were only two choices: wallowing in misery or the opposite. Construct a new life so delicious that it could only be said that the best thing that ever happened to you was to get rid of the old ball and chain.

Clarissa tried to feel enthusiastic as Kate emptied the contents of her bag on the desk: a binder labeled MMPI, a spiral notepad, a Scantron and stapled test form, and a pile of Rorschach-style cards which she placed blot side down on the desk.

True, she would feel better if she got a new job. She wouldn't feel so adrift. It would give her something to focus on; she could throw herself into her work. And yet, the enthusiasm just wasn't there.

"We're going to start with the inkblots. I'm going to hand you ten cards, and I want you to say aloud the first thing that comes to your mind about what you think the blot represents."

Clarissa folded her hands in her lap. "Okay, I'm ready."

Kate handed her the first card. "What is this?"

It looked like a large black spatter. "Um . . . a small furry animal?"

"Could you please be more specific?"

"I don't know . . . say, a guinea pig?"

"Mmm . . . this?"

This looked a little more familiar. "Ah . . . a gun?"

"This?"

This one looked a lot more familiar. Clarissa yawned. "That would be a penis."

"This?"

"Palm tree?"

"This?"

"Oooh. Um. A . . . a . . ."

"First thing that pops into your head."

"Okay, sorry. A butterfly."

"This?"

"A noose?"

"Mmm. This?"

"A moose?" she blurted out and forced herself not to laugh. Kate narrowed her eyes.

Clarissa sighed wearily. "Why is this so important to you? If it's not important to me, then what's it to you?"

"It's important, okay?"

Clarissa blinked in surprise at Kate's rather sharp tone. "Okay. What now?"

Kate stacked the cards up and gave them a brisk tap against the edge of the desk and then handed Clarissa a large manual. "I'll log your answers into the computer while you review these questions. You're going to want to answer them directly into the program, though."

Clarissa stared down at the five-hundred-question booklet and began. Did she have lots of friends or just a few very close ones? Did being around others sap her energy or enhance it? Did she like to go out to parties or stay inside with a good book? In essence, was she a prom queen or a geek?

Oh, god. I'm a geek. Not a promising start.

An hour later, she'd finished answering the questions and

entering the data while Kate lay on the bed reading a romance novel and snacking on chocolates.

Almost eagerly, she pushed ENTER for the last time. "Okay, I'm ready."

"I was just getting to the good part." Kate dropped the book and came over to the computer where she hit a couple of keys and then squinted down at the screen as the machine hissed and whirred. "Oh."

Clarissa was watching Kate in profile and saw her friend's face fall for a moment, just before she caught herself and turned the expression into a beaming smile. "Yes?"

"Mmm."

"What does it say?"

"Well . . . it says it has distilled the analysis down to its essence by using a simple formula for the information provided, and has come to the conclusion that—" She stopped abruptly and looked up. "You know, truth be told, the instructions say this all works much better with a qualified psychologist around to, er, troubleshoot and double-check the results. Perhaps you should consult a professional."

"What does it say?"

Kate licked her lips. "Well, it's really . . . very good news. I think you'll be pleased. It says . . ." And yet she hesitated once more, clearly stalling, then finally gestured to the screen with a flourish. "As a borderline hysteric with subdued schizophrenic tendencies, you are ideally suited to . . . a career with a low stress threshold such as rabbit breeder or passport application stamper." She pulled her hands away from the keyboard. "And there you are. Problem solved. Your, er, destiny is before you."

Silence.

"I'm sorry, I thought you said rabbits," Clarissa said, and began to laugh in a voice much higher than normal.

Kate shrugged. "It's not so far-fetched."

"Rabbits?" Clarissa shrieked. "Are you joking?"

"Not at all." Kate just sat there calmly and blinked. "You do own at least four angora sweaters. Say, Clarissa?"

"What?"

"No offense, but a mere few weeks ago, had you not essentially been planning to settle down and breed with Kieran in the first place? Isn't this sort of the same thing, but with rabbits?"

Clarissa just put her head down on the desk and moaned.

Chapter Four

What do you do when your best-laid plans are shot to hell? What do you do when you have to start over? On the plus side, you have all roads in front of you open—you can do anything, be anything. The deal is, you have to know what you want. Unfortunately, Clarissa still wanted the life she and Kieran had planned together. Or at least she wanted the feeling she got when she thought about how it felt to know everything was all figured out. To have her future shattered in one blindsiding instant, well, that wasn't something she'd prepared for. There was no Plan B. There was no alternate course of action. There just hadn't been any point.

Clarissa sat in the car with the ignition still running and gave herself a moment to collect the sort of superhuman inner strength normally required to handle Kate and Delilah at the same time.

Delilah Aranahi was the founder of a growing online teenage cosmetics company. First impression proved her to be one part glitter, one part air, and one part luck, but she had a whole lot of business savvy that she rarely got credit for based on her brunette bombshell good looks and tendency to dress like "the girlie one" in an all-female pop group.

Kate's black Range Rover pulled up beside her in the parking lot. Clarissa rolled down her window, and Kate got out of the car and came around. "Hi."

"What am I doing here, again?"

"Um, well, Delilah needed some help testing a couple of new products, that's all. And I thought it would be good to get you out of the house. Not to mention . . . *free makeup!*"

"I think it's too early for me to be out in public. I don't want to shock my system." Clarissa sniffed and pressed her enormous Gucci sunglasses back against her face like some cosmetic surgery patient feeling overprotective of a recent eyelift. "I might see something unpleasant, something that wouldn't be healthy for me. Like happy married people. Or babies. Or giddy couples in the throes of first love—oh, god, see? I'm not a well person."

"Not likely inside the building." Kate reached through the window and turned off the ignition. "So the sooner we get in there, the better. Now get out of the car and move your ass."

Clarissa looked at her in shock.

"This is tough love, baby. Out."

Clarissa meekly complied, and she and Kate approached Delilah's home base together.

The company was located in a retrofitted warehouse just around the corner from the city stadium. In fact, if you sat in the high part of the bleachers, you could actually see the pink neon logo surrounded by flashing marquee lights from a distance. Once inside, you had the sensation of being on set in a revival of *Xanadu*. The walls were painted in shades of pink and purple and accented with lots of mirrored tiles. All the conference room doors featured retro-looking silhouettes of girls with shopping bags in high heels and miniskirts. Everything flashed, everything sassed. Bowls of brightly colored candy perched on every kidney-shaped communal working space. Pop music played over the loudspeaker. Clarissa could see Delilah's administrative assistant roller-skating down the hall with her cell phone and PDA hanging from a hip holster.

Kate took Clarissa by the hand and dragged her to the testing room, which featured a giant disco ball swaying below a gyrating ceiling fan.

Delilah sat at the table in a low-cut sweater trimmed with white feathers. A notepad and a large array of numbered, generic-looking silver pots and tubes covered the table. "Hi, guys. It's so good to see you out, Clary. So, do either of you think my hair smells like a Snickers?" She held out a chunk of hair and tried to get one of them to smell it.

Both Kate and Clarissa took a step backward.

"Okay, whatever. I'm just worried about our new candy-scented fragrances." She gestured to the table. "We're test-driving some new concepts in lipgloss. Have at 'em."

"Do we get to keep the ones we try?"

"Sure."

Kate sorted through the colors and made her choice.

"So, how's it going over at your parents'?" Delilah asked. "We've been worried about you."

"Actually, Kate and I are worried about you," Clarissa said.

"Um, no, that was just something Kate and I made up to convince you to get out of bed and come over here."

"Oh, my god. You double-crossed my double-cross. This is a ruse." Clarissa gasped. "A sneaky *St. Elmo's Fire* bring-Demi-Moore-to-the-homeless-shelter-for-lunch maneuver."

"I don't see any homeless people in this room, do you?" Kate asked.

Clarissa narrowed her eyes. "This is a setup. It's not right. I don't like surprises and . . . and trickery. This is an outrage."

An uncomfortable silence fell over the table.

"I think I have glitter in my nostril," Delilah finally said.

"Well, then," Kate responded. "The fact is that I actually wanted to speak with both of you about your futures, and if Clarissa doesn't want to share with us, we can move on to Deli—"

"It's not working," Clarissa blurted out, suddenly unwilling to miss her turn. She sighed. "I think I'm too old to be at home. Plus, the whole concept is depressing. Unemployed, living with parents, dumped by boyfriend . . . I'm just . . . it just . . . it all just screams 'pathetic.' I'm like a twenty-something after-school special." She hung her head.

"Absolutely not. You're not pathetic, and everyone knows you weren't the problem. You were much, much too good for him."

Clarissa smiled weakly. "I know that's what I'm supposed to think."

"I'm telling you the truth. Kieran was like . . . he was like . . . one of those high school football stars who peaked too early. Mark my words. In five years he'll have lost half his hair and developed a huge beer gut. He won't even be able to speak in complete sentences and you'd've had to develop an entirely new form of communication based on multitonal grunting. Just think how that would have impacted your children."

Good lord. Clarissa put her hand to her mouth.

"I say good riddance. You're much more interesting without him."

"Oh, well . . . thanks so much, Delilah."

"Frankly, I never liked Kieran," Kate said. "I thought he was a complete loser the first time I met him and just being in the same room with him made me want to stick an ice pick through my eyeball."

Delilah smiled. "To be totally honest, I couldn't stand him either. He was like nails on a blackboard."

"When the person in front of you pulls out a checkbook instead of a credit card."

"When you find a mystery hair in your hamburger."

"A slow dripping sound at one in the morning and you have no idea where it's coming from."

"A paper cut!" Delilah squealed. "He was like a paper cut."

"No, a yeast infection! An insidious, bothersome, painful—"

"Okay, thanks! I get it." Clarissa smiled too brightly. "Thanks for the support."

Clarissa knew these comments were intended as kindnesses meant to make her, the dumpee, feel better. But they really just proved she'd exhibited horrendous judgment choosing him in the first place, and reminded her that she'd managed to waste almost a decade of her life with a guy who would play absolutely zero role in the rest of it. How depressing. And what are you supposed to say in response? "Yes, I never liked him either"? Well, that wasn't true. Perhaps something a little more backhanded, a little snider. "Yes, well, I had no idea I came off as such a boring person when I was with him. How nice that I shine so brightly for you now"?

"Say, Clary," Delilah said. "You never said who he left you for."

Clarissa looked first at Delilah, then at Kate. "Luna Fong," she said with as much dramatic flair as she could muster. A gasp went up from the table.

"The Chinese girl with the perfect hair," Kate intoned, wide-eyed. "White guy dumps white girlfriend for exotic Asian chick with perfect hair. Bummer. What? It's true, isn't it? Can we not speak the truth? These are facts. The very same thing happened to me in college. It was terrible. I couldn't eat any sort of Asian food for a month. Not Chinese, Thai, Vietnamese . . . nothing. Couldn't touch the stuff. It was just too painful."

"Well, that's not very PC, is it," Delilah said matter-of-factly. "I went to Berkeley, and that's definitely un-PC."

"Yeah, the facts may be the facts," Clarissa conceded. "But it's not the sort of thing you talk about, is it."

"Why not? I'm willing to bet at Berkeley, the Asian *guys* are talking about this. I bet the Asian *girls* are talking about this. Besides, at Berkeley, you say something bad about salmon mousse and the fish-spread enthusiasts call you un-PC," Kate said.

"Are you suggesting I'm some sort of a fish bigot?" Delilah asked. She looked really confused.

"Um, no. Of course not." Kate flashed Clarissa an incredulous smile.

Delilah shrugged. "Well, I think if my boyfriend dumped me for an exotic Chinese girl I'd be pretty upset. You're taking it well, under the circumstances."

"I guess," Clarissa said.

"What . . . what *happened?*" Delilah asked. "I don't understand what happened. What does she have that you don't?"

"It could have been anything. How do I know? I've spent many a night wondering. She does have better shoes than me. I can say that for sure. She has these incredible shoes that go with her outfits—and not in that creepy Southern sort of way."

"Ooh, that *bitch,*" Kate muttered.

"Yeah." Clarissa sighed. "She gave me her hairdresser and took my boyfriend."

Delilah huffed. "Your hair looks terrific; I'm not so sure it wasn't a fair trade."

Kate slammed her hand down on the table. "Wait a minute! Wasn't Luna Fong supposed to be Kieran's *platonic* friend?"

"No!" Delilah's hand flew to her throat. "She was his *platonic* friend? That's outrageous! That's beyond the pale."

"Does it matter?" Clarissa asked.

"Does it matter? Does it matter? Of course it matters." Kate appeared to be genuinely enraged. "It's like the ultimate betrayal. We're talking about the platonic friend who happens to have all of the same hobbies and interests as the guy you're seeing. The platonic friend who pretends to like you and all the while is just biding her time. *That* platonic friend. She has gone—or rather, he has taken her—where you just don't go. It's not right. It's not right at all."

"I'm not sure I grasp . . ." Clarissa's voice faltered.

"What is a platonic friend, really?" Kate asked. "A member of the opposite sex who either didn't want to have sex with you or desperately does but hasn't, which means the idea of having sex is always out there, hovering in the air. Will they? Won't they? Why haven't they? Do they want to?"

"When you put it like that . . ."

"It's an excuse. An excuse to date someone else without getting in trouble."

"Absolutely," Delilah chimed in. "If your boyfriend claims to have a platonic friend, either the women in question refused to sleep with him, which is why she is still just a friend, or else she desperately wants to but hasn't—yet. Either way, she's not a woman you want to have around."

Clarissa gulped.

"Or else the woman finds the man in question sorely lacking in some department, which should make you take pause and wonder why. If he's not good enough for her, why is he good enough for you?" Kate said.

"Well, you know, according to *The American Heritage Dictionary,* 'platonic' is derived from the philosopher, Plato," Delilah said blithely.

Kate and Clarissa hit twin double takes.

Delilah rolled her eyes. "Just because I'm beautiful doesn't mean I'm stupid. If I may be allowed to quote, the definition states that platonic is 'essentially that which transcends physical desire and tends toward the purely spiritual or ideal.' If my boyfriend told me he had a girl who was a 'friend' who transcended physical desire and tended toward the ideal, I'd be very concerned, I can tell you that."

"I disagree," Kate said huffily, quite likely because overt displays of intelligence not arising from her own mouth tended to make her very uneasy. "It may mean one thing in the dictionary, but the word 'platonic' . . . well, the word itself has transcended its own meaning."

Delilah fluttered a bit of loose glitter off her eyelash. "How so?"

"Rather than platonic being a state in which you transcend the need for sex, in reality platonic is just another name for sexually unsatisfied."

"I don't see that. How does that work?"

"Okay . . . like 'underdog' is just another name for pathetic?" Kate explained. "They put a positive spin on a negative situation."

At this point, Delilah seemed to notice the increasingly disturbed expression Clarissa knew was plastered on her face. "Ease up, Kate," she said. "Let's not harp on what's in the past."

"I have no problem with that. Let's concentrate on the positive spin. What's next, Clary?"

Clarissa carefully dabbed a pearly pink shade of nail polish on her left hand, too embarrassed even to look at her closest friends, and said in a small voice, "Um . . . I don't know . . . maybe a . . . spa day?"

Kate folded her arms across her chest and looked at Delilah, who merely shrugged. "A spa day. That's your recovery plan."

Clarissa just looked at her helplessly. "What do you think I should do? I'm in a really bad way." She quickly held up her palm. "And if you say anything about rabbits—"

"No rabbits," Kate promised.

"Did you ever take the test?" Clarissa asked suddenly.

"Me?"

Clarissa rolled her eyes. "You did. What did it say? What's your best-suited job?"

"Prison guard," Kate said sharply. "The software was obviously a beta. But we're not talking about me, we're talking about you. I think we ought to brainstorm some options."

"We really are worried about your future," Delilah added.

Clarissa stared intently at Delilah, and it suddenly occurred to her that she could see some of her own confusion on her friend's face. She clasped her hands in front of her on the table and took a deep breath. "I don't think it's just 'Clarissa at a crossroads' here, is it? Would you like to share with us?"

Delilah started in surprise, then made a show of testing some lipstick on the back of her hand. "What on earth do you mean?"

Clarissa reached out and patted Delilah's hand. "Is something . . . bothering you? Are you upset about something?"

Delilah didn't look up. She merely put the lipstick down and began applying magenta mascara to her long eyelashes. "Oh, I'm not upset. I'm just a little . . . unsettled. Corporate is planning to remodel, and it's just a huge bother."

"What do you mean, remodel?"

Delilah waved her hands in the air a little wildly. "Deconstruct, assimilate, corporatize, you know, remodel. They don't like the . . . design . . . the gestalt, you know? They think it's not professional enough, not representative of the company line."

"What are they going to do?"

"They showed me samples. It's . . . oh, god, it's . . ." She abandoned her façade and went speechless for a moment, then managed to utter, "Blue-and-navy striped wallpaper. Very . . ."

Kate gasped. "Very Republican First Lady!"

Delilah exhaled loudly, almost relieved, it seemed, that she'd shared the information. "Precisely. It's not me at all. Not an ounce of me."

"Why don't you just tell them no?" Clarissa asked.

Delilah lifted her chin, her cheeks burning rather brighter than normal. "Because I don't have quite so much control over that sort of thing anymore."

Kate and Clarissa looked at her sympathetically.

Delilah smiled brightly, but her voice trembled as she said, "Well, I did sell out. Literally and figuratively. I'm not sorry. It made sense. It's just that things are . . . different, now."

"Lots of things are different now," Clarissa muttered, going a little *verklempt* herself.

"I mean, I have oodles of money now, I realize that. And I'm not complaining, exactly. It's just surprisingly unsettling to have something that was yours . . . not."

"There's nothing wrong with going mercenary every now and then," Kate said, rubbing Delilah's back. "Nothing wrong with it at all. Sometimes it just makes good business sense."

Clarissa could see Delilah was working hard not to let her expression crumple into something rather more desperate. "It's just not mine anymore, that's all. I don't know what I'm doing here anymore."

Kate suddenly stood up and leaned over the table, almost, it seemed, almost as if she'd been waiting for the opportunity. "That is a very reasonable question. And I'm here to put things in perspective for you. You see the writing on the wall, and I'm going to read it out for you, loud and clear."

Clarissa pushed her chair back to give Kate a little more space for her performance.

"Delilah, you're an artist. We respect that. But ever since Loralline Cosmetics bought you out, they've only let you dodder around the office like somebody's really old mentally disturbed relative. You realize they'll have you 'product testing'"—she put her fingers up in the air and bent them in the shape of quotation marks— "makeup with your friends for the rest of your life just to keep you out of the management meetings. We can't have that. It's the corporate equivalent of cruise ship shuffleboard."

Delilah contemplated that statement for a moment and then suddenly reared back as if the significance of Kate's words had just hit her in the face. "Oh, god. That's just . . . that's grotesque."

"Well, I didn't mean it quite—"

"Shush," Clarissa said. "I don't think she's done yet."

"I'm beginning to think it's time . . ." Delilah trailed off and began to smear crème blush on her cheeks to hide her emotion.

"Time for what?" Clarissa urged her on gently.

Silence. More blush, way too much at this point, even for Delilah.

"Move on," Kate said quietly. "Time to move on? You can say it, Delilah."

"I'm not sure I can." Delilah looked distinctly flustered. "You know, I think Clary's idea had real potential. Day spa?" she suggested weakly.

Kate reviewed her own nail polish and released a world-weary sigh. "Been there, done that. And I can say from experience that all the chanting and seaweed wraps in the world don't make a difference. You can't try to escape. You've got to meet this tragedy, this debacle, this trauma, head on. Both of you. *Be* your trauma. *Own* your trauma."

Something began to dawn on Clarissa at this point. It was almost as if Kate were not merely giving the pep talk to the two of them. It was almost . . . almost as if she were trying to convince . . . herself?

Clarissa leaped to her feet. "Kate!"

Delilah and Kate both reared back.

Clarissa pointed at Kate. " 'Fess up, Kate."

"What?"

"You heard me. 'Fess up."

Delilah's cares seemed to evaporate. "Ooh, Clarissa. Does Kate have a secret?"

"I think Kate *does* has a secret." Clarissa turned back to Kate. "Does she?"

Kate cleared her throat, affecting much annoyance. "As a matter of fact, I do have some . . . news."

She had their full attention.

"I've been fired. Kaput."

Clarissa's bravado deflated. "*Excuse* me?"

"You heard me. I saw you to your car. I walked back inside. The boss called me to his office to say our department had been downsized." Kate suddenly frowned and smooshed her lips together. "Do anybody else's lips feel odd?"

Delilah poked at her lips. "Mine do. They're sort of stinging, actually. I'll have to take another look at that formula."

Kate swallowed hard and wiped the lipgloss off with a tissue.

Delilah looked at her with exasperation. "Well, we can't test on animals. That would be wrong."

"But it's okay to put toxic chemicals on *my* lips?"

"What in god's name do you think Botox is?"

Kate gasped. "I would *never* use Botox . . . say, do you think this stuff reacts with collagen?"

Delilah rolled her eyes. "I swear, Kate, it's not going to kill you. It says so in the company mission statement."

Clarissa tapped her foot on the ground as she crossed her arms over her chest. "Don't try to skirt the subject. What do you mean, downsized?"

"Downsized. I was downsized. Oh, whatever you want to call it. The point is that I am currently at loose ends. Ready for a change, if you will—"

"Loose ends?" Clarissa's lips twitched and she started to giggle. "We're in crisis but you're merely 'at loose ends'? I love you, Kate. Your logic is just so . . . delightful."

"I'm pleased I amuse you in some way. But you're missing my point in your anxiousness to make a point about my delivery. What I'm getting at is that it just so happens that all three of us may be ready for a little something different."

The word "different" felt like a bullet. Irrationally so. But there it was. "I don't want different," Clarissa said, her giggles gone, once again on the edge of tears, struggling to get a tissue out of the box. "I want what I had. I want the same. I want . . . normal. I don't want different. There was nothing wrong with my life. It was all making sense. And now nothing makes sense."

The mood once again shot, Kate and Delilah stared downcast at the makeup sprawled all over the table as Clarissa started to cry. Then they looked at each other and transmitted some more nonverbal communication. And then Kate pulled something out of her purse from under the table and placed, in the center of everything, a rusty, dented can of curried tongue.

Clarissa reared back. "Don't remind me. That was a horrible night." She swallowed hard, fighting with the tears.

"I'm not putting it there to upset you," Kate said softly. "I'm putting it there as inspiration."

"Inspiration!?"

"Oh, dear," Delilah muttered. "I knew this was a bad idea. Symbolism is all well and good, Kate, but I think it's too soon."

"It's not too soon. You must *reclaim* the curried tongue. You must draw inspiration from the curried tongue. Let the curried tongue be the catalyst for change."

"You just like saying the phrase 'curried tongue,'" Clarissa said wearily. "Okay, I'll bite. What do you have up your sleeve?"

"Seeing as how the three of us are all on the crux of something really great, something huge, I thought it would a nice idea for us to go to one of those planning seminars."

Clarissa slumped even farther down in her chair. "My mother put you up to this."

"She did not put me up to this."

"No?"

"No. She merely provided the brochure. Let's go."

Chapter Five

Two hours into the seminar, even Kate looked ready to commit a random act of violence. The girls bailed out of the session during the first break and snuck into an empty conference room.

"Who has the notebook?"

Clarissa and Delilah looked at Kate blankly.

"The notebook where I wrote down our goals! Who's got it?"

More blank looks.

Kate rolled her eyes, then rummaged around in her totebag and found the tiny spiral notepad she'd been looking for.

She flipped the lid. "Great. So, I've written down our goals, all distilled and condensed from past conversations. Right here in this notebook are the reasons we're here. Let's review." She trailed her finger down the page. "I want to be a chef. If I don't get my act together I'm going to be slinging hash and complaining about how I can't afford to make long distance calls on fifteen percent tips for the rest of my life. I want to cook. And that's what I'm going to do."

Her finger trailed some more. "Clarissa, you want to break

into the L.A. TV and film production scene. No one in their right mind would hire a dot-com vapor strategist directly into a decent Hollywood producing position, so you're going to pursue a gig to get an awesome reference to take to L.A. with you."

Clarissa opened her mouth to protest, but Kate silenced her with a palm in the air.

"Delilah, unless you wish to retire, and I don't think you do, then your job is to find your muse. We'll be expecting a business plan for a brand-new line of cosmetics." She flipped the notepad shut. "Right. So, that puts us all on the same page."

"I think I'm depressed," Clarissa said.

"What about the boys?" Delilah asked.

Kate lowered her arm. "What about the boys? We don't need specific goals for boys. I thought boys were a given."

"Boys are never a given," Clarissa said in a rather hostile tone.

"As far as I'm concerned, we can be expanding our sexual horizons the entire time. I'd even go so far as to encourage it."

Delilah leaned over and whispered in Clarissa's ear, "What exactly does she mean by 'sexual horizons'?"

With as straight a face as she could muster, Clarissa looked at her and said, "Flat on your back."

Delilah nodded sagely. "Of course, of course."

Kate walked to the front of the room, stuck a disk into the computer setup, and snapped open a pointer. A PowerPoint presentation loaded, accompanied by the theme to *Rocky*. The first slide was a picture Clarissa recognized, with the three girls at a party, arms around each other—plus the addition of a large penguin doctored into the spot from which Kieran had been cropped.

In her presentation voice, Kate began. "Looking for a change? Wishing you had more adventures in your life?"

Clarissa just stared woefully at the screen.

Kate swapped the slide out to one of the three of them bundled up in ski clothes in a lodge bar in Lake Tahoe. She cleared her throat. "So, the way I see it is you're single now, and you get to do whatever the hell you damn please. You can sleep with who you want, you can go wherever you want, and it seems you ought to take advantage of a situation like that. Especially now that we're all single at the same time, for once. This is classic female bonding stuff. We need jobs with access to the highest possible ratio of men."

"It's June. We've missed the ski season," Clarissa said.

"We're not going skiing. We're going to Antarctica."

"I'm sorry, what did you just say?"

"Antarctica. The three of us. We're going to Antarctica."

There was a long pause. Delilah cocked her head. "Oh. Oh, it's a joke. Right. So we'll do *that* right after we summit Everest."

"Summiting Everest is so yesterday," Kate said in a bored tone. "Do you realize how many men there will be at the South Pole? Willing and able?"

"Cancún, I can see. Paris, I can see. Even Las Vegas, I can see. Antarctica, I'm not seeing. Give me one good reason why we should go to the coldest, driest place on earth. I mean, have you considered what the climate would do to your skin?" Clarissa asked.

Delilah rolled her eyes impatiently. "Don't be dense, Clarissa. We'll bring a good moisturizer. Think of all the men. The men!"

"The men? I'm against men. Down with men!"

"Do you realize what sort of male-to-female ratio we're talking about here?" Delilah asked.

"That's sad."

"It's not sad at all. Not in the least. It's a very, very happy thought, if you ask me," Kate said.

"Okay, how about this. Let's assume for the moment that

there are, oh, I don't know . . . four men for every female. What on earth makes you think we'd be compatible with the sort of men who'd go there?"

"Who cares about compatibility! You haven't even done your rebound guy."

"It's not me. Antarctica is definitely not me."

"Who are you?"

Clarissa suddenly felt horrified. She used to be Kieran's wife-to-be. And employed. And going somewhere. Now she was . . . who the hell knew?

"Consider this," Kate said. "We'd get *paid*. Mmm?"

"I could get paid to do a lot of things."

"Could you get paid to hang out with a lot of single men?"

"I doubt that would be my job description."

"Think about this. You don't have a job at the moment—"

"I don't have this one either."

"Stop interrupting. They need women. With equal employment opportunity, we'd have no problem."

"That's lame. We should get hired on our own merits, or not at all."

"Let's just ignore that for the moment. You could have an adventure, meet men, get paid, and return home to real life all without one of those unsightly blank spots on your résumé. What do you think? Shall we go for it?"

"I think it's asinine." At the same time, she couldn't help thinking that there was something appealing about going away. Far, far away. To someplace that had cachet and seemed unusual, impressive, and unique to other people. As opposed to, say, going home with her tail between her legs and living with her parents for the next six months while she looked for another job. But it was ridiculous. She simply wasn't the sort of person who could get on in Antarctica.

Antarctica was out of the question. "You know, some of us aren't adventurers. Some of us aren't leaders."

Kate took one hand, Delilah took the other. "We're not telling you to lead, Clary. We're telling you to follow. See? You don't even have to leave your comfort zone."

"Besides, you've been wanting to make a career change for a while," Delilah said.

"Yeah, and if you do a good job, maybe it would springboard you into the Hollywood space," Kate added.

Delilah nodded. "And just think, you can show Kieran what a loser he is. He always hated the idea of you going to work in L.A. He discouraged you. And I distinctly remember him saying that L.A. would eat you alive."

Clarissa shrugged, halfway to being sold on the idea, though the path from Antarctica to Hollywood wasn't entirely obvious to her.

She wasn't sold when Kate pointed out that there would be a ratio of about five to one, men to women. Or when she pointed out that they were not likely to ever bump into these people again in their lifetime, and that what happened there, could stay there. She certainly wasn't sold when Delilah pointed out that it was the perfect opportunity to indulge in slutty behavior without being judged in the real world and that it was an opportunity to "sample" different kinds of men in one convenient location. And she wasn't sold even when they all realized at the same time that it was a perfect excuse to buy a pair of those really cool Prada hiking boots.

Clarissa was sold when it occurred to her that her friends were serious. And that if both Delilah and Kate went away without her, she'd be completely and totally . . . guyless, friendless, and jobless. Anchors away.

* * *

I am a cog in the wheel. I am a cog in the wheel. Okay, that works. I'm fine with that. There are all kinds of people that make up a team. If we were all Kates and Delilahs, there would be no one to give instructions to and nothing would actually get done. I'm good with instructions. I can follow instructions. I'm impressive that way. Give me instructions and you won't have to ask me about it twice . . . hmm, but maybe it's too soon to get a new job. I need rest. I need perspective. I need time to think . . . of course, one could perhaps assume that there would be time to think—space to think—in Antarctica. It's a big . . . wide . . . empty sort of place. Yes, the sort of place where one could just clear one's mind of clutter. I've been through a rough patch. No, I'm not even out of it yet. I'm still in a rough patch. It's been a very difficult month. Has it been a month? Come to think of it, I wonder what day it is. The thing is, I've been traumatized. I don't want to overexert myself. I don't want anything too taxing. Don't be tempted by a prestige job, Clarissa. That's just a trap. A recipe for stress. Just go for a job with as little responsibility as possible. You'll be better off that way. You'll be good at that.

My god, Clarissa. What is it you're so afraid of?

"Clarissa, we're falling out of line," Kate hissed. "Move up."

Clarissa blinked and looked around her. The three of them were standing in an impossibly long interview line. The first thing Clarissa noticed was a small table filled with small rubber squeezie penguins. The second thing she noticed was that the room had gone deathly silent and that approximately three hundred men were staring at them.

There were men everywhere. Men with T-shirts and tattoos and lots of facial hair. Men in jeans with dirt on them and men with their arms crossed, looking sullen, bored, or amused.

"These are definitely men," Kate said. "Men."

"Grunt," Delilah said.

"Scratch," Kate agreed.

"Snort," Clarissa conceded.

"Men," the three concluded simultaneously.

"I've never seen so many variations on the soul patch in my life. Some of these guys look like they have lint glued on their faces," Kate said.

Clarissa checked her watch, sighed, and looked around the room.

They reached the front of the room and the three girls were shunted into booths with three different recruiters. It was obvious these weren't actual, trained human resources employees. Rather, they seemed to be fellow employees. Or the employees who would be their fellows once they arrived in Antarctica.

Clarissa's recruiter had on a pair of extremely dark sunglasses, shorts that looked like he'd unzipped the bottom part that made them pants, Teva sandals and a stained T-shirt that read SOUTH POLE: THE MEN, NOT THE BOYS.

Clarissa sat down and slid her résumé across the desk and he studied it for a moment. "I'm Mitchell Kipling. I'll ask you the stock questions first, and then we can just relax and talk."

Clarissa smiled. "Great."

"Are you comfortable operating heavy machinery?"

Clarissa paused, a little taken aback. She was expecting the strengths-and-weaknesses mumbo jumbo for which she had articulate, packaged answers that she'd practiced just enough to sound unpracticed. "Sorry, come again?"

"Do you know how to operate heavy machinery?"

"Um, do you mean like a blender?"

He didn't laugh at the joke; he just blinked and wrote something down on a piece of paper he held curled over at the top the way smart kids in school do when they don't want anyone cribbing their answers.

"Oh! Oh, I'm sorry, I misunderstood the question. The answer is yes. Yes. My friend owns a Range Rover."

He coughed not-so-politely. "Ever install insulation? Do some plumbing? Heavy lifting?"

She shook her head in the negative.

"Do you know how to build . . . or maybe just, uh, fix . . ." —here, he let his gaze follow her body down to her shoes— ". . . *anything?*"

"Not really." Clarissa shifted uncomfortably in the orange plastic chair.

The checks came faster now, were larger, like big F grades . . . he was pretty much checking the NO boxes before she'd even answered.

"What experience do you have with the outdoors?"

Clarissa chewed at her bottom lip. Gardening was probably not the answer he was looking for.

"Do you feel you are adaptable to extremely cold environments?"

Clarissa thought of that last ski trip. Sure, it was freezing, the temperature having dropped to something like twenty degrees in springtime, for god's sake, but she'd done just fine. A couple of hours by the lodge fireplace with a mug of hot chocolate tipped with Kahlua and she was ready to go right back out on the slopes. "Absolutely."

"Do you become easily depressed?"

"No, I—"

"Are you easily bored?"

"No, it's—"

"Do you have a problem with a two-minute shower?"

Clarissa looked at him askance. "What sort of problem would there be?" she asked cautiously, making sure to sound upbeat.

Did he mean two minutes of heat? Or two minutes of water? Or a two-minute wait before showering? Or a two-minute increment?

"Depending on where you might be deployed, you may need to restrict yourself to two-minute showers, and in some cases in the field, you may not be able to shower."

A pause passed between them as Clarissa waited for him to finish the sentence. Finally she said, "May not be able to shower for . . . ?"

"At all."

"At all?" she breathed.

He tipped his head.

Clarissa went for the quick recovery. "Oh! No problem. It's not good to wash your hair every day anyway."

"What we recommend, actually, is that you stop washing your hair for two weeks. After that, your scalp won't produce so much oil."

Gross. "Two days," Clarissa corrected. "I think you meant to say two days."

"No."

"No, I mean, I understood what you meant, it's just that you said two weeks instead of two days."

"Riiight." He leaned back in the chair, slowly put his hands up behind his neck and smiled patronizingly. "Two weeks is what I meant to say."

"Oh."

He looked like he was trying not to laugh . . . or at least not to smile. A muscle at the corner of his mouth twitched. "Okay, well, thanks for coming by." He slid her résumé across the table. "Here's this back . . ."

Clarissa's jaw dropped.

". . . and the good news is that *Bachelorettes of Alaska Two* is holding auditions just down the hall to the right."

Dear lord. He was rejecting her. She hadn't botched a job interview in . . . ever. She leaned forward, looked him square in the eye, and said in a confident yet not arrogant tone, "Mitchell. I think I'd be a really good match for your company. And I'm really excited about the experience."

He cleared his throat and stared at her for a few minutes. "I don't really know how to say this . . . okay, here it is. A lot of people like the idea of going to Antarctica. There's something sort of . . ." Here he leaned forward. Clarissa found it hard to concentrate on what he was saying. Dirt had never smelled so good. ". . . sort of romantic about the idea, I think, for people like . . ." He shifted uncomfortably, like a guy who wasn't really okay with using the word "romantic" in a sentence.

"Yes?" Clarissa asked eagerly.

"You just seem very . . . can we go off record here, Clarissa?"

"Yes," she repeated, wide-eyed.

"Like you. People like you who . . . hell, I'm just going to say it. People like you who are completely unprepared for the reality of the environment."

Clarissa lurched back, completely out of his spell. "That's a gross generalization. What exactly do you mean by 'people like me'?"

He scrubbed at his hair until it stood on end, a messy mop of bedhead. It was devastatingly attractive. He sighed and rested his chin in his hand, staring at her.

This man, this rugged, outdoorsy man, didn't think she was good enough. Didn't think she had what it takes. Clarissa wasn't used to being unimpressive. She wasn't used to being . . . well, wrongly qualified. And she didn't like her femaleness translated as stupid. "If we're off the record . . . Mitchell . . . then we can speak frankly?"

"Absolutely."

"You're in this for science."

"That's right."

"To support the scientists you need a big support staff and then, of course, you need what you need to support a big support staff. So really, some of the staff is just there to support the staff supporting the scientists. It's entirely possible you have more support staff for the support staff than you do scientists."

He conceded with a curious grin.

"And with all those people, you don't have one opening that could make use of my skills?"

"Your skills . . . riiight." His pen malfunctioned at this point, leaving a streak of black ink on his thumb. He absently rubbed the ink into his palm. "I'm sorry, your qualifications in general are excellent, but they don't really match . . ." His sentence trailed off and he peered more closely at her résumé, then peered at her over the top of the paper, then back to the paper.

Clarissa took the opening. "I'm looking for a little . . . grit. I tell you, I'm ready to get down on my hands and knees with some serious tools in twenty below zero and . . . and . . . and weld something together," she ended enthusiastically.

"You don't look like the sort of woman looking for grit."

"How would you know?"

"Does this bother you?" To her combined horror and sick delight, he actually swiped the pen on the thigh of his jeans, leaving a black stain running across the blue denim.

Clarissa just stared beyond the corner of the desk at his leg in fascination. Kieran would never have done that. Kieran didn't like stains. Well, to be honest, neither of them liked stains. Stains were bad in her old life. Stains and sweat and dirty clothes—these were things you constantly were at war with. She stared at the stain, then up at Mitchell, who waited patiently for an answer.

Of course it bothered her. Which was precisely why she wanted to go. This was absolutely for her. This was exactly what she needed. A hundred and eighty degree turn toward a latitude of ninety degrees south. If this wasn't a character building experience, what was?

Mitchell started to chuckle before she could even answer him. "I'm going to get them to hire you, Clarissa. If only because I can't wait to watch you react to things out there."

He swiveled in the chair and picked up the phone. "It's Mitch. Did you decide to fill that Hollywood req? Uh-huh . . . uh-huh . . . right. Well, as a matter of fact, I do." He looked up at her again, then pulled a form from the stack of manila envelopes next to his elbow. "I can fax you a résumé. Uh-huh. Clarissa . . . Scheck— no, that's Schneckberg. Clarissa Schneckberg. Yeah, I think she'll be perfect for that special requisition. . . . Well, I do. She's sitting right here. Okay. Then, if that's all you need to know . . . terrific." He hung up.

Clarissa's eyebrow flew up.

Mitchell held out his hand. "Congratulations, Clarissa. And welcome to the team. You're our new distinguished visitor liaison. Basically a press contact and escort. USAA is trying to put a more . . . attractive face on its polar operations. You're the new face of Antarctica." He flicked a glance over her and chuckled. "It's going to be a hell of a season."

They shook hands, and he slid a folder as thick as a phone book across the table. "All you need to do now is pass medical."

Clarissa took the folder and headed back to the meeting spot where Delilah and Kate already were waiting. "I'm in!" she shrieked.

"Me too!"

"Me too!"

A huge man in overalls and a ski hat looked at them over his shoulder, his eyes widening in horror as he caught a glimpse of the girls. He quickly looked away.

They giggled and swapped offer letters.

"Vehicle operator?" Clarissa choked on her laughter. "Delilah, you've accepted a job to drive?"

Delilah grinned. "This is just the soul-searching sabbatical I've been waiting for. And when I get back, I can use the inspiration as means to put together a whole new line of makeup." Then suddenly the grin disappeared. "You don't think I'm going to have to drive stick, do you?"

"That sort of depends on the vehicle."

"I'm driving the town bus! Can't you just see it? Too delicious."

Clarissa could see it. And it wasn't a pretty sight. She had flashes of Delilah driving busloads of scientists into ice crevasses, derailing the entire national research process, and sending the future of American science into an irreversible tailspin. Delilah was a horrible driver.

"Let me see yours."

Clarissa handed over her slip.

Delilah squinted at the page. "Media liaison." She looked up at Clarissa, a look of pain on her face. "That's sort of what you do now. The idea was to, I don't know, expand our horizons."

"You think driving a bus is going to expand your horizons?"

"You never know. Think of all those captive males. I can pick and choose from the rearview mirror."

"I should hope under the circumstances, you'd be looking in front of you."

They headed back outside to the parking lot.

"Oh, god! What are we going to wear down there?" Kate started to panic. "What should we pack?"

Delilah smoothed her eyebrows. "We have an allotment of only forty pounds. Forty pounds of personal belongings to survive for six months on the Antarctic continent. What *do* you take? We're going to have to make some tough choices."

"Okay, pick one. Those gorgeous navy strappy sandals or two pounds of freshly ground Peet's Coffee?"

Clarissa licked her lips, which were becoming drier by the second. "Um . . . the navy strappy sandals? I don't know what sort of coffee-making facilities we'll have."

"Well, someone can always mail us a French press. But for now, agreed. The navy strappy sandals."

Kate flailed her arms out. "I've got one. What's more important . . . a hair dryer or the two pounds of Peet's?"

Delilah nervously clasped her hands. "Oh, that's a good one. Um . . . um . . . can I think about it?"

"Yes. Moving on," Kate said. "What's more important, the beaded sweater or the sandwich grill?"

Clarissa lifted her chin. "You guys, I have to hand it to you. This was a brilliant idea. Already, I feel better. I think my self-esteem is coming back. I have what it takes to do this. The will, the sense of adventure, the courage—" She did a double take and stared down at the list of medical requirements stapled to the top of the folder in her hands. "Good god, does this involve needles?"

"Antarctica is a very dangerous place. People die."

Clarissa looked up in alarm. It was an excellent point. "You know, if we're going to stare death in the face, there are two things we must do before we leave."

"Make a will," Kate said.

"And buy new underwear," Delilah added.

So off they went to Bloomingdale's to prepare for their collective demise.

Chapter Six

The Bloomingdale's lingerie department seemed light-years away as Clarissa, Delilah, and Kate lined up single file down the aisle of the aircraft to prepare to disembark.

Clarissa took stock once more of the baggy black bib pants with wide suspender straps, the long underwear tops that smelled faintly of sweat, cigarettes and fruit punch, the gigantic white military-issue rubber "bunny" boots that seemed to weigh about ten pounds each, and as a crowning glory, the massive orange feather-down parkas that made them look like a backup trio for some sort of ill-conceived citrus-themed song and dance troupe.

Delilah had personalized the ensemble by crowning herself with a hat that gave the impression her head was under attack by crazed wildlife. It was the sort of hat one used to see on Peter Jennings during one of those old "Live From Red Square" specials, except this one was much larger, fluffier, and, well, more pink.

Clarissa had brought her own sunglasses along as moral support and was sort of able to get around the sheer horror of the garb by pretending she was wearing a costume.

But Kate had not yet even recovered from the trauma of the previous night's cold-weather-gear issue responsible for saddling them all with these wearable atrocities. She kept wrinkling her nose and pulling the neck of her long underwear away from her body. "My god. Did they even wash these after the last season? Mark my words, one of us is going to end up with some sort of skin disease. Who knows what these people have been up to . . . and orange?! Who looks good in orange?"

Delilah shuffled closer to the exit as a wave of excitement compressed the line even more. "I'm with you," she said. "Frankly, I thought the clothes would have more of a Suzy Chapstick savoir faire."

Clarissa looked down at her gear and frowned. "I know what you mean. Do you remember that ad campaign the last time those shearling and suede jackets were in style?"

Delilah perked up. "I do, I do! Those models romping around in the snow in sherpa jackets, furry boots, and white lacy underwear? They were *so* pretty. That's exactly what I thought it would be like too."

"I don't feel attractive," Kate huffed. She pulled at the turtleneck again, looking faintly nauseous.

The sound of hydraulics doing, well, something different, sent an excited buzz through the passengers, all dressed in exactly the same way as the girls, with hats and sunglasses being the only true differentiators.

Suddenly, the plane's loadmaster reached forward and opened the door. Cold, white, bright light streamed into the plane.

All three of them instinctively gasped and reared back. Clarissa half expected a burst of triumphant religious music to start playing on a loudspeaker.

Kate took Delilah's hand, Delilah took Clarissa's hand, and they slowly trundled down the aisle toward the exit.

Cold became colder, white whiter, and bright even brighter as they stepped out onto the top of the rickety metal stairs and had their first look at the place that for the last month or so had been more a figment of their overactive creative imaginations than a real location.

Antarctica was cold enough to take Clarissa's breath away. It practically hurt. And the sun really was unbelievably strong, glancing off the whitish-bluish foreverness with a blinding force that made Clarissa want to say a small prayer of thanks for the extra-wide amber lenses Gucci had provided in last season's sunglasses models.

In spite of the jostling and jockeying going on in the plane behind them, the girls took their time. After all, Clarissa considered, one only comes to Antarctica for the first time . . . once.

As if to psych themselves up, Delilah adjusted her enormous hat with a firm hand, Kate threw off her parka hood altogether, and Clarissa clutched at her zipper.

"Keep it moving!" the loadmaster shouted, giving Clarissa a shove toward the doorway. She fell against Delilah and Kate and without further delay, they headed gingerly down the stairs in a line, like children on the way to the zoo.

At the bottom of the stairs, Clarissa looked out into the distance, across the vast, white landscape. It made her feel very, very small. Of course, the Kieran Debacle already had rendered her two sizes smaller than usual, at least inside, so small was a relative thing.

She licked her lips nervously. When it got right down to it, she might be in Antarctica, but she wasn't the sort of girl who would go to Antarctica. It was obvious she wasn't a good fit.

In fact, even as she stood there, she was probably sweating into her cashmere sweater and lord knew they didn't have a dry cleaners and she had only brought one large bottle of Woolite which she'd obviously have to ration carefully to deal with all the hand washables the three of them had brought down.

Clarissa took a gingerly step forward and her foot skidded. She looked down in puzzlement. The ground was tinged blue, hideously slippery in the bunny boots, and had the corrugated look of snow that had been tamped down by a ski resort grooming machine.

Delilah jabbed an elbow into her side. "Where are the penguins?" she asked in a disappointed voice.

Clarissa pointed to the ground. "Look. We're standing on the ocean. On the frozen ocean." She had just enough time for a last glance around her as a bullhorn-toting parka-wearing gal started herding them to the transport buses.

"What's that?" Kate suddenly said in a voice that meant trouble.

Clarissa looked closer, then reared back. Delilah and Kate looked again and did the same. Off in the not-far-enough distance next to a flag, some guy was peeing into the pristine white snow. He was whistling. Whistling and peeing. Right there.

The three girls looked at each other in horror.

Clarissa instinctively tightened her grip on their hands.

"Oh, dear," Delilah said, one eyebrow raised.

"Oh. My. God." Kate clutched her chest. "I am SO sure."

Chapter Seven

The three girls stood clustered outside the door while Clarissa fiddled with the key. Under the layers of issued clothing, her cashmere sweater was definitely, at this point, clinging to her like a small, damp animal.

Kate was practically dancing. "Hurry up, Clary. Let's see our new home." Delilah just watched, wide-eyed, with her hands clasped tightly in front of her.

One more jiggle and the latch clicked . . . the collective sucking in of breath as she swung open the door . . . and . . . and . . .

"Oh, my god. It's the Gulag Archipelago." Delilah barreled into the room and dropped her luggage in the middle of the floor.

Kate followed her in with Clarissa on her heels.

Three rickety metal bunk beds with wafer-thin mattresses in pale green plastic that looked like something one might find in a hospital in the Ukraine. Some mattress ticking–fabric pillows so flattened by continuous use and so greasy you could probably fold them down to the size of your palm and fry up a cheese sandwich. Three brown wool blankets that smelled like dog and smoke, and three pairs of mismatched sheets so transparent they could have been used in place of plastic wrap were it not for the issue of hygiene.

Delilah stared at the bunk beds with a horrified expression. "We are not alone," she intoned. "My incredible powers of deduction tell me that with six bed spaces and three people in the room at the moment, there may be three more coming." She looked around wildly. "They can't put anyone in with us."

"They wouldn't stuff six people in a tiny room like this, for god's sake," Kate said with an imperious snort.

"You make it sound like we belong in quarantine," Clarissa said with a weak laugh.

"We do belong in quarantine. We're new." At this point, Delilah was running to and fro examining everything in great detail with her enormous pink fur hat bobbing like a beacon in the dull gray ocean of the nearly empty room. "We haven't had time to build up the proper immunities. It's critical that we shouldn't be exposed to . . . to . . ."

"You are perfectly healthy." Kate folded her arms. "There's absolutely nothing wrong with you. We sat for six hours on a plane. Whatever was going to be exposed one way—or the other—has been."

All three of them contemplated that for a moment. Clarissa looked at her enormous white bunny boots and wondered if anyone was wishing they were back at home.

"Huddle," Kate said.

The three girls moved in close and slung their arms around each other's shoulders.

Even Kate looked shaken. But Clarissa knew that since the whole thing had really been her idea, she would do her best not to show it. In fact, any moment now, Kate would begin rallying the troops and putting together a game plan.

"Okay, we definitely need a game plan," Kate said.

"How about we get back on the plane and leave?" Clarissa suggested, only half joking.

Delilah looked like she was willing to entertain the notion, but Kate made it clear it was out of the question. "I am NOT going to fly back INTO San Francisco and have to explain to EVERYONE that we couldn't hack our big adventure as of day one. That's not an option. We're going to develop a plan and we're going to stick to it, and we're going to prove that we are just as good as everybody else here and that we have what it takes."

"Why?" Clarissa blurted out before she thought about what she was saying.

"I wish I'd thought of delving into that question in more detail earlier," Delilah said. "But then, I'd pictured it all more sorority-like and less Russian prison novel."

"You thought this was going to be like the sorority?" Clarissa asked in a slightly higher pitch than usual.

The huddle collapsed. Delilah put her hands on her hips. "Oh, don't start that with me, Clarissa. It wasn't an unreasonable assumption. I mean, *really.* You saw the same brochure I did. A dining area for group meals, seventies theme parties, a giant nonfat frozen yogurt machine . . . the recruiter even told me there would be a sing-along at Christmastime. We've been given the old bait and switch. It's like going to the Army recruitment center and they don't come right out and tell you you're going to have to wear the puce-colored trousers and get dirty!"

"You went to the Army recruitment center?" Clarissa asked. "*I* could have told you you should have gone Navy. They wear the most pristine white uni—"

"Ladies!" Kate stepped between them. "Focus, please. There's much to be gained by this experience. Much to be gained. Remember what we talked about? This is a growth opportunity, for all of us. We're going to go beyond our . . . our . . . stale, pathetic, yuppie existences and—"

Clarissa raised her hand.

"What?" Kate asked.

"Just because you got fired doesn't mean you need to go around and disown all those years, saying it was a pathetic, yuppie existence. It just means you got fired and feel bitter. But go on," Clarissa said politely.

"No, please. Continue."

"I think it's better just to be honest about our life experiences. I mean, I was dumped. It doesn't mean my relationship with Kieran was pathetic, it just means . . . it just means . . . oh, god, maybe it does." She flopped her head down in her hands.

"As I was saying," Kate continued. "We have big futures ahead of us. So let's get started."

Apparently making the bed was the first step in the big game plan. Clarissa and Delilah looked at each other, then followed suit.

"It's like prison," Delilah said with delight, as she unfolded a dingy gray sheet. "It's all so deliciously . . . unpleasant! I mean, I've always been curious to know what it would be like to suffer. There's something sort of romantic about it." Her open palms swept the air, as the far-off look in her eyes indicated she was just able to picture the Victorian charm of teatime at San Quentin.

"I'm not feeling the romance," Clarissa said morosely as she examined a faint rust-colored stain on her pillowcase.

It wasn't long before the bed-making segued to the luggage-unpacking, and within fifteen minutes, the gray blah of the room was dotted with splotches of color as the girls ran about setting things up, grabbing fistfuls of belongings out of suitcases, with glitter, fake fur, high heels, toiletries, and CDs flying through the air.

The sound of a female third party clearing her throat brought everything to a crashing halt as the girls swiveled around.

Clarissa nearly had a heart attack and she was sure Delilah and Kate were having a similar reaction, because one of them actually gulped and the other squeaked.

Three blondes hovered in the doorway in perfect V formation. It wasn't just that they were blondes. Or that there were three of them. Or that they were willowy and tall, but appeared to have Amazon-like strength. It was the kung-fu-Sandra-Bernhardt-sneer aura about them, a sort of we-could-crush-you-like-a-tin-can sensibility about them that Clarissa found a wee bit disconcerting.

The sinking feeling taking root in her insides only got stronger as the girls barreled into the room and dropped a pile of their own luggage on the floor.

While the wingmen looked around the room, the middle one turned and gave Delilah, Clarissa, and Kate all a long look up and down.

"Who—who are you?" Delilah asked.

"We're the Death Squad."

"The Death Squad?" Kate bleated out.

"Just kidding," said one of the wingmen, totally deadpan.

But as they say, it was out there.

A small pink feather wafted to the ground. The middle blond girl stopped it from flying up again with a thud of one muddy boot.

"She killed it," Delilah said in a very small voice.

Kate drew herself to her full height, which was still several inches shorter than the shortest Death Squad Girl, and with as much dignity as she could muster, looked the middle blonde square in the eye and said, "Unconscionable."

Clarissa cringed, but with that, it appeared that some sort of war had been declared. She had no choice. To demonstrate her solidarity, she lifted her chin. Delilah sneezed and Kate cleared her throat. And thusly they held their ground, wilted finery, bits of glitter and odd feathers, tufts of fur still bobbing a bit in the air, and all.

The Amazon Death Squad had returned to formation, now standing legs braced apart, arms folded over chests. Rather than the standard orange parkas and black bibs issued to everyone, they wore the dull brown "supplemental" parkas issued only to outside workers involved in some sort of labor.

On the right girl, two blond pigtails perched perkily high up on the side of her head. "Mindy," she said. The left girl had two braids poking out jauntily from under her earflap wool cap. "Emily." And the middle girl had dyed black streaks in her streaming platinum hair. "Bette."

Kate cleared her throat again. "Kate."

"Clarissa."

"Delilah."

They exchanged glances amongst themselves, and then with maximum disdain, Mindy murmured under her breath, "Ice Princesses."

"From Hell," Bette added solemnly.

Delilah clapped her hands in glee. "Oh, that's good!"

All five remaining girls looked at her like she was insane.

"That was an insult, Delilah," Clarissa explained.

"Sorry, I thought we were doing gangs . . . what? . . . It's a cute name."

Clarissa, for some reason, decided enough was enough. "I beg your pardon," she said politely to the ringleader. "But we've already been assigned to this room."

"We live here," Bette said.

"I beg your pardon?" Clarissa repeated, a little lamely this time.

"This is our room," the one on the right with adorable tiny little pigtails said abruptly.

"I'm afraid there's been some mistake," Kate said. "This is *our* room."

"We're your roommates."

"We don't have any roommates," Delilah said, obviously forgetting she'd pointed out the likelihood of roommates only half an hour prior. "There's obviously been some mistake."

Emily almost looked sympathetic. "Everybody has roommates."

"Mmm. It's not for everybody." Bette looked Clarissa up and down. "So, can I have your bed?"

"Excuse me?" Clarissa reared back in horror. "You may not have my bed. I'm very sorry."

"But you're packing up, already," Mindy said casually.

"Packing?" Clarissa repeated indignantly. "We're not *packing*. We're *un*packing."

Bette peered into Delilah's suitcase. She picked up a leopard print "just in case" negligee on the hook of her pinkie finger. "That's strange. It looks distinctly as if you were . . . *packing*. As if you just sort of stuffed your clothes in there in a hurry."

"I can't imagine why you would say that," Kate said, snatching the teddy back and handing it to Delilah.

"Well, it's either that or you're starting the South Pole's first gay disco," Emily said.

"We just got here, why would we be leaving?" Delilah asked.

"They're suggesting we can't hack it," Clarissa said with a maximum display of outrage, suddenly overwhelmed with the need to make it clear that she and her friends were not weak or incompetent in any of the ways these mean Death Squad Girls were implying. She lifted her chin. "I find that extremely offensive."

"Oh, my god," Delilah said to Kate. "What's gotten into Clarissa? She's so aggressive all of a sudden."

"Did I say anything about hacking it?" Bette said to Clarissa. "I'm just saying you shouldn't feel embarrassed if you decide to turn around and go home."

Clarissa started forward, got nervous on the way, and ended up smooshing the forward step into only a half step. "Who's embarrassed? Nobody's embarrassed. In fact, nobody's going home."

Bette shrugged. "Okay."

An uncomfortable pause descended over the room. "Clary, are you okay?" Delilah whispered. "You're so agitated."

Emily cocked her head to one side and sort of squinted through one eye at Clarissa. "Interesting."

Kate narrowed her eyes. "You be quiet."

"Feisty," muttered Bette with an appraising glance. "Which is good. But definitely out of their league, here."

"We're not out of our league!" Clarissa yelped. "I can't imagine what would make you assume such a thing."

All three blond heads swiveled to the sight of the glitter and high heels and feathers covering the floor and the beds.

"Oh, nothing," Mindy said.

Clarissa strained like an irate prisoner trying to throw off her jailers as Kate and Delilah each held her back by one arm.

"Look, we've got to go check in with the boss, so we'll unpack later. The good news is that our day off is Wednesdays. Maybe we'll barely run into each other. But it would be great if you could just move some of this . . ."—Bette dismissed the girls' precious belongings with a wave of her hand—". . . business out of the middle of the floor."

"Of course we will," Clarissa said, trying to muster up a little dignity. "Since we're just *unpacking*."

The Death Squad Girls took another moment to survey the damage, then just walked right back out the door.

Another long silence transpired.

Delilah and Kate looked at Clarissa. "Are you okay?" Kate asked.

Clarissa nodded and managed to smile. But she wasn't really okay. She felt like a fraud. Like an incompetent. She felt exactly like what the Death Squad Girls were implying. Because she believed they were right.

Chapter Eight

The Death Squad Girls were already gone by the time Clarissa, Kate, and Delilah finished showering the next morning.

In a brilliant stroke of foresight, Clarissa had spent some time prior to the trip mastering the art of fifteen-minute makeup application. She'd seen it in *Cosmopolitan* and had practiced it over and over until she really could do it as well as Charlize Theron in the example. She glanced at her watch. Judging from the quantity, duration, and speed of the spritzing, glopping, and plucking sounds coming from Delilah's corner, and the fact that Kate had only just begun reading her morning inspiration passage from her dog-eared copy of *The 7 Habits of Highly Effective People,* Clarissa figured she had about fifteen minutes before her friends would be ready.

"I'll be right back!" she shouted over the revving up of Delilah's hairdryer.

"K!" Kate shouted back.

Clarissa grabbed a map of the station, opened the door and stepped out into the hall, trying to ignore the pit-of-the-stomach feeling as she headed for the building exit. Sleep hadn't changed anything. Her aggressive behavior toward the Death Squad Girls was a symptom of the fact that she simply wasn't comfortable out here. And it had nothing to do with being forced to sleep on a green plastic mattress.

"What was I thinking?" she muttered almost angrily to herself. She was angry. And not irrationally so. They said you couldn't leave your problems behind, and it wasn't taking Clarissa long to find out that they were right. Your problems were the same whether you were in the northern or the southern hemisphere. They just rotated around you, adjusting location to wherever you were, like the earth around the sun.

She'd let the other two talk her into something as if it were a cure, a correction, a solution, an answer. It just wasn't that easy.

Sighing, she consulted her map and walked briskly down the main "street" toward the edge of town. Clarissa wasn't a small town girl. What the hell had she moved to a small town for? Was that all this really was? Was this Antarctica, the subject of so much interest and envy, nothing more than a sort of a larger Alaska? If so, what made any of them think something special could happen here?

Palmurdo Station was comprised of a series of long, rectangular, brown and olive green buildings. Aside from those that were used as work centers and science facilities, there was the gym, the bar, and the complex that contained both the administrative offices and the dining hall where she and Kate would be working. According to the map, Delilah was in another building which, Clarissa noted with well-suppressed amusement, required walking up a large snowy hill. The entire station was supposedly nestled at the bottom of an active volcano on a vast plateau of lava rock and snow.

Of course, the presence of the volcano didn't make her feel unsafe. Given how many scientists per square foot were living here, she figured that if they didn't have a problem with it, she shouldn't either. Besides, there were probably hundreds of ways to die out here. Hot lava was the least of her worries. Humiliation ranked a lot higher on her list.

And then more than the cold took her breath away. Poised on a smallish bluff was a signpost that read PALMURDO STATION, ROSS ISLAND, ANTARCTICA. And as one looked out into the distance, it was nothing short of spectacular.

A long, long stretch of flat, bordered in the distance by intermittent rocky mountain blobs of various shapes and sizes. White, so much white. The brown of the mountains. And the surprising accent of robin's-egg blue where cracks in the flat had tipped up slabs of ice showing off color-drenched cross sections. Little flags crisscrossed the snow, marking safe travelling routes in faded reds and greens. Well, that was helpful. If she just managed to stay within the flags, she'd be fine while she was here. She'd be perfectly safe.

Hmm . . . white, brown, red, green . . . robin's-egg blue.

Robin's-egg blue. Clarissa couldn't help but smile. If Kieran could see her now . . . well, he wouldn't believe it. And even if he did believe it, it would be all about how he had to help her along with everything. How he had to do everything for her because she wasn't doing anything right.

Well, just because she was used to following Kieran's lead, and just because the Amazon Death Squad had gone and made assumptions, didn't mean Clarissa was actually incapable of taking care of her own business out here. She'd simply have to figure out how to do things right on her own, take a leadership role in her own life. And that was what this adventure was all about anyway.

With a start, Clarissa realized she'd been gone for longer than "right back," and headed for the dorms. When she returned to the room Delilah and Kate were having a heated discussion.

Kate whirled around. "Good lord, we were about to mobilize a search-and-rescue team. I can't believe you just . . . you just . . . went *out* there without us."

"I'm perfectly fine." Clarissa held up her map. "It's a small-ish place, really."

"Clarissa, you know how you are," Kate said.

"I think you coddle me!" she blurted out. "And I'm not sure it's healthy anymore. You're . . . you're . . . enabling negative behaviors."

Delilah and Kate looked at each other. "I beg your pardon," Kate said, as she slipped into her parka. "Was there some sort of transition sentence I missed? Some segue? A connecting phrase, even?"

"Did we do something to her?" Delilah asked in a worried tone. "Is she blaming us for—"

"No, no! It's just that I'm beginning to think—" Clarissa sat with her hands gripping the rails of her bunkbed, thinking perhaps she was on the edge of some sort of epiphany, her mind racing. *I think I'm losing my mind. There's something clearly wrong with me but I don't know what it is. Kieran must have seen it, though. I'd really like to go back to bed right now. In San Francisco.*

"Clary?" Delilah asked, peering nervously into Clarissa's face. She looked at Kate with a frown. "Do you think it's the lack of oxygen?"

"We're at about the same elevation as Denver. If she wouldn't drop dead in Denver, she wouldn't drop dead here."

"Well, that's comforting," Delilah said cheerfully. "You're not going to die. That's a bit of good news!"

"Well, I think so," Kate said, slapping Clarissa on the back. "Let's go."

She and Delilah headed right past Clarissa out the door,

down the hall, and out the exit in a wave of perfume as she trailed after them.

"Oh, my god, it's bright," Delilah said.

Clarissa peeked under her sunglasses.

Delilah panicked. "Don't do that! The hole in the ozone will fry out your eyeballs."

Clarissa dropped her sunglasses back on her nose. "What? Who told you that?"

"I think I read it somewhere."

The girls headed for the orientation building, but it was slow going as Delilah's stilettos kept getting stuck in the snow. Finally she had to put one arm around each of the other two and hop across the ice on the balls of her shoes.

They walked on, just the sounds of Delilah squealing with each step and the crunch of snow under Kate's and Clarissa's designer cold-weather hiking boots (which Clarissa was beginning to realize bore no relationship to the kind of boots that were actually meant for hiking in cold weather).

A plume of white wafted up from their mouths as they breathed into the cold air. "Oh, my goodness, it's cold," Delilah said.

Kate tugged at the collar on her parka. "This isn't Palm Springs."

"I'm aware this isn't Palm Springs, thank you very much," Delilah snapped.

Two seconds later from Kate: "Oh, my GOD, it's cold."

Delilah snorted.

"We're in Antarctica," Clarissa said, with a wink. "It's a harsh continent."

"It's not really that harsh, is it?" Kate said, frowning up at the sky. "Maybe we're just overcommercialized, overmarketed, overeverything. Maybe it's us, and it's only in a relative sense that things seem harsher than they really are. Maybe we need to suffer more. Maybe we need to really know what it's like to be one with the . . . the masses, or whatever. Maybe we should have gone to India."

"Oh, lord," Clarissa muttered. "With all due respect, I don't feel up to suffering more."

"We'll just have to try to be Zen about it," Kate said authoritatively. "It will be much easier if we can just be one with the cold."

"You've never managed to be Zen in your life. You haven't an ounce of Zen in you. And if we don't walk a little faster, we *are* going to be ones with the colds. My nose is running already," Clarissa said.

"Are we there yet?" Delilah asked as she stumbled and had to right her hat which was taking over her face.

Kate stopped in her tracks. "I think this is it. Wait a minute. Are we lost? This can't be it. Where's that map?"

They stared up at the front of a long, brown Jamesway building.

Clarissa took the map from her parka pocket. "Here are the dorms all in a row—there's ours . . . and here's the dining hall, here's the post office, here's the wastewater treatment plant, the mechanics . . . the three bars, here, here, and here . . . and this is the main building. We're at the right spot."

Apparently orientation was to take place there, in the dining hall, whilst the previously oriented finished their institutional breakfast and read the morning gossip rag. The prison metaphor was becoming more and more apt.

"I'm having visions of grandeur," Kate said, as they settled into their seats for the presentation. "This is going to be big, for me. A big experience."

"What makes you say that?" Clarissa asked. Even from her orientation seat, she could see orange and green plastic trays with little cutouts on one end so four people could sit together at one small table with the noses of their little plastic trays pointing in and fitting everyone together like a orange, yellow, and green mosaic tribute to the Design School of Bad 1960s' Ski Cabin Decor.

"I'm already thinking revolution." She pointed to a glob of congealed cream of wheat sitting on a nearby tray. "Look at that. Just look at that."

Delilah and Clarissa looked, then winced.

"I'm going to revolutionize the institutional culinary experience."

"It needs it," Clarissa muttered.

Delilah took a long look around the room. "Kate's on to something. There's inspiration here. I can feel it. I don't know what it is yet, but I think my muse is here somewhere."

Clarissa managed a weak smile. She'd been hoping, of course, that her friends would reveal some similar internal struggle, some like reservations, some inherent discomfort with their new surroundings, any evidence whatsoever of even the smallest amount of panic that would put the three of them on equal ground rather than Clarissa always feeling . . . well, lesser.

Of course this feeling was not something she could possibly blame on Delilah and Kate. Any decent self-help book (there was such a thing, wasn't there?) would tell her that these feelings of inadequacy were something she was responsible for, something she conjured in herself, for herself, but somehow she was beginning to think that she was always projecting her behavior on to the other two. The more helpless and uncertain she behaved, the more they'd respond to that by amping up their own competencies. And the more Clarissa would sit back and feel rather sorry.

"Can I have your attention, please?" A short, balding man stepped to the front of the dining hall wearing the absolute latest in outdoor gear done up in shiny techno-fabric and impossibly tight ski pants which showed off way too much of his . . . package. It was horrifying. The three of them noticed it at once.

"You can see which side it's hanging down on," Kate hissed. "If an innocent bystander can tell which side—"

"Maybe they're not so innocent!" Clarissa snorted with glee.

"No, it means the pants are too tight. Do you think I should say something to him? I'm going to say something." Kate immediately raised her hand.

Clarissa grabbed it down. "Are you insane? You can't announce in front of the assembly that the speaker's member is too prominent."

Kate blinked. "Why on earth not? It's like having spinach in your teeth. I'd want to know. It's going to overshadow his announcement. Everyone will be staring."

"At you, maybe, if you say something! It's *not* like having spinach in your teeth. Believe me, he doesn't want to know."

The speaker dinged on a water glass. "We know you're all still tired from yesterday's flight and you have a long workday ahead of you. So I'm going to make this as quick as possible." He held up an empty plastic water bottle. "Antarctica is the driest place on the planet. It's dryer than the Sahara Desert . . ."

Kate gasped. Delilah nodded knowingly. "We'll definitely need to import more moisturizer. These poor, poor people."

". . . so, drink a lot of water or else your internal body organs will shut down and you'll die. Okay, next. Safety first. Do not run when outside. Do not go outside of the flagged areas. Do not wander off without checking in with the firehouse. If you fall into an ice crevasse, you're going to get cold. If you get too cold, we're talking hypothermia. And basically that means that your internal body organs will shut down and you'll die. Great. That's covered. Next. You may see some wildlife come into town . . ."

"'town'?" Kate hissed. "That definition pushes the boundaries of reasonable."

Clarissa shushed her.

". . . and as you know, harassment of wildlife is prohibited under the conditions of the International Antarctic Treaty. If the animal reacts to you in any way, it means that you're too close. If you are observed harassing wildlife, this means that we'll shut down your internal body organs for you and you'll die. Obviously, we will not lay claim to the kidneys and glands of grantees and other members of the scientific community working on projects with the animals out here. They would be the exception to that rule. In summary, safety first and keep your hands off the animals . . . or you die. Any questions? No? That's it, then. Have a nice day."

An odd moment transpired in which everyone wondered if they were supposed to applaud, and then the meeting simply dispersed and the newcomers were greeted by their clipboard-wielding supervisors.

"Clarissa Schneckberg?"

A pleasant-looking man stood behind her wearing just about the warmest smile she'd seen since she'd arrived. Clarissa heaved a sigh of relief. "Yes, I'm Clarissa."

"I'm your supervisor," he said. There was something so comforting about him. Something so gentle. He wore a white short-sleeved collared shirt, a clip-on tie, and khaki trousers with pleats that unfortunately accented his rather pronounced paunch. She could see his undershirt below the thin white fabric. His hair was receding and he wore small rectangular glasses. There was something a bit Bill Gates about him, although this man was clearly shorter and less wealthy. But there was nothing scary or creepy about him. He looked like the sort of older man who usually got handpicked by the network to fill the "father figure" slot on a reality TV show.

She looked up at him and gave him a genuinely bright smile. This was going to be fine. She was going to be fine! She would do her administrative duties, take things easy, treat it all like a vacation. They were always sending people away to the countryside in the old days to fix them up. Taking the air, they called it. Really, this was a brilliant idea. Fresh air—probably the freshest in the world—time to think away from the rat race and the evil specter of urban dating, or the specter of a lack thereof. It would be like a giant, no-stress, mental restoration event. Without any of the Frances Farmer–like unpleasantries.

Clarissa shook his hand. "I'm so pleased to meet you . . . Mr . . . ?"

He gave her another one of those really warm smiles, and extended his hand in a perfectly acceptable handshake—not too hard, not too limp—and Clarissa began to imagine him exactly as that sort of comforting father figure, a supplier of personal advice, even, if the place got too rough, or—

"Actually, I'd really prefer it if you could just refer to me in the third person as the Lord High Priest Demon of Vengeance."

Or not.

Clarissa stuttered for a moment without actually generating a word. "I'm Clarissa," she ended up repeating lamely. "It's great to meet you."

"So, just Clarissa, then?"

"Well, sometimes my friends call me 'Clary.'" *Or if you were really so inclined, you could call me Sweet Peaches of the Order of the Angry Goddess Lulu.*

"That's a lovely name," he said with his hands clasped angelically in front of him. He looked like he absolutely meant it. Totally sincere. "Why don't I show you your office."

Clarissa picked up her notepad and trailed after him out of the dining room and down the hall to a row of tiny rooms.

Everyone going Hollywood had to pay their dues. Clarissa

was more than willing to pay hers, and as she looked at the tiny office to which she'd been assigned, it appeared she was about to pay hers sooner rather than later.

He pulled out her chair for her and once she was seated, he sat down across from her. "I'm going to explain to you how things work. You see, I don't really . . . want to have to do anything."

He paused and seemed to be waiting for a response.

"Well, I'm here to facilitate things," she said, sounding chipper and enthusiastic, sort of like a soccer coach for seven-year-olds. Take it down just one notch.

"No, I don't mean that I want things easy. The thing is, I have my own interests. I don't really want any of this"—he gestured to the piles of paper on the desk—"at all. It's not really my bag."

"It's not your bag," Clarissa repeated, a smile frozen on her face.

He crossed one leg over the other and clasped his hands in his lap. "Right. I kind of feel like . . ." He frowned, really thinking about the words. "I feel like I'm just not all that interested in doing this anymore. So I've decided I'm just going leave it up to you. You're going to do a great job, Clarissa. I have one hundred percent confidence in you. Do you have any questions?"

"Are you leaving the continent?" Clarissa asked, hoping it didn't sound too rude. But then, it was a little rude to have everything dumped in her lap in the first place.

"No, I think I'm just going to stay in my room and play Lethal Death Strike Three."

"I see. Well . . . that's great. That's . . . I'm really happy for you, Lord . . . High . . . Priest . . ."

"Demon of Vengeance," he prompted.

Clarissa cleared her throat, crossed her ankles, and very politely repeated, "Demon of Vengeance."

He smiled back at her and then . . . silence.

"Are you going to be okay in your room by yourself?" Clarissa asked pleasantly.

"Yeah. This, um, this whole business . . ."—he gestured to the office—". . . this just doesn't really suit me. I'm going to plug my computer into the Net and stay online for a while. That just feels right for me. And that's what I'm going to do."

He smiled at Clarissa.

Clarissa smiled back and pulled her collar away from her throat. "So, um, what exactly is it I'm meant to do?"

He leaned forward. "You've got to get this documentary off the ground. Talk to Lenny and Squiggy. They're targeting PBS, and we want them to come away from here with a piece that's going to do justice to the organization. Something that will really make us shine."

"Okay. So, where might I find this, um, Lenny and Squigg—"

"Everything's right here. What you need to know. They're going to need direction, leadership. I understand that you have an interest in the entertainment industry. Well, think of yourself as executive producer." He pushed a single piece of paper containing a short bulleted list across the desk. "This project will be your only responsibility for the season. Here's a list of station phone numbers."

"There's nothing else I need?" Clarissa asked.

"Well, they'll teach you everything else at Snow Survival School. You'll go next week."

"Snow Survival School? Nobody really mentioned anything about that." She shifted uneasily. "Will, um . . . will I be going outside a lot?"

He thought about that for a long time. "Yeah. Yeah, I think you will."

"Oh!" Clarissa squeaked.

"So that's it. And I think I'm going to go to my room now. And I'm not planning to show up to work again. So, I'll see you around. Maybe the dining hall."

He got up, wrestled himself into a thick navy blazer, and walked out.

Clarissa sat there on the verge of panic for a moment, staring at the exit from the dining hall. Some people might have been excited by the prospect of playing what was essentially a producer role on a major documentary theoretically slated for PBS.

She *should* have been excited. She should have been elated. Because her chance to prove everything had just been handed to her on a silver platter. And now she had to deliver and she had no idea how to go about it. She'd imagined she'd be one of a staff, working according to memo requests and e-mailed instructions, basically executing someone else's plans like she always did.

Well, there was nothing to be done now. Except sit at her desk and look busy and knowledgeable while she waited for Lenny and Squiggy to show up.

Chapter Nine

When Clarissa dragged herself through the door, she found Kate in bed with the sheets pulled up to her chin and something strange on her head. Delilah was sitting on a ratty couch that looked suspiciously similar to one that used to be in the second floor lounge. One hand covered half her face as she stared glumly up at Clarissa.

"Oh, dear," Clarissa said.

Kate turned her head and blinked at her, then went back to staring intently at the springs in the top bunk.

A giant ethereal mess of yellow safety tape, some camouflage netting, a roll of PVC, a toolbox, some plastic goggles and a canister of WD-40 indicated that the Amazon Death Squad episode was not a group hallucination.

If Clarissa wanted a shoulder to lean on—or cry on—and a sympathetic ear focused entirely on her, she would probably have been better off hunting down the station nurse.

"Are you okay, Kate?"

"I'm fine," she said gruffly.

Clarissa looked at Delilah, who answered with only a half-hearted shrug.

"Maybe you were right all along," Kate blurted out. "Maybe we don't belong here."

Clarissa shrank back into the couch. In spite of her lousy day, in spite of her own misgivings, she simply wasn't certain whether she wanted to agree with that statement or not. Odd. She would have thought she'd be sighing with relief and helping Kate pull out the suitcases. Most likely she didn't want to be a quitter. Again.

Kate had gone silent once more, still clutching the covers up around her.

"Kate?"

"Yes?"

"You're really acting peculiar."

"I've had a difficult day." Her voice seemed thick. "In fact, I have something I really should just come out and tell you."

Clarissa quickly sat forward.

"We had a situation. Another run-in with the Amazon Death Squad. They made it clear to me that we weren't wanted here."

Kate had a way of being preemptively abrasive; it wasn't impossible that she'd driven the members of the Death Squad to that point. "I see. Are you sure that's what they really thought? Or did you, you know, sort of put words in their mouths?"

That didn't go over so well. "Excuse me? I didn't wheedle, cajole, or goad anybody into thinking or saying anything. They barged in, fussed about, and ultimately insulted me when I . . . when I . . ."

"When you?"

"When I revealed my dismay over a certain thing. They called me a prima donna. Me!"

"Oh, dear."

Kate whipped her head around and gaped at Clarissa. "'Oh, dear'? This is bigger than 'oh, dear.' This is a conspiracy against our kind. I'm beginning to suspect we were hired for sport.

These people are trying to prove us unworthy, incompetent, UNFIT. They mean to run us out!"

"I'm sure we were not hired just for sport. I mean, it was expensive to even fly us out here. But I will agree with you that perhaps expectations were not set as well as they could have been." She turned and looked at Delilah. "You're awfully quiet. Were you here?"

Delilah nodded. "And I've had an absolute shocker of a day, myself, to boot."

Kate turned woeful eyes on her but didn't say a word. Something about her expression told Clarissa that maybe, just maybe, Kate's trauma wasn't really about the Death Squad Girls. Not really. Kate looked way too emotional for it to be the result of some territorial dispute involving outdoorswomen. "What exactly happened?"

Kate's voice wobbled as she spoke. "They stole Delilah's moisturizer and now we're all paying the price."

Clarissa frowned. "Okay, let's not start accusing people. How do you know they stole it?"

"It's hard to *misplace* a four-gallon jug of moisturizer," Delilah pointed out.

"I know you didn't take it," Kate added. "And we certainly didn't take it."

"Maybe they just borrowed it. Maybe we've given them an interest in proper skin care procedures and they couldn't help themselves. I'm sure there's a reasonable explanation. Why don't we just talk to them and see if this can be cleared up?"

"It's gone beyond that," Kate said. "As I said, we had a situation."

There was no such thing as a good situation. Or a neutral situation. A situation was inherently bad.

Clarissa rubbed her forehead, trying to muster up the extra patience she suspected she was going to require in order to make it through this conversation. "Let me get this straight. We're still upset about these girls being our roommates."

"Yes."

"Because they're competent."

"Yes."

"Outdoorsy."

"Yes."

"They seem to hate us as much as we hate them."

"Yes."

"And worst of all, they're unexpectedly good-looking."

"Yes!" Kate said. "Do you understand what this means?"

"They're tall, they're blond, and they can weld."

"Yes! I knew you'd understand."

"Aside from this business of insufficient moisturizer, what exactly is our beef here?" Clarissa asked.

"I think they may be starting some sort of smear campaign against us," Kate said, going unstable all over again. "I tried to tell them not to hate us because we're beautiful, but it only seemed to fan the flames of hatred."

Clarissa's jaw dropped. "You told three blond girls who can weld not to hate us because we're beautiful? Oh, god. What else?"

"Well, they're aggressive." Kate pulled a notebook out from under the covers and flipped it open, careful not to let the covers sag away from her chin. "And due to the nature of this blatant act of kleptomania, I've taken steps to . . ."

Delilah let loose with a giggle at this point. Clarissa managed to suppress hers, but Kate didn't seem to notice. She kept talking, even held up a hand-drawn map of the station where she'd marked possible Death Squad strongholds. Both bars and the weight room had huge Xs on them.

"So, we must use cunning," Kate was saying. "We must appeal to our strengths. You see how it is. If they go military/cargo, we must go feathers and glitter. An equal but opposite show of force to neutralize their offensive. I'm also thinking we should move the furniture around, create some sort of barricade between the two sides."

Delilah looked fairly alarmed. "I'm not sure that's a good idea."

Clarissa agreed. She looked at Kate. "Don't you think that sort of, er, separatist policy will only alienate these girls further?"

Delilah nodded. "I think Clarissa is right. Prejudice and hate are born of misunderstanding and lack of communication."

"Thanks for the input, Gandhi," Kate said.

"Why don't we just invite them to the bar and buy them some beer?" Clarissa asked. "We can clear everything up and that will be that."

Kate slapped her forehead. "You weren't there when they ganged up on me. It's too late to engage in talks. What we've got here is an . . . an . . . uprising. I swear to god, I wanted to do something, but what were we to do? These girls are twice my size. Maybe Delilah could have taken them on, but I think she was worried about chipping a nail."

"Well, Clarissa's the blonde of the group," Delilah said. "Maybe she can find some common ground with them."

Clarissa sighed. Something just wasn't adding up. The overwrought reaction to the Death Squad Girls bespoke of much deeper things. Clarissa turned back to Delilah. "Um, do you feel like talking at all?"

Delilah moistened her lips and gestured glumly to her face with her free hand. "I get here and within a matter of days, I've totally degenerated. I'm like a scab, a walking lesion. I finally understand why they have such a large fire department here. I'm like kindling."

"Did you know that the Antarctic is actually dryer than the Sahara Desert?" Kate asked rather unnecessarily.

"Let me see what's going on under there," Clarissa said, trying to get a peek under Delilah's hand. "I'm sure you're exaggerating."

Delilah shook her head. "Here I am, so dry that I'm at risk for spontaneous combustion. And yet there is one part of me that seems to be sucking up all possible grease and moisture from the rest of my body."

"Move your hand away and let me see. It can't be that bad."

At last, Delilah moved her hand away to reveal an enormous pimple, of a circumference and breadth Clarissa would have to admit she had not seen before. "Wow."

Delilah whimpered and prodded the pimple. "Please, *please* go away," she pleaded desperately to the offending bump. She looked at Clarissa, her voice on the edge of tears. "I can't take it. I'm not emotionally equipped to handle this. I may have to stay away from work until I'm cured . . . oh god, what if it's indefinitely unresponsive?"

"You have a zit, not a terminal disease," Kate muttered.

Clarissa looked at Kate in surprise, then put her arm around Delilah's shoulders. "Are you sure it's the pimple that's bothering you?"

"It's the pimple," Delilah said, glaring at Kate.

"Are you sure?" Clarissa asked, definitely suspicious at this point.

Delilah darted a quick glance at Kate. She cleared her throat. "Oh, well, Kate was just referring to a little mix-up at work. I've been reassigned to a position of less authority, if you can believe it. But I'm sure it will be good for me. You know, free up extra brain cells to think about makeup."

Clarissa patted her back. "I'm so sorry, Delilah. I know it's a shock, this less-responsibility business, but you'll get used to it. You might even enjoy it."

Her sympathy seemed to undo Delilah a little bit. Her friend crumpled and confessed. "Oh, it's more than that! I was using the Internet the other day, and I went to the company Web site, and I saw that the new Loralline line is out. It's all glittering and girlie . . . and, oh, it's so delicious! I mean, not as delicious, of course, as the ones *I* had full control over, but really good stuff. And it's the first line where I had only marginal input."

Delilah started to get a little watery at this point; Clarissa reached over the side of the couch and ripped a length of toilet paper off the roll they'd been using for tissue. "Well, you should feel very, very proud of yourself for what you've accomplished," she said, dabbing gently under Delilah's eyes to control the mascara that had begun to run.

"Then why do I just feel like I've lost a part of myself? And if I miss it all so much, why can't I come up with anything new so I can start over?"

"It will come."

"I don't know." Delilah sighed. "Maybe I've just used up all my good ideas. Maybe I should just do something else. It's not as if I didn't make a success of it. I did what I originally set out to do, and maybe it's time I turn to something else."

"But you love what you do. Would you really be happy without it?"

"I don't know."

"Maybe you're putting so much pressure on yourself that you're stifling your creativity."

Delilah shrugged sadly. "I've lost the muse." She put her palm up to block off any further discussion. "I don't quite think I can discuss this anymore today."

"I understand." Clarissa turned back and gave Kate a long look, then got up and walked over to the bed.

She cocked her head and focused on the gauzy business on Kate's head and the likely source of her friend's trauma suddenly dawned on her. "Get out of bed, Kate."

"I can't!"

"You can. It can't be that bad."

"It can! You'll laugh . . . Oh . . . fine!" Kate closed her eyes as if to steel herself, threw back the covers and leaped to her feet, fully clothed in . . . in—

"Sweet Jesus." Clarissa couldn't help it; she recoiled.

"Nobody's laughing," Delilah said, leaping up for a better view, in a suddenly better mood than just moments earlier.

Clarissa successfully suppressed a chuckle, but Kate could see where things were going. She held out her arms and turned in a slow circle. "Go ahead and laugh. Just go ahead and get it all out of your system. Yes, it's true, ladies . . ." She drew herself up to her most outraged height and brought home the kicker: "I've been issued a *uniform.*"

She said the word "uniform" in a hissing breath accompanied by the kind of exaggerated lip movements she used to gossip about acquaintances who'd contracted some unpleasant disease or slept with their sister's boyfriend.

Clarissa's jaw dropped as the odor of partially hydrogenated oils and processed lunch meat wafted off Kate's garb. "Oh, my *god!*" That really was more than any girl should have to put up with. She didn't blame Kate in the least for being so upset. But it would be more helpful to make her feel better about it than to reconfirm that it really was horrible.

Clarissa stroked her chin as she assessed the damage. It was really that bad. That could not be denied. But she did her best to be objective about it. "Let's all please try to remain calm. Okay, um, let's process this. What I'm seeing is Hot Dog on a Stick meets Ralph Lauren."

Delilah nodded her agreement.

"But I don't know what to say about that business on your head . . . is that a . . . good lord, that's not a do-rag is it?"

"My goodness, Clary, I had no idea you were so street," Delilah said in a tone of clear admiration.

Kate rolled her eyes. "If she were 'so street' she would know this in no way resembles a do-rag. She's probably been dying to use that word in a complete sentence for months now. And thanks, Clary, I knew I could count on you for support."

Delilah reached over and patted Kate on what had now clearly revealed itself to be an enormous swath of a gauzy-looking hairnet that seemed part hospital wear, part toxic waste prevention. "It's really not that bad. We're not going to laugh at you."

"I really don't understand why you don't get to wear one of those cute double-breasted sous-chef jackets like the other sous-chefs," Clarissa said. "Have you asked them about it?"

"Of course," Kate said in a clipped tone. "And besides, like Delilah, I've come to realize that the job requires just a bit less responsibility than I'm used to. Just a bit, though! The thing is, unfortunately, you see, they've . . . well, they've run out of sous-chef uniforms . . . at my level."

"Oh, dear," Clarissa said. "How very . . . odd."

Kate's shoulders slumped a little farther. "The word I'd use is 'wrong.' This is just wrong in so many ways. Can you believe the hairnet?"

"No," Delilah and Clarissa chorused in unison.

"I *know*. When you consider what they put in that food, it's insulting to think that they are concerned that *my* hair is going to taint anything. And you think the hairnet is bad," Kate said glumly. "Did you take a gander at the shoes?"

Clarissa looked down, had enough of a gander that when she opened her mouth to speak nothing came out.

Delilah looked closer and registered an equally strong measure of shock. "Are those orthopedic shoes?"

"Okay, let's just get it all over with. It's not fair that I'm in the only occupation that requires a uniform, but there you go. Obviously, it's some Larger Being's way of trying to make me a stronger person. So am I going to run off to human resources and quit simply because I'm being forced to wear MC Hammer pants, a polo shirt, orthopedic shoes, and a hairnet? No. No, I'm not. Because I'm here for a reason. I'm here to learn about myself as a person and hit adversity head-on."

Clarissa went ahead and made the mistake of trying to lighten the mood by saying, "I thought you were here to get a good piece of ass."

Wrong thing to say.

Kate glared at her. "Do I LOOK like I'm going to get ANY SORT of ass? I'd be lucky to get SUB-PAR ass with this getup."

Clarissa opened her mouth, intending to make nice, but Kate jumped the gun. "Don't mock me, Clarissa. I'm not in the mood."

"Nobody's mocking."

"Hmph."

Clarissa tried, but she couldn't help it. Kate would have done the same. "Okay, I'm mocking. But in the nicest possible way. Besides, orthopedic shoes aren't exactly what I would call extreme adversity. There's a kid with headgear out there somewhere taking exception to your representation."

Suddenly, Kate's mouth twitched and she looked like she might conceivably burst into tears, which would, of course, have been totally outrageous.

Clarissa ran forward to pat, pet, and soothe. "There, there. I was just kidding. Orthopedic shoes are absolutely just as bad as headgear, we promise. You have every right to be upset. I'm sorry I hurt your feelings. If it's any consolation, the eighties are back. The eighties are in . . . no, no, I see, it's no consolation whatsoever. Of course not."

Of course, why Kate insisted on wearing her uniform after hours was beyond Clarissa. Perhaps she wanted to acclimate. Perhaps she was operating under the principle that multiple exposures would render the ensemble less potent in its ability to offend.

"Hey!" Delilah wheeled around. "You know what's funny? Clarissa suddenly has more responsibility and we have—"

"Really cush jobs," Kate blurted out, interrupting Delilah with a fairly transparent Meaningful Look.

"What's with the look?" Clarissa asked.

"Nothing," Kate said. "We just don't want to gloat. You know. Since this is all new for you, this extra responsibility, it's probably going to be a lot of hard work. It seems inappropriate to . . . gloat over a cush job."

"Oh. Well, that's very considerate of you," Clarissa said. "It is going to be a challenge. The thing is that while I've always liked the idea of working behind the scenes in the film industry, I don't really know what anyone actually does."

"What do you mean you don't know what anyone does?" Delilah asked. "You rent so many DVDs! Surely—"

"It's not the same. If it really gets down to it, I'm basically unqualified for film jobs."

"You're not unqualified," Kate said indignantly. "You're just wrongly qualified. But that can be fixed. Besides, it's your boss's job to point you in the right direction."

"I don't really have a boss, per se."

"Well, the filmmakers you'll be helping must have some idea of what they need done."

"Yeah. And I'm sure they'll be very nice. They'll help you. And you're so sweet they'll give you references even if you mess up."

Clarissa managed a weak smile. Just barely.

Chapter Ten

"'You know we're goin' to the YyyyyyMCA. The YyyyyyMCA.' Dudda-d-DUH . . . Dudda-d-DUH . . .'"

Clarissa froze, her hands suspended over her keyboard as two men wearing baseball caps and brightly colored nylon parachute pants suddenly entered the room, still singing.

Lenny. And Squiggy. There was no question in Clarissa's mind.

Thank goodness they hadn't caught her twiddling her thumbs waiting for them all afternoon. She'd cleaned her desk, made coffee, surfed the Net, and essentially did everything she used to do in her cubicle in her office building in her boring life back home. This could have been any cubicle in any office in any life in the world. The possibility that she'd come all this way only to realize that nothing had changed had been dogging her all day.

Needless to say, Lenny and Squiggy's arrival was something of a relief. Not to mention something of a scaled-down two-person production number.

Taking big steps and bending at the knees, the two men bobbed a bit before each step while they sang. When one stood up, the other bobbed down. All this included jazz hands, shoulder shimmies, and some Sir Mix-a-Lot ass-bouncing, the latter of which Clarissa could have particularly done without.

They assembled around Clarissa's desk on a final high note they really should not have attempted, and removed the Robert McKee–logo messenger bags strapped diagonally across their backs.

"Gotta make an entrance, eh? I'm Lenny," said the blond, snapping his fingers and pointing to Clarissa in a bastardized Sinatra sort of way.

"Squiggy," said the dark-haired guy, pointing to his chest with his thumb.

"Lenny and Squiggy," Clarissa repeated with a straight face.

"That's all you gotta know," Lenny explained. "We've branded ourselves, sort of like Madonna. Just Lenny and Squiggy. It really works. People seem to remember us."

They leaned so close over her desk she thought she might go into convulsions on the strength of Squiggy's Drakkar Noir alone. Forced back in the recesses of her chair—which unfortunately wasn't far enough—Clarissa cowered while they crouched down on either side of her.

"Okay, so, we're really psyched you're finally here. That dude wasn't happening for us, you know. Your boss? Yeah, um, not so much."

"He seems very sweet," Clarissa said diplomatically.

"Right, right. Very sweet. Especially for a demon of vengeance," Lenny said, rather more sarcastically than Clarissa thought warranted under the circumstances. But then, she hadn't really had a chance to get to know her boss, and it didn't look like she was going to.

One more chorus ensued of what Clarissa could only imagine was some sort of theme song, and then the boys went immediately into pitch mode.

"Very people-oriented. People, right? Big picture . . ." His hands went up as if framing a far-off piece of art.

"Big picture," Squiggy echoed.

"It's a harsh continent." Lenny looked at Clarissa. "You still with me?"

She smiled politely. "Absolutely."

"A harsh continent. And . . . and things . . . well, things go on. Right?"

"Uh-huh."

"Right, so what we want to do is to really capture the flavor, if you will, the flavor of the Antarctic experience here on-station. You get what I'm saying. Big picture, the flavor." He made a fist and shook it to emphasize the intensity of it all. "The *flavor.*"

"The flavor," Clarissa agreed.

"The flavor," Squiggy repeated, totally unnecessarily. Lenny gave him an impatient look and Clarissa felt an odd sort of sympathy for poor Squigg.

"We're looking for, say, six to ten major segments," Lenny was saying. "We'll start editing once we get some footage together, and then wham, HBO, PBS, you name it, we're there. And you'll be there too! We're ready to start filming anytime. So, if you could get subjects for the segments locked down, that would be great. I've got a lead on a segment with the greenhouse, and we've shot some material out at the airstrip, but other than that, it's all you."

Clarissa started to breathe a little easier. Here was a little more direction. "So, you want me to . . . book some filming opportunities."

"Exactly," Squiggy said.

"All science?"

"Oh, no. We want a cross section. A variety. And some, you know, eye candy," Lenny explained.

"Eye candy."

"Some visual excitement," Squiggy explained. "You know. Get us some . . . some . . ."

Lenny belched loudly and said, "Some *ass.*"

Squiggy looked a little apologetic. "Well, not all of it should be ass. Just *some* ass." He swiveled around and had a look at Clarissa behind the desk, his expression indicating that he wasn't unimpressed with what he saw.

"Ass." Clarissa beamed enthusiastically. "Absolutely."

"Terrific. We've got this guy, Mitchell Kipling. He's the instructor for Snow Survival School. He's available to escort us into any areas of questionable safety."

"I know him. I'll sync up with him," Clarissa said authoritatively, a little unnerved both by the phrase "questionable safety" and by the fact that they seemed to know so much more about what she should be doing and setting things up than she did.

"Fan-damn-tastic! We'll see you tomorrow morning, then," Squiggy said. He tipped an imaginary fedora to her and the two men were out the door.

Clarissa cranked up the Web browser, waited for the impossibly slow connection to show signs of life, and proceeded to Google "Lenny and Squiggy," actually coming up with an entry, a bio from a Hollywood e-zine put out some years prior.

This job might just really be the start of something. A whole new direction, a whole new career. With "Lenny and Squiggy" as references and a documentary with producing credits, she might just launch herself farther than she'd even imagined on the first try alone. Clarissa started to feel almost ebullient about it all. Eagerly she clicked through the screens.

"Lenny and Squiggy" established a private television production company in 1998. They produced pilots for 32 shows in the last decade, all considered "unique" and "original" and "laughable," but have

so far been unable to secure a contract for additional episodes.

Prior to the partnership, Lenny worked on the acclaimed Sundance Film Festival grand prize winner, Fellini Ate My Truffaut. *Unfortunately, he walked off the set in a alienating rage after only the second week of production and was unable to capitalize on the success enjoyed by the film's other production principals, who all received multimillion dollar film budgets and new homes in Beverly Hills.*

Lenny is an aficionado of the art-house film and his work has been described in the highly complimentary terms, "pretentious, needy, and obscurely obtuse."

Squiggy worked in craft service on a series of important slasher films including the underground blockbuster Halloween Night of Living Horror in the Haunted House on Elm Street.

Squiggy's work has been described as "fresh," "well-conceived," and "low-carbohydrate."

Clarissa put her head in her hands on the desk. "I think I need a drink."

Chapter Eleven

"I t doesn't even say 'bar,'" Clarissa noted as she stared up at the building and tucked the map away.

Kate elbowed between them and pushed open the heavy wooden door. A huge cloud of smoke burst free. All three girls reared back in horror. "Do you think we should turn back?"

Delilah wrapped a curl of hair around her index finger. "Maybe we should. I mean, I haven't actually seen a cigarette up close since nineteen eighty-nine. Smoke is hell on the complexion. Have you ever seen Rene Russo in person? She looks, like, a hundred years old!"

The three of them looked at each other, Kate chewing on her lip, Delilah nervously running her hand over her cheek . . . Clarissa suddenly felt an odd need to assert her newly minted leadership qualities as if to prove they really existed. She just squared her shoulders and walked through the door with the other two quickly following behind her.

They sidled up to the bar and Clarissa had a look around while Kate ordered up three rum and Cokes. The place was decorated in U.S. Navy meets Fish and Chips Restaurant, with the ubiquitous foosball and billiards tables, the dartboard, the photographs of hearty young men in uniform (always a plus), and other random memorabilia from when the military had run the station as a base in decades gone by. On primitive wooden shelving sat rusty tin cans with peeling labels that looked so cute and retro one could almost forget they were really old, possibly explosive, canned food. Clarissa thought of the can of curried tongue she'd bought at the auction. How long ago it seemed.

The crowd at the bar was varied, to say the least. Clarissa's eyes went first to the center of the room, where the Amazon Death Squad sat blithely playing poker with some equally hearty-looking guys.

The place was packed with guys, in fact. Guys who looked young enough, and dressed appropriately enough, for a rave. Guys who looked old enough to have to have relied on nepotism to pass the medical requirements to get here. Guys who looked like hippies, guys who looked like doctors, guys wearing gym shorts and T-shirts from the basketball league, guys wearing striped red-and-white tube socks from the bowling league. Guys wearing stained shirts from the ceramics room, and guys wearing grease from the auto shop.

There were sleepy-looking old guys with trucker caps and flannel shirts hunched over their drinks at the bar. There were outdoorsy guys in the latest gear, and firefighters in T-shirts that proudly identified them as, well, firefighters.

There were members of the kitchen staff still wearing stained chef's jackets. There were scientists in loafers and university logo sweatshirts crowded around laptops.

Guys. Guys. Guys. It was almost Total Male Overload.

And suddenly, it seemed like the entire room noticed they were there.

"Is that buzzing in my ears the sound of testosterone ramping up?" Kate asked.

"I think it's the can opener behind the bar," Clarissa said.

"Everyone's watching us," Delilah hissed. "Fantastic!"

"Glasses up, please!" Kate said loudly, swinging her drink up wildly in the air. "Here's to a successful mission!"

"Cheers!" Clarissa said, feeling a little self-conscious.

Delilah lifted her drink as well and they gulped in solidarity.

"Well, what do you think?" Kate said, looking around openly as if they'd all ordered steak and it was time to pick out their respective cows.

"I think I'm overwhelmed," Clarissa murmured under her breath. There were men everywhere. This had nothing to do with her leadership qualities and everything to do with suddenly wondering if it was simply too soon to be out and about as a newly single woman.

"I actually see people I recognize from the plane!" Delilah squealed with delight. "And from work. We know people!"

"We don't know bupkis," Clarissa muttered.

"I wouldn't mind a fling," Kate said, her eyes darting from one possible candidate to the next. "And Clarissa, I think getting right back into the game would be good for you. You might consider even two flings, just to take care of that inevitable rebound business."

"Two flings?" Clarissa shook her head. "I'm a lousy slut."

Kate looked back at her and giggled. "Oh, right. Maybe just one."

"You know I've tried," Clarissa said, giggling along with her. "But I just keep accidentally having long-term relationships!"

"Maybe you haven't tried hard enough," Delilah suggested, downing her drink and finding another one in its place courtesy of the fellow sitting next to her before she'd even finished raising her finger to alert the bartender. "Oh, thank you," she said, nudging Clarissa as if to say, "Look how easy this is!"

"Besides," Clarissa said, nearly choking on her own drink, "I don't think that getting a reputation for being known as 'the girl in Antarctica who sleeps around' would do much for my self-esteem."

"Mmm. Point. You're probably right," Kate said. "I think it's just this being surrounded by so much . . . prey that has me getting ahead of myself . . . yes, you're definitely right. Because this is real life, and real life is gossip, and bad reputations, and people telling other people 'how last night went.'"

Delilah nodded. "Yeah, I think it's best to find one person with whom to have a fabulous, passionate fling."

"Which means that it would not be wise to choose a subject precipitately," Kate said. "You can't go for the first guy who shows interest."

"Absolutely not. Big mistake. Especially you, Clarissa," Delilah chimed in. "You know how you always regret it."

Given that Clarissa had been with Kieran for years, the term "always" seemed a bit odd. But she *was* regretting it. So maybe she was "always" regretting . . . it. And the meet-cute with Kieran at a financial district newspaper kiosk *was* a sort of first-guy-who-shows-interest scenario. Clarissa's cheerfulness flagged a little, and she quickly pushed thoughts of regret and "always" and Kieran and jumping on the first guy who showed interest out of her head in order to concentrate on enjoying the evening.

"You are absolutely right," Clarissa said. "As I have found more than once in my dating history, it is common to develop a huge crush on a guy early in a situation only to find two weeks later that you can hardly stand the sight of him, not to mention the sound and smell. So, we should make a stipulation. No kissing *anybody* for at least three week."

"And no drunk first encounters," Kate added, clearly beginning to get drunk. "Mmm. Clarissa, I think you have quite a point. Really, when you get down to it, there aren't going to be that many to choose from when you take away the married ones, the ones who are ugly or smell worse than average, and the ones who are boring." She waved her drink in the air, gesturing to the bar population. "It brings the eligibility percentage right down."

"Hey, there's that scuba diver who sat next to me on the plane," Delilah said. "I think he's got his eye on you, Kate."

Kate's head shot around. "Oh! He's hot."

Clarissa and Delilah looked at each other and started laughing.

Kate's first impression had been correct. The guy was . . . hot. Except for one problem. It seemed that tonight, at least, he had come straight to the bar in some sort of specialized cold-water scuba-suit long underwear, a beige one-piece suit with extra woolly fur on the ass and knee sections. That, and his giant white rubber bunny boots.

Kate studied him with the keen eye of a connoisseur. "I'm not sure I quite understand what he has on. Although, if it weren't for that . . . that getup . . . oh, what the hell."

Delilah snorted. "He's wearing Garanimals or something."

Kate winced at the term. "They're not Garanimals. They're some sort of fish-larvae scientist-diver-person cold-water long underwear used in pursuit of scientific excellence."

"Kate."

"Mmm?"

"The guy is wearing the equivalent of footie pajamas. In public," Clarissa stressed.

"Do you think they'd be better in private?" Kate asked with mock innocence.

Delilah laughed into her drink. "I don't know, but I will say that if you can wear footie pajamas in public, well, you can do anything."

Clarissa wheeled around and looked at her. "You know, Delilah, I think you're right about that."

Delilah made a clucking noise as she assessed the situation. "Although . . . having said that . . . I just don't know. The bottom line is that the man is wearing a *onesie*."

"You couldn't sleep with a guy who wore footie pajamas?" Kate asked.

Clarissa grinned. "It's hard to say. Depends on the guy. And the pajamas. Although I really have to say that he's carrying them off admirably. Someone who can wear footie pajamas in public *can* probably do just about anything. Maybe I should get a pair."

"I think I see something." Delilah had fixed her gaze on one of the firefighters who sat with his almost identical T-shirt-wearing fellow firefighters in a clique over by the pool table.

"Out of the question," Clarissa said. "They don't even look legal."

"You know you're old when you have to worry about the legal age of your sexual partners," Delilah said.

Kate gave her a look. "We've been that old for many years, now. It's more a question of a meeting of the minds."

"Oh, do you think they're dumb?" Delilah asked.

"That's not what I mea—"

"Because I've always fantasized about a big, dumb, hot . . ." Delilah was already getting a little drunk, because she'd kind of bent at the knees a bit, wobbling on her high heels as she mimicked grabbing firefighter ass.

"Good lord. Delilah, everybody is looking at you," Clarissa whispered.

She shot upright, delighted. "Really?"

"Really." Not that it should have been surprising. The girls were decked for an evening out. Clarissa had on a pink miniskirt with matching pink shearling boots. The fitted white T-shirt she wore didn't exactly keep her warm, but that problem was handled by a heavy white feather-trimmed jacket.

White was always so impractical, but she'd found it on sale at Loehmann's and Kate and Delilah had convinced her that it was just the sort of thing that would look really excellent while frolicking in the snow with boys.

Delilah was temporarily fixated on the idea of using "dirt" as the inspiration for her new line, so she'd dressed completely in neutrals to see if it triggered any ideas. She wore tan suede pants with impossibly high-heeled brown leather boots with pointed toes, and a lacy, cream-colored top with a low neckline. There was something very Indian Squaw meets Victoria's Secret about the look, and she somehow managed to carry it off.

Kate had covered herself from head to toe in black with the exception of a few yellow, white, and red striping accents and was going for a motocross-babe look complete with tiny rhinestone barrettes in the shape of NASCAR autos.

"Okay, incoming," Kate muttered, as the fish-larvae diver-scientist person headed in their direction. "Act normal."

"So, uh, how was work? Are you feeling better about it?" Clarissa asked, trying to act normal.

Her question was met by pointed silence from both parties. Surprised, she gave the girls her full attention, looking from Delilah to Kate. "Was it okay?"

"It was fine," Kate said super-cheerily, then turned away as Garanimal reached her and gestured toward the bar behind them and the two melted away to secure a new drink.

Delilah and Clarissa made a point of not watching them, playing it cool. "Mine was fine too," Delilah said quickly. "But it would be much more interesting to hear about yours. Do you have a better sense of what you'll be doing?"

Clarissa frowned. She knew a hedge when she heard one. Her friends were both probably still torqued by the less-responsibility thing. In her opinion, being Sous-Chef, Level I instead of Sous-Chef, Level II wasn't such a bad thing. And since Delilah was a horrible driver, it seemed that things would be much less stressful for her if she didn't have to drive at all.

"You don't have to talk about it if it's unpleasant," Delilah said.

"Oh, no! It's fine. I met the two guys I'll be working with for the rest of the season, Lenny and Squiggy, and they're just . . . so . . . L.A. I'm responsible for helping identify and develop segments for this cable documentary, and I have to make sure that I handle all of the logistics and make sure that the filmmakers get where they need to be . . ."

At this point, Clarissa was reminded that she didn't really know what else the job entailed, which in turn reminded her that she didn't really know what she was doing. She tossed back the rest of her drink and tried to sound more enthusiastic than desperate when she blurted out, "And stuff like that."

"That sounds easy enough," Delilah said. "So, you're okay with that level of responsibility, then?"

Clarissa felt inexplicably annoyed by that statement. She knew that Delilah hadn't meant it in any put-down sort of way, but it bothered her nonetheless. Perhaps because it implied that she was perilously close to being in over her head.

As a sort of preemptive strike or perhaps merely to convince herself, she went on. "Well, it's not necessarily easy to wrangle things like that. And it's super important that this documentary comes out fabulous, because it's basically all I'll have on my résumé to show for real, participatory experience in some sort of cinematic venture. This is really going to put my leadership skills to good use."

Delilah tore her gaze away from the firefighter and looked Clarissa square in the eyes. "That's exactly what Kate and I think." She suddenly hugged Clarissa in a drunk-sorority-girl-after-the-big-boyfriend-drama-at-the-party sort of way, an almost defiant, going-into-battle look in her eye when she pulled away. "Good for you, Clarissa. Good for you. It's just what Kate and I wanted for you."

"Gee . . . thanks, Delilah." At this point, Clarissa was smelling a plot, a plan, some sort of hijinks in the air. Just a faint whiff of it, but she'd known Kate and Delilah long enough to be suspicious.

Unfortunately, her thoughts on that score were derailed as Mitchell Kipling—the very Mitchell Kipling who had landed her in this situation in the first place—waved at her from across the room.

Letting bygones be bygones, and since she'd thought she wanted the job in the first place, she waved back. He crossed the bar, looking attractive in that same vaguely unkempt and outdoorsy sort of way, and Clarissa's heart rate actually sped up for a moment.

He looked like the sort of guy you'd want to wake up to on a camping trip, assuming you wanted to wake up on a camping trip at all. Yes, the sort of guy who'd hold a tin mug of steaming coffee with a shot of whiskey at five in the morning as he watched the sun rise over a lake in Minnesota.

Really, the thing was, she didn't want to be interested. It was too soon. It was too . . . much. She wasn't even sure she really felt like having a fling, wasn't positive she was up to the task. It wasn't clear she had enough emotional cycles left to spin what with handling the end of a long-term relationship and the pressure of performing at a job that required more proactive behavior at work than she'd ever had to display in all of her past job experience combined.

Clarissa simply wasn't a proactive sort of person. Not everyone was; and did they all have to be? Who was left to follow if everyone insisted on leading? What on earth would poor Delilah and Kate do in such a world, with everyone jostling and jockeying for supremacy all at once? Why, Clarissa's reticence was almost a public service to the rest of the world. Maybe she could think of it as a sort of contribution to group dynamics and team harmony.

Delilah hip-checked her, nearly spilling both their drinks. "Don't be so obvious," she hissed. "You're staring."

"Worry about your own love life," Clarissa hissed back, hip-checking Delilah back in place as Mitchell finally made it through the crowd.

"I may not have anything to worry about," Delilah said as her firefighter stood up from the table and waggled his barely legal fingers at her.

Mitchell raised his glass and smiled, drawing Clarissa's attention back. She looked down and smiled shyly into her drink. Part of her didn't want to deal with it; part of her knew that if she indulged she'd experience an uptick in self-esteem. She sighed. That wouldn't be so bad, would it?

"How you getting along, Clarissa? Is it what you'd expected?" he asked, suddenly in front of her.

"I'm great. It's great," she said.

"I hear you're going to be one of my pupils at the next Snow Survival School."

"Yeah," Clarissa said. "I think so."

"Great! I'm really looking forward to it," he said, and smiled. Clarissa smiled back.

They smiled at each other.

Smiles all around.

This wasn't so hard. She'd find love again someday. See, she'd been apart from Kieran a mere matter of months and she already had new interest. And she hadn't had to do much to get it either. She was still lovable. Good god, what a relief. She looked up and fed him a huge, perky smile that she meant every bit of.

He studied her, then studied the label on his beer bottle. "Well, it might get bad, but it'll get better."

Clarissa felt her smile fall down a notch. "What do you mean?"

"Just what I said." He gestured casually with his beer bottle. "You'll cry or whatever and then you'll get over it and you'll probably enjoy the experience."

"I'll *cry*? One doesn't make a nonchalant gesture in the air and tell a girl that she's going to cry without explaining why. Are you planning to make me cry?"

He unveiled a slow, easy grin. "Not if I can help it."

"Thanks! So, what do you do off The Ice?" she asked, quickly changing the subject.

"I'm an outdoor adventure guide. You know, kayaking trips, rappelling, camping."

"Oh."

He raised an eyebrow. "You don't know, do you?"

"No," she said matter-of-factly with a big smile. "Not at all."

"Do you have a boyfriend?" he asked.

Clarissa blurted out a laugh. "Well, get right to the point. No, I do not have a boyfriend."

Mitchell laughed and took a swig of beer. He glanced up and as Clarissa's gaze locked with his, he reached over to her drink and very deliberately stole her little red cocktail straw and stuck it in his mouth. He chewed slowly on the tip.

"That's hard to believe."

"Sweet talker."

"I'm just the talker, you're the sweet."

"Oh, please. Quit while you're ahead."

"Am I ahead?" He gave her one of those slow, Southern grins, the Dennis Quaid kind that she could imagine one might get while perched on the back of some sort of John Deere machinery with a picnic basket and a gingham tablecloth in one's lap, perhaps even singing a two-part harmony of "Surrey with the Fringe on Top."

"So, what happened with your boyfriend?"

"He dumped me for somebody else." She shrugged carelessly. "Better shoes. You know, the usual."

"Are you kidding? He dumped you?"

"I know, I know," she said with a don't-care wave of her hand. "He was clearly off his rocker."

They smiled at each other, and Mitchell leaned forward in the way those people who like to debate issues do, and said, "So it's his fault, you're saying?"

Clarissa felt her smile falter. "Well, yeah . . . it *was* his fault," she said. "He left me for his platonic friend, you see. He went where one doesn't go."

Mitchell nodded as if he found this all very interesting. And it occurred to Clarissa that perhaps he actually *did* find it very interesting. That it wasn't an act. That he wasn't trying to impress her.

"I'm not defending it," he said, "but women don't seem to realize that they're always blaming the men for relationship disasters."

"Do go on." She was now working harder than usual to keep some semblance of a smile on her face.

"Well, when a relationship doesn't work out, the woman always blames the guy, regardless of who calls it off. The guy doesn't blame anyone—it just 'didn't work out.'"

He'd met his match. Two could play this game. Clarissa gestured broadly with her plastic cup. "And you see this as evidence of male superiority? The fact that men prefer to ascribe failure to something vague instead of digging down and figuring out exactly what went wrong?"

"I said nothing of male superiority," he said with amusement. "Though an argument could be made. No, I see it as evidence that women and men have completely different brains."

"I don't know what kind of control group you were using in

whatever experiment you were running, but I see it as evidence that not all men *have* brains." She was definitely getting drunk, and slightly belligerent. She suddenly stuck her drink up in the air. "No! No, wait a minute. I'm not being fair, am I? You may have a point. Perhaps it *is* better explained by the fact that men have different brains. More simplistic brains, men's brains. Which does make it hard to blame them for their own stupidity."

He leaned over on the bar, right up next to her ear. "I'm just kidding, Clarissa. The guy was a real bastard to dump you, however you look at it." He actually chucked her gently under the chin. "Oh, and if you just need someone to talk to, you know, about that crying thing, well, I'm happy to be that guy." And with that, Mitchell Kipling tipped his baseball cap and disappeared into the bar scene.

Clarissa stared after him, horrified. After all, she'd ranted and lurched like a drunk, baggage-laden harpy. She might as well have screamed out that she wasn't over Kieran yet. How unappealing. On the other hand, she probably should have been annoyed by the implication that she was headed for some sort of nervous breakdown. Some sort of inevitable, inescapable crying jag—what did he know? Instead she found herself swept up in a flash fantasy of riding between the rows of corn on a farm somewhere, as she snuggled against Mitchell on the back of his dirt bike.

"How did it go?"

Clarissa turned around to face Delilah. She swallowed hard. "I acted out."

"What do you mean?"

"I mean I acted out. I don't think it's fatal or anything. But I think I'm experiencing trauma byproduct from the Kieran Debacle. I'm going to bed." She put her cup down on the counter and looked around for Kate.

"Well, I'll go with you. I've been hit on so many times I think I've got bruises," Delilah said, grinning. She looked over her shoulder. "Kate, you coming to—"

"Good god," Clarissa and Delilah blurted out simultaneously.

Clarissa raised an eyebrow. "It's like making out with a mascot."

"That's the nicest thing you can say about it," Delilah said, as she tapped Kate on the back.

Kate looked over her shoulder, pink lipstick smeared all over the lower quadrant of her face. An equal amount of pink lipstick was smeared all over the lower quadrant of the Garanimal-wearing fish-larvae diver's face. Both of them looked slightly dazed.

The girls gave her the signal. Kate said something to the Garanimal and followed them to the door.

"Did you find your muse?" Kate asked Delilah.

"No, but it looks like you found your moose."

Clarissa and Delilah dissolved into hysterical laughter, Kate choking and spluttering as the last of her rum and Coke went up her nose. She tossed the empty plastic cup in a bin and the three of them stumbled out of the bar, immediately disoriented by the bright sunshine.

All three of them stepped forward in opposite directions. Then noticed the other two hadn't followed. Then collided as they stepped back toward each other.

Clarissa suddenly stopped short. "Do you realize where we are?"

Kate stopped short too, swaying somewhat more than the rest of them.

Delilah obviously had no choice, since Kate needed support on both sides.

Clarissa stared off into the distance at the mountains. "Sometimes I can imagine, with those mountains, that I'm just in Lake Tahoe, and that I can go home anytime. Sometimes I look up and I focus on the miles and miles of flat, and I realize this is definitely not Lake Tahoe."

"S' very deep, Clary," Delilah said sincerely. "Sometimes I look up and think, all this space to breathe and all this space to think, and yet I can't come up with one decent idea for eye shadow."

Clarissa contemplated that, noting that robin's-egg blue was a perfectly reasonable color for next spring. But it was probably more complicated than that. "It will come. I look up and I think something different every single time. So I think eventually it will just come to you. It's almost like a sounding board, this place."

"Like a person," Kate said, oddly serious all of the sudden.

"Maybe he or she will tell me something, then," Delilah said. "Maybe one day I'll wake up and this place will just hand over one brilliant idea."

They stood there, staring out at the icy landscape, almost unconscious of the cold. Until Clarissa could no longer feel her big toes, anyway. At which point she linked arms with the other two and managed to Laverne-and-Shirley them as a group all the way back to the dorm.

Kate fell face-first on the bed and immediately began to snore.

Delilah went through a twenty-minute skin care regimen in front of the mirror with a remarkably steady hand and climbed into bed with a pleased sigh.

Clarissa didn't have the heart to tell her she'd just given her reflection rather than her face a really thorough spa treatment.

The room was dark and silent for approximately six seconds. Suddenly, Delilah blurted out, "Is anybody else having Girl Scout Camp flashbacks?"

Kate's only response was a heavy wheeze.

"I don't recall being able to hear anyone having sex in the next cabin over at Girl Scout Camp," Clarissa said.

"Good point, good point."

Silence.

"Clarissa, wake up."

"I never fell asleep."

"Wake up," Delilah repeated urgently.

Clarissa sat bolt upright. "What's the matter?"

"I don't think we brought enough moisturizer."

"Excuse me?"

"I don't think we brought enough moisturizer."

It occurred to her to mention that they were definitely not going to have enough moisturizer if she used half of it on the mirror, but it was much too late to embark on the sort of conversation a comment like that would spawn. "Can we discuss an emergency skin care plan in the morning?"

"Sorry, it's just that I can feel my skin turning already."

"We can order some stuff online tomorrow and have it flown in. Okay? Good night."

"Good night."

Silence.

"Clarissa, are you still awake?"

Clarissa tossed her arm over her eyes and mumbled, "Yes."

"Have you seen my flip-flops? The one with the yellow daisies on top?" Delilah asked. "I so don't want to contract a foot fungus. I really don't."

"We can look for them tomorrow."

"Okay. Good night."

Silence.

"You know, I *like* men who wear footie pajamas. It shows a certain lack of self-consciousness. Footie pajamas imply a comfortableness with the self," Delilah noted, garbling the pronunciation of "comfortableness."

"Indeed," Clarissa said politely.

"I wish I were going with you to Snow Survival School. I bet there's inspiration there."

"I wish you were going too." Clarissa sighed. "I'm not hoping for inspiration so much as survival."

"It's going to be great. I bet you'll end up loving it. By the way, the Amazon Death Squad is going to be there with you."

Clarissa's eyes flew open. "No way! What a nightmare . . . they might do something to me. I mean, Kate's been ranting since we arrived about how the ADS are a soul-sucking, self-esteem-killing trio from hell."

"Oh, you always get along with people better than she does. You'll be fine." Delilah suddenly began snoring like a banshee.

Clarissa stared at the metal slats that held up the top of the bunk bed and wondered if she was really going to make it to the end of all this.

You're not going to get me down, Antarctica. You're not going to beat me. This is my big chance. This is where I show my stuff. I can be a leader. I can stand on my own. I'm not even sure I need anchors anymore!

She made a fist under her covers and shook it for emphasis in the darkness. "You go, Clarissa," she whispered. "You can be a footie pajama sort of person, too, you know. You . . . you . . . you show them all you've got . . . *moxie!*"

And then she made a mental note to wipe moisturizer off the mirror first thing in the morning and finally fell asleep.

Chapter Twelve

"Moxie" feels different when one is drunk and lying in one's warm bed than when one is standing in a semi-circle in the middle of Antarctica with the Amazon Death Squad, surrounded by a network of those death-inducing ice crevasses, and no bed in sight. Clarissa had just learned this lesson and was concentrating hard on not losing her nerve.

The participants in this escapade stood in their cold-weather gear in a circle eyeing each other. This was where she could begin to find her inner adventurer. This was where she could build some confidence. This was where she could prove that she was more than just an aimless, unworthy dumpee.

There was a lot at stake here. A guy to impress, her own self-respect, her ability to perform under the watchful glare of the Amazon Death Squad, AKA Emily, Mindy and Bette; in fact, she had the entire stereotype to break down. Stiletto-wearing, adorable-handbag-toting girls throughout the United States were depending on her!

"Do we all know why we are here?" Mitchell asked the assembled group of participants for Snow Camp Emergency Training.

Clarissa pondered the question, making a point not to make eye contact with the three Death Squad members lest she be psyched out before she'd even begun.

Here she was out on the tundra: flat white all around, with glaciers and mountains and volcanoes in the distance. A couple of hut-type structures dotted the landscape.

A shuttle had dropped them off with some food supplies next to a lonely little shed containing an assortment of tents and tools.

Clarissa took comfort in the fact that with all this gear on, her fellow participants would not be able to make snap judgments about her level of competence based on the fact that she wore, say, glitter eye shadow or strappy high heels back at home base. That, of course, did not prevent her from making snap judgments about everybody else.

Clarissa took the opportunity to eye and assess the other participants. Aside from the Amazon Death Squad, there was a couple wearing amber-colored parkas that signified they'd be moving on to a different research station who looked a) oddly similar to each other and b) had twin cases of the worst bedhead Clarissa had ever seen, so much so that it hardly seemed possible that it wasn't on purpose. There was a woman with a flattop who looked ready to kill somebody. Other than that, she seemed really friendly.

There was a squirrelly little guy who stood with his arms crossed with an air of self-confidence that was both surprising and impressive given his rather alarming bad looks. Clarissa couldn't tell much about his body, which might have been spectacular for all she knew.

There was Clarissa, of course, who hoped she was not projecting "Terminally Incompetent Yuppie From Hell." At least not to those who hadn't met her yet.

There was a guy with a redhead Afro that the others called 'Vegie.' Whatever the peculiar smell was, wafting over from the opposite side of the circle, it was most likely coming from him.

And then there was Mitchell, who looked like something from a "Hot Mountaineers of America" calendar.

Mitchell was clearly in his element. He stood tall, proud in his cool, non–standard issue gear. He took a deep breath through his nose and exhaled, looking very much as though he loved the smell of napalm in the morning.

Clarissa and Emily looked at each other wide-eyed, and Emily let loose a low whistle. "The Robert Duvall of it all," she whispered.

Clarissa nodded, put her hand on her heart and echoed reverently, "The *Robert Duvall* of it all."

"Gortex cowboy," Squirrelly Boy muttered, clearly disgruntled.

"You know what they say about men with big noses," Mindy said.

Clarissa snickered knowingly and felt irrationally pleased she'd bonded, even if it was with members of the Death Squad, and even though she could only assume that what people said about men with big noses was the same thing they said about men with big feet and hands.

Mitchell cleared his throat. "Anyone? Do we know why we are here?"

Everyone shuffled a bit and flapped their arms against the cold.

Clarissa raised her hand for a little clarification. "Do you mean right now, or in the abstract?"

Nine pairs of eyes glanced over at her, looked down, looked up . . . and looked away.

Clarissa quickly tucked her hand back into her pocket and

willed herself to be as small as humanly possible, such that she might actually just up and disappear.

Christ, it was cold. In truth, she wasn't exactly sure what made her qualified to handle this degree of cold. As a native Californian, her closest brush with cold was when she'd stood in a meat locker for two hours at ten below zero counting frozen Chinese pot stickers for an accounting class during college. Now she was the dumpling.

Mitchell walked over to the supply shed and swung open the double doors. He handed each participant a paper bag. "Okay, we're ready for the first exercise in our survival training course," he said. "Everyone except Clarissa and Vegie, go ahead and get in two single-file lines . . . great . . . now put the bags over your heads."

Clarissa looked at Mitchell in terror. What was he thinking? Was this his idea of special treatment? Or was it the opposite? "I'm sorry . . . um, Mitchell, why am I not in a line? And why don't I get to wear a bag over my head?"

"You're better looking than those guys," he joked, elbowing her. "No, seriously. You two are the team leaders."

"Oh, no. I don't think so." She backed away a few steps, starting to panic, thoughts of empowerment and the importance of appearing competent vanishing. "I'm not management material. I'm a team player, a bag wearer, if you will. I work best in groups. You know . . . in collaboration."

Mitchell put his arm around her and rubbed her shoulder vigorously. "You'll do fine. It's good to get you out of your comfort zone."

He was smiling. There seemed to be no evidence of malice . . . what the hell comfort zone was he talking about? Her pinkies were numb and she was sweating violently under the giant parka.

"Okay, Clarissa and Vegie, take a look around you. You'll

see a couple of flags out in the distance. Your task is to lead your blind team members to the flag. They have to trust you, just as they would have to trust a leader in a whiteout situation. Make sure you don't go outside of the perimeter of our campsite. If you do, you might just lead your entire group into a particularly nasty ice crevasse, and believe me, we don't want that."

No, we certainly don't, thought Clarissa, licking her lips nervously.

"So, team members, take the hand of the person in front of you . . . and *trust* them to take you where you need to go."

She took Mindy's hand, gritted her teeth, and headed off to her flag with true purpose, even instigating a sort of drill instructor "Left-right, left-right" to prevent everyone from slowing things down with the blindman shuffle. The flag in her sights, she looked over her shoulder, noting that Vegie was almost to his flag, off in the distance. She picked up the pace on her chanting, and the group responded.

She'd done it! She wasn't a loser after all! She was as outdoorsy as Vegie, and she smelled better, too.

Or did she.

Actually, something smelled odd, and since Vegie was over yonder, she couldn't quite place its provenance.

The team started to grumble about it and everyone took their bags off.

"Oh, my god," Mindy said, in disbelief.

The other members started to laugh.

"What?" Clarissa asked, bewildered. "What's wrong?"

Mitchell came running over, the funniest look on his face, like he was trying desperately not to laugh at her. "Clarissa, I don't even know what to say."

Clarissa suddenly noticed everyone staring down at the ground. She was afraid to look . . .

"The red flag, Clarissa," he choked out. "I meant the red flag." Mitchell pointed at a red flag flapping merrily about ten meters away.

Slowly, very slowly, she looked down at the snow only to discover that the snow was as yellow as . . . the flag around which they all stood. She felt the color drain out of her face. She'd led them to the pee flag. Oh, dear god.

"Hey, no big deal," Mitchell said, his stoic façade crumbling and a burst of laughter piercing the air. Hardly able to get the words out, he added, "No, really, it's good you brought it up. I'd almost forgotten to point it out to you all."

Clarissa stared at Mitchell in horror, trying to calculate how she was supposed to feel about it all, about him. And then she realized that the only possible recourse was to laugh at herself. Dying inside, she burst out in peals of fake laughter. "I'm such an idiot! Oh, my goodness, I'm so sorry, you all!" Heh-heh, heh-heh. Heh. Hah. Ugh.

"Seriously, it's no big deal." He reached over and tugged at both sides of Clarissa's hat, establishing a sort of intimacy (relative to instructor/participant, anyway) that almost made Clarissa forgive him for putting her in this mess in the first place. At least he was showing favoritism, for god's sake. He wasn't pretending one thing in private and one thing in public. At least there was that.

Mindy had to ruin the moment by producing an enormous, put-out sigh of disgust. "No big deal to you, maybe." And then she began to literally distance herself from Clarissa as if she wanted to make it completely clear that just because they were the girliest of the bunch, they were not *friends* by any stretch of the imagination.

Like a mass exodus, everyone else likewise slowly backed away from Clarissa, off the yellow snow.

"Since we're here," Mitchell said, "this might be a good time to recommend that before going to bed you wait until the very last minute and then go for the Big Pee."

"The Big Pee." Uh-huh.

Everyone else nodded wisely as if they knew all about the Big Pee.

"You want to wait just as long as you can until you can't hold it any more and then go for the Biggest, Longest Pee ever. The Master Pee." Mitchell was actually enjoying this bit. He was reveling in it, as men seemed to do often when speaking of bodily functions.

Clarissa tried to control her eyebrow, tried to prevent it from elevating as he went on and on, but old habits die hard, and there it went.

"I'll be happy to show you how to use a funnel," Flattop Killer said, nudging Clarissa. "The trick is to get a good seal. You can share mine."

"Ew," Mindy said.

Clarissa's sentiments exactly, but it was a friendly offer from the friendliest person in the bunch. "Thanks. Um, maybe some other time."

The next task was to prepare a variety of sleeping options. They circled around the giant pile of belongings they'd brought with them. Mitchell handed out shovels and they began to cover their stuff with snow. Clarissa began to hallucinate that she was part of some sort of chain gang, but she was being paid, so it wasn't really that bad. No, this was more like digging for a mass burial.

It had warmed up substantially and was, by most opinions, a "nice day." By Clarissa's estimation, that would make it something like thirty degrees above freezing. Due to the warm weather, Vegie decided it would be appropriate to remove his shirt.

Which he did, and accordingly, the entire group simultaneously reared back in horror.

"What, is he housing a pair of dead hamsters in his armpits?" Bette muttered.

Clarissa realized that determining the direction of the wind was actually a fairly important survival technique.

Squirrelly Boy had no such qualms. "Jesus, Veg, how can you stink already? We haven't done anything yet."

"We haven't?" Clarissa asked weakly. They hadn't done anything yet? They'd built a snow cave, which involved more snow shoveling than Clarissa had cumulatively done in her entire life to date which, compared to the shoveling everyone else was doing, was fairly inconsequential. And it didn't go unnoticed. Squirrelly Boy leaned on his shovel. "Uh, Clarissa, why don't you drag one of those supply sleds over here. I'll finish shoveling this side."

Clarissa enthusiastically surrendered her shovel and went over to the sleds. She put one of the straps diagonally over her shoulder and tried to channel the spirit of a Clydesdale workhorse. The sled didn't budge.

The rest of the team looked at her in silence. Finally, Vegie scratched his left hamster and said, "Clarissa, I bet you're a really good cook."

And with that, she was banished to the kitchen. Or the snow trench they'd declared the kitchen, anyway. Brilliant. A brilliant idea to hand the most incompetent member of the team matches and a flammable substance. But at least it was a manageable sort of thing with a clear-cut goal. While the rest of them finished striking tents and crafting trenches that looked like horrible little claustrophobic graves, all she had to do was keep the water hot, keep the fire burning.

Keep the fire burning. Four words, easy to remember . . . maybe this really was her calling. "Keep the fire burning," she hummed to herself, mentally adding a funk track. She poked at the pot to keep it upright on the rickety burner. This was fun.

Everybody had their strengths. Hers was fire. She was doing just fine.

"Keeeeep the fire buuurning, baaaybbbeeeeeeee."

Clarissa looked over. Mitchell was doing a bit of air guitar with the snow shovel. He grinned, then went back to work.

Clarissa suddenly felt better. Like she belonged.

There was room for all kinds of people here. Obviously they needed girlie girls as much as outdoorsy types. There were all kinds of people in this world. All kinds. If everyone were the same, how boring would that be?

The pot finally managed to muster up a bubble or two, and within half an hour, Clarissa had found her calling, passing out sporks and packets of dehydrated soup and ladling water into the envelopes. It had all the romance and glamour of battlefield operations, with Clarissa imagining herself as a sort of cold-weather Florence Nightingale, ministering to the troops.

Finally, she took her own soup and sat down next to Vegie, who seemed to have a lot of space on either side of him. Vegie pointed to her packet and said, "One trick is to zip the envelope back up and put the soup in your bib pocket . . . helps you keep warm while you're waiting for it to rehydrate."

"Thanks," she said, grateful to be bonding with someone, anyone at last, and did as he suggested.

"Did everyone get a couple of chocolate bars?" the instructor asked. "If you want to stay warm, you got to keep eating, right? So, make sure you take a couple of chocolate bars from the ration bag to bed with you, and if you wake up in the middle of the night and you're cold, go ahead and eat one."

They sat around the cluster of tiny camping stoves which held giant pots of boiling water and spooned rehydrated meal packets into their mouths. Clarissa felt substantially less tired, dirty, humiliated, and stupid than she had earlier, but it was all still a lot for one day. And she couldn't help the fact that "What was I thinking?" and "What am I doing here?" kept popping into her head.

She sighed and contemplated her spork. Some people just weren't hardwired for . . . for . . . igloo-building, dry ration–eating sorts of days.

No, that wasn't the right attitude, now was it. *I'm game. I'm a team player. I have a positive mental attitude. Can do.* In fact, it wasn't even so cold anymore. She was already starting to warm up.

"Clarissa, is that soup running down your leg or are you just happy to pee here?"

Clarissa looked down at the curry soup pooling in the snow around her ankles, slumped against the ice wall they'd built bordering the "kitchen," and prayed that a small but dedicated penguin would drag her off to feed its young.

She wasn't used to feeling incompetent. At home, she didn't bungle about like this. At home, she was smart and accomplished and pretty and men actually liked her (in varying degrees) and her friends and family said she was a catch. So there. Here she was a catch more like "catch of the day" or "to catch a disease."

It took a while to recover from the disaster. And only after she retreated to her tent for the night, gnawing on one of her chocolate bar, did she have time to really contemplate what it all meant.

She'd brought it upon herself. She'd set herself up for the fall. *I'm not cut out for this sort of thing. I'm not meant for bigger things. I'm meant for a nice, focused, small-scale life . . . the sort of life I was supposed to have with Kieran. Maybe Kieran dumping me didn't mean I was meant for something bigger and better . . . maybe it just meant that Kieran dumped me.*

Luckily for her, thinks looked better in the morning. Well,

she was feeling about as haggard and unwashed as it was possible to feel, but things definitely looked better. Perhaps with the exception of the fact that the Big Pee apparently hadn't been big enough, and it was obvious that it would not be possible to wait for the shuttle back to town where she could take advantage of the privacy.

It was still early when she stepped out to the pee flag. She had no idea what the actual time was, but it seemed early enough—and was quiet enough—that she thought she could drop trou without anyone around to see her ass hanging out in the wind.

She jogged quickly to the pee flag and proceeded to get down to business. "Ha-ha! I'm in Antarctica with my ass hanging out in the wind! Look at me!" She shook her fist at the sky. "I am woman, hear me roar!" She finished peeing, cackled triumphantly, and then headed back to camp to pack, her spirits high.

Her tentmate had already dressed and vacated the premises, which had Clarissa worried whether or not she was expected to have cranked up the stoves for boiling water prior to everyone else waking up. She quickly looked around under her pillow and sleeping bag for the chocolate bar she'd slept with last night, thinking it would be a better breakfast than whatever it was possible to rehydrate. But it was gone; her tent mate must have eaten it in the middle of the night. Great.

She clambered out of the tent and almost ran straight into Mitchell, who'd leaned down to knock on the side.

"Good morning, Clarissa," he said.

"It *is* a good morning."

"Listen, before everyone gets together for the morning class, I wanted to pull you aside."

"Yes?" she asked, with ill-concealed dread.

"No, no, no. It's nothing bad. It's just that when we do the timed camp setup exercise later, I want you to pretend to be dehydrated and disoriented."

"I beg your pardon?"

"It's a test to see if the other team members are looking out for each other. In a survival situation, it's important that everyone be aware of any strange behavior—it may be a sign of hypothermia."

"Um, couldn't I just be a team member?" Clarissa pleaded.

"No, it's part of the drill. Just go out there and wander around . . . you know, like you're a little crazy."

"I'm sorry, you want me to act *insane?* Why do *I* have to be the one pretending to be insane?"

Mitchell looked puzzled. "Well, I thought you'd be good at it."

"You thought I'd be *good* at it? At the rate I've been going, I could run around screaming like a madman, and it's not like anyone would be able to tell the difference."

At this point the conversation was interrupted by the sound of Vegie running around screaming like a madman.

"What the hell?" Mitchell split.

Clarissa heard various shouts and assorted other chaotic noises coming from the direction of the . . . of the . . . kitchen?

Oh, no. Oh. No.

Clarissa froze at the sound of her name being yelled at the top of someone's lungs.

She clambered out of the tent. Everyone was clustered in the area near the kitchen. Bad sign. The fact that they were shoveling snow like mad onto a cluster of sleds, didn't seem too good either. Vegie, in fact, was like a man possessed, muttering something about how the world was being destroyed by, well, "mankind," and how man was responsible for everything, everywhere, being totally wrong.

How could you go wrong boiling water. *How could you go wrong boiling water????* Clarissa steeled herself and clomped over. They all stopped shoveling and glared at her. Mitchell looked distinctly unhappy.

"Um, Clarissa. Next time, screw the cap back on the gas."

Clarissa sucked in a breath. "I did . . . didn't I?"

His radio crackled. "Snow Camp Three, we've mobilized an environmental spill squad and will meet you down at the transition. Over."

Her heart sank. "It couldn't have been more than a quart."

They looked at her with disgust and then peeled away silently except for Squirrelly Boy, who waggled his eyebrows and punched her arm. "So, what was it like sleeping next to a lesbian?"

Clarissa just slowly turned to look at him. "I'm not going to dignify that ridiculous question with an answer, especially at a time like this. Besides, do I look remotely desirable to you?"

"No," he admitted.

She glared at him and clomped off toward the shuttle.

"By the way, Clarissa," Mindy called out after her. "I wasn't sure I should say anything, but I really hope that's a chocolate bar on the side of your head."

Clarissa's stomach dropped as she put her hand up to her matted hair and felt what could only be her missing breakfast squashed into the right side of her head. Tears pricked her eyes. But there was nothing to be done except hold her chin up as best she could . . . and start figuring out how to get the hell off the continent.

She'd learned a valuable lesson. You don't take a person who's just been crushed and put them in a place where they're just going to get more crushed. It's really bad for the self-esteem. And if experience was any indicator, things could always get worse.

Chapter Thirteen

*C*larissa had never quite achieved this level of self-disgust before. She didn't care if the other girls thought she was a quitter. She didn't care if the other girls thought she was weak. She just wanted to get away from this place, get away from constant reminders that she couldn't hack it, wasn't good enough.

And with that in mind, as soon as the shuttle off-loaded at the entrance to the main building, she grabbed her bag and shuffled in her bunny boots straight to human resources. Because if she talked about it with the girls first, something would get in the way of the one thing she wanted the most: to go home.

Which led her to this moment, where she sat in the chair in the human resources office and dabbed at tears of humiliation and frustration with a bandanna that still smelled like musty trail mix.

"I'm very sorry to have wasted the company's time, but I'm here to resign my position."

The HR rep froze, her left hand hovering over the strings of a battered old banjo. The twang of the last chord she'd played still hovered in the air.

Clarissa cleared her throat. "I know it's very inconvenient in terms of getting a replacement, but I think this is best for everyone."

"You want to quit?"

"That is correct. I'd like to leave immediately. I understand that I will have to forfeit my end-of-the-season bonus." They were welcome to it.

The HR girl folded her hands together on the desk and looked down at them quietly, almost as if she were praying or gathering strength. After several minutes had passed, it occurred to Clarissa that something might be very wrong. She was about to lean over and check her pulse when the HR girl looked up with a start and sat bolt upright.

"Are you okay?" Clarissa asked.

The girl looked at Clarissa and blinked vaguely. "I'm fine. Just fine." She looked up at the ceiling and studied the tiles. "I've been here for twelve months."

"Oh?" Clarissa said politely.

The girl didn't answer. In fact she kept staring up at the tiles and then suddenly her lower jaw dropped and she actually started to snore.

Clarissa contemplated the girl's grown-out bleach job and began to cycle through her options as she slept.

A giant snort later, the girl stood up and took Clarissa's hand and pumped it vigorously up and down. "Clarissa, right? Let's see . . . what were we discussing?"

Clarissa sighed. Well, it was all the more reason to leave— she had no idea how long it took for the transformation to get started but she didn't want to be reduced to a similar vegetative state. Maybe it had something to do with the elevation, the amount of oxygen. Or perhaps they put something strange in the food to keep people sedated over the winter.

Clarissa figured the girl could have one of two strategies at work—"I'm out of here in a few weeks and I don't care about policies and procedures anymore so I'll do whatever you want me to do," or else "I'm out of here in a few weeks and I don't give a goddamn about your problem." It was really hard to tell at this pace. She wondered if violent tendencies lurked beneath the placid exterior.

"I'd like to leave this place."

"What? Oh, sorry, not gonna happen." She picked her banjo off her lap and began to strum at the strings.

Clarissa froze. "What do you mean, 'not gonna happen'?"

"'Someone's singing, my lord . . . *kumbayaaaaaa* . . .' I mean you can't be spared . . . 'Someone's laughing, my lord . . . *kumbayaaaa* . . .'"

"Of course, I can be spared!" Clarissa shrieked a little desperately over the strumming. "I'm worthless. Useless. Entirely expendable and . . . and . . . woefully unhelpful." Good god.

"I'm sure you're not that bad."

"You know how when somebody's on the sidewalk dying and the person applying the tourniquet turns and points to someone and goes, 'You. Call an ambulance'?"

The drama of Clarissa's story seemed to have captured her interest. She stopped with the banjo business. "Yeah?"

"I'm not the person they're pointing to."

The girl blinked like a lizard in the sun. It seemed like it took half a minute for her to finish the revolution of her eyelids.

"Can't we just . . . oh, I don't know . . . make an exception?" Clarissa smiled conspiratorially.

The HR girl appeared uninterested in conspiring. "The thing is, even if we wanted to send you back, the thing is that weather has cancelled all flights for the next week and the press came in yesterday and the plane left last night so see, you have no choice but to get to work. That's the thing."

"What? No planes for a week? Was some sort of dispatch sent out to station personnel?"

"Um, no. That's not normal policy. And another thing, even if a plane becomes available, you wouldn't have first priority to fly out."

"Why not?"

"For the very reason you implied; you're not mission critical."

Clarissa winced.

"Research comes first and if we have enough scientists to fill the plane, that's who goes."

"Oh, dear."

Suddenly, the girl's eyes closed again and her mouth dropped open.

"Excuse me," Clarissa prompted tentatively.

A gargling sound came out of the HR girl's mouth, as if water was being forced through a coffee filter, and then the girl woke up with a start. She looked puzzled for a moment and then seemed to become irrationally annoyed, at least as far as Clarissa was concerned. "Do I look like I'm in charge of the weather? Have you ever heard me break into song with 'I'm Mr. Icicle, I'm Mr. Snow'?"

"I haven't known you that long." *But it wouldn't surprise me at this point.*

"Say, aren't you Clarissa Schneckberg?"

Clarissa sighed. "Yes, I am."

"I understand that you have an injury report to complete. For future reference, an injury report should be filed immediately after the incident occurs, assuming you still maintain consciousness."

This miffed Clarissa a bit considering the HR girl didn't seem to be in much of a position to bark orders about one's consciousness. "I'm fine. I don't have anything to report."

She shuffled slowly through a stack of paperwork. "Something about minor burns in the crotch area due to a . . . this is a bit hard to read . . . a 'boiling soup burn incident'? That can't be right . . ." She rifled through some papers. "Well, that's what it says. I guess this would be before you caused the environmental damage for which you will need to file a spill report."

Clarissa sat back in the chair and tried to breathe as deeply as she could as the offending unaddressed report slid across the desk at her.

Maybe she could petition for some sort of special emergency airlift. Perhaps she could feign insanity. She'd be willing to bet the weather report would miraculously clear up if she were to feign insanity.

She'd heard all about the guy who insisted aliens were coming to Antarctica. The whole town made hats out of tinfoil and stood outside waiting with him on the appointed day. Apparently, the firefighters had to restrain him at some point and put him under house arrest until they could ship him out. And then there was the guy from the heavy shop who tried to murder a coworker by bopping him on the head with a wrench.

She was quite certain they managed to deport those people quickly enough.

Chapter Fourteen

As Clarissa limped down the hall toward her room, she could hear her friends laughing. Laughing! She slowed down at the open door and peeked around the doorjamb into the room.

Delilah and Kate were lying on their beds talking about Kate's progress with Garanimal Boy. It hardly seemed fair to walk in from snow school with her tales of woe and bring down the mood when the girls were obviously starting to have some fun with all of this. Of course, they didn't have as much at stake as Clarissa did. They were talking about *flirting,* for god's sake.

Flirting was really the least of her worries. She was trying not to self-destruct as a human being, not worry about whether a romp in the snow would be followed by a phone call in a reasonable period of time.

Clarissa stood there, holding her gear bag limply in one hand, and listened for a moment. The familiar voices were controlled, even, relaxed . . . happy. There was something distinctly disconcerting about the fact that they seemed to be totally acclimating to their new situation while Clarissa floundered about.

One minute she'd convinced herself she was qualified to belt out "I am woman, hear me roar" on the bar karaoke machine and in the next minute she'd convinced herself she wasn't qualified for anything. She couldn't get comfortable in any state of mind. She was beginning to feel like a stranger in her own skin.

Clarissa decided not to try and hide what she had just done. Or, rather, tried to do. A straightforward confession without apology seemed to be about right under the circumstances. So when she finally made it back to the room, she dropped her bag outside the door, raised her chin, and flung open the door to deal with the fallout head-on.

"Clarissa! You're back!" Delilah cried out.

"Hey." Kate leaned toward her, sniffed loudly, then wrinkled her nose. "What's—"

Suddenly, Delilah screamed at the top of her lungs. "Oh! Oh, lord! What's that in your hair?" She leaped up from her bed and tiptoed toward Clarissa, her fingers twitching as she raised her hands up toward Clarissa's hair. "Tell me it's one of those mud pack deep-cleansing conditioners. Although it really should be applied evenly across the scalp."

"It's chocolate," Clarissa said in a most woeful manner.

"Clary, are you all right? You don't seem very happy. Did you have a bad experience?" She looked at Kate, who just shrugged helplessly.

Clarissa headed toward Kate's bed, but was stopped in her tracks as her friend reared up, a look of sheer horror on her face.

"What the hell is that?" Kate asked, looking around the room wildly. "What's that bizarre sme—" She honed in on Clarissa who marched right up and sat down at the foot of the bed.

"Oh, okay. Okay, um. Right. So, Clarissa," Kate said nervously, climbing out of bed and approaching all nervous and fidgety-like. "Um, could you not . . . it's just that . . . well, I just washed my sheets . . . and I don't know how else to say this but the thing is you smell strongly of curry, and I'm just not sure how that's even possible, but it can't be a good thing."

Clarissa looked at her woefully, but refused to move. "I'm on the comforter. No part of me is touching the sheets. And besides, the curry has already dried."

That seemed to appease Kate a little, but she couldn't help hovering and twitching her fingers as if she were dying to just physically remove Clarissa from her sleeping quarters.

"I think you need a change of clothes and something to eat," Kate said abruptly. "Besides whatever you're wearing."

"Eating would be good," Clarissa mumbled hopefully, and began to strip off the layers of her snow school gear, dumping it on the floor by the bed as Kate went to the bookcase to fetch the sandwich grill.

Clarissa took a deep breath, feeling it rattle a bit in her throat. She could let it all out. She could indulge. But, no. There would be no indulging in self-pity today. She was stronger than that. She lifted her chin. "Snow school was a little . . . rougher than I expected." Her voice wobbled, so she paused and then finished up as strongly and as brightly as she could. "I'm just really tired, that's all. But I sure learned a lot!" Then for some reason she lost control of the calibration and in a squeaky high-pitched voice added, "What doesn't kill you makes you stronger!"

Delilah and Kate did that wide-eyed-look-at-each-other thing again, and it was obvious that they weren't totally buying it. A silence. If Clarissa were the paranoid type, she would assume that they were waiting for her to crack. Which was, of course, a ridiculous notion. Clarissa might be down. She might be struggling, but there was no way she was going to crack.

They sat there waiting. So Clarissa indulged, but just a little bit. "I started by leading everyone to the pee flag in the whiteout drill," she explained, using monotone to illustrate the sheer hell of it all in addition to wanting to control her pitch. "And I ended by causing an environmental spill. Everyone who was there hates me . . . there were quite a few people there. I'm afraid we may even have to chalk it up as another 'situation' as far as international relations with the Death Squad Girls go."

"You've only been gone one and a half days," Kate said.

"No, but . . ." It occurred to her that she didn't used to be quite so sorry-for-oneself-esque. She wasn't normally a complainer, a downer. True, she wasn't exactly the go-to girl when some sort of crisis leadership was required, say if someone had a flat tire or required an eyewash or something, but if she did say so herself, she was solid. People wanted her around. And if she really thought about it, it could almost be said that she'd let Kieran's disappearing act excuse some pretty sorry behavior in the last month or so. There'd been the wallowing in self-imposed bed rest, the increasingly introverted behavior, the quitting, for god's sake, and the assumption that she'd never find anyone to love her again . . . good lord, all this because of Kieran?

"Hello? Clarissa, are you still with us? I said you've only been gone a few days."

"Yes, I know. It's amazing what you can accomplish when you really put yourself into it," Clarissa said, trying to muster up a smile. "Anyway, there's something I really need to tell you."

Carefully enunciating so that there could be neither misunderstanding nor an indication that she was somehow ashamed of her actions, Clarissa said almost belligerently, "I think you should know that I've just been to human resources. I tried to quit."

Kate whipped her head around, brandishing the spatula she was using for the sandwiches. "You WHAT?"

"I said I tried to quit. But I didn't. They wouldn't let me."

"How could you?" Delilah said, aghast. She'd moved to the

floor and wrapped herself in a down comforter with only her toes sticking out in preparation for a nail polish change. "I thought we were in this together," she added. "If there was going to be quitting, it should have been a group decision."

"Delilah," Kate said in a warning tone.

Delilah harrumphed petulantly. "Well, we've all made sacrifices here."

"So you tried to quit. You went to HR?" Kate asked.

"Mmm. I did. And a banjo-playing narcoleptic refused to put me on the plane."

A pause. "Did you say 'banjo'?" Kate asked.

Delilah looked at her. "Why wouldn't she put you on the plane?"

"She claimed the weather was bad, if you can believe it. I mean, of course, the weather was 'bad.' We're in the Antarctic for god's sake. But it's not like that's going to stop us from getting home at the end of the season," Clarissa said. "The bottom line is that I tried to quit and a banjo-playing narcoleptic told me I couldn't go home."

"I beg your pardon," Kate said, still not quite comprehending. "I don't think I heard you right. A what?"

"A banjo-playing narcoleptic. The HR girl."

"Oh. I did hear right."

Delilah looked at Kate in confusion.

Clarissa flopped back on the bed, ignoring Kate's squeals of protest. "This has been a *very* trying experience. My only consolation is knowing that I'll have one fabulous piece of work on my résumé. It all comes down to the documentary. There's nothing else here for me."

Kate frowned. "Why didn't Mitchell help you at Snow Survival School?"

Clarissa turned her head and gave her friends a suitably

muddled look. While she was really wondering if his refusal to steer her clear of the pee flag suggested some sort of serious internal flaw, instead she said, "Maybe he was trying to empower me."

"I think that means he *respects* you," Delilah said.

"Right," Clarissa said, wanting to change the subject. "That could very well be. And speaking of men, how *are* things with your Furby, Kate?"

"The term is anthropomorphic, thank you very much."

"Anthro-what?" Delilah asked, choking on her laughter.

"A Furby was a hideous trend in children's toys popularized in the last decade. An anthropomorphic is a person who happens to enjoy 'humanized animals.'"

"'Enjoy humanized animals.' I see. As in a human person who likes to wear animal suits?"

Kate cleared her throat a bit. "That would be one manifestation. Might I take this moment to remind you that *Bill* is wearing long underwear that only happens to resemble an animal suit. He is not actually in costume."

"Actually, I shouldn't laugh," Delilah said. "After you started seeing the Garanimal, I actually had a full-fledged, well-rounded idea for a new cosmetics line, packaging and all."

Both Kate and Clarissa squealed with delight. "That's wonderful, Delilah!"

"Footie pajamas strike again!" Kate said.

"To an extent," Delilah said. "While it's undeniably a small success, it's unusable. It's a safari theme. It smacked of Sunday comic inserts. Something along the lines of an insidious shade of hot pink lipstick packaged in animal print tubes being sold for four dollars next to the ad for the Hummel plates from the National Mint."

Clarissa and Kate made knowing sounds.

"See? I can't use it."

Clarissa gave her a sympathetic pat on the back. "Well, it was just your first idea. There will be others."

Delilah smiled brightly. "I know. I have a good feeling about all of this."

Clarissa could only wish she had that kind of confidence.

Chapter Fifteen

Once Clarissa accepted that she couldn't leave Antarctica, the progress of the documentary began to consume her thoughts. The thing was, she felt like she wasn't really contributing—that Lenny and Squiggy didn't really expect anything from her. Which would normally be fine, except for the fact that the segments Lenny and Squiggy came up with were, well, sort of lackluster. If the documentary was really going to shine, Clarissa was going to have to get more involved. What had they said they wanted? Eye candy . . . visual excitement. . . .

Ass.

Clarissa discretely eyed Delilah and Kate over the top of her completely blank notepad. The three of them were sitting together on the floor with Kate engrossed in one of her craft projects and Delilah with her nose buried in a magazine. Clarissa was (theoretically) sketching out a documentary segment idea to pitch to the boys. She was going to have to bite the bullet and broach the subject. Because if it came down to "ass," to make this documentary a success, she wanted to be prepared. "Ass" wasn't the sort of thing you blindsided your friends with on the spur of the moment. Best to start blindsiding them early.

"Um, guys? Can I ask you a favor?"

"Of course," Delilah said. "As long as it's not gross."

"Well, for variety, Lenny and Squiggy would like to film a couple of segments featuring, ahem, smart, beautiful, accomplished women. And, obviously, you two immediately come to mind."

This actually worked. Both of them perked up substantially.

Kate stood up, her eyes wide and hopeful. "That's perfect! Let's . . . let's put on a show!"

Delilah clapped her hands, "Oh, this is just what I needed! A little pick-me-up! I can re-create the romping-in-sherpa-fur-jacket-and-lacy-underwear look. But it will be very tasteful. Very art house. The makeup will be glossy neutrals . . . how fun!"

Clarissa hated to disappoint them, but this was just the time to stand firm, to really state and go for what she needed. And what she needed was not a "show" in the way Kate and Delilah thought about putting on a show. "No, that's not quite—"

"Oh! Oh! And for Kate, I'll do Heroin Chic meets Dying Inuit. You know? Like in that famous film where the Eskimo girl dies but her beauty is preserved in the ice forever?"

Kate nodded happily. "Cool!"

Delilah leaned forward. "That *is* a real movie, right? Or was that just something I read in a book? Oh, it doesn't matter. I'm thinking slutty-chic eyeliner in thick charcoal and smoky blues. You'll look fabulous, Kate! I mean, Eskimos are North Pole, not South Pole, but who ever gets that straight? Even *I* was looking out for polar bears the first few weeks we got here. *So* embarrassing."

"No!" Clarissa barked. She hated to burst their bubbles when it was the first time in a long time she'd seen them so totally "up." But she had no choice. Expectations were spiraling out of control here. "No," she reconfirmed.

"No? But—"

"No. You're to be filmed on the job." Not that Lenny and Squiggy would have objected to lacy underwear or slutty eyeliner, but that's not what would make for a great documentary. Clarissa needed a great documentary. "I'm talking about more of a, you know, a sort of day in the life in Antarctica . . ." She trailed off. Delilah and Kate had turned absolutely pale.

"What on earth is going on with you two?" Clarissa asked.

"Nothing," Kate said.

"Nothing," Delilah echoed.

"So can we do it?" Clarissa asked.

"Absolutely not," Kate said immediately. Clarissa just stared at her. Since when had Kate turned down any sort of attention-getting venture? She loved being the center of attention.

"How about you, Delilah?"

"Um . . ." Delilah didn't make eye contact, which was odd. "Um, I don't think that's such a good idea. I mean, they might accuse you of cronyism or something."

Since when had Delilah turned down an opportunity for a little publicity? "But once you do find your inspiration for a new line of cosmetics, how perfect would it be to gain this sort of publicity?"

"Why don't you just consider us . . . backups," Kate said firmly. "We'll just be your backups in case of total emergency."

Clarissa sighed. "Okay. It's just that this is really important to me. It's something I can really turn my focus to. I mean, it's my new anchor. This documentary better be good, that's all I can say. I've going to brainstorm some really great segment ideas of my own to pitch to Lenny and Squiggy. You know, so I can show that I'm proactive."

"It's going to be great," Kate said.

"Absolutely," Delilah chimed in. "You really don't need us. It will be great all on its own."

She stared back at Delilah. "Riiight. Okay."

An enormous blank pause filled the room. And in the span of that moment, Clarissa made a decision. If they were unwilling to give her a decent reason why she shouldn't film them on the job, she would simply show up, producers and cameras at her side. She would simply show up and film the segments. She could sit in during the editing and make sure they came out of it looking fabulous. And that would be that.

That was certainly proactive decision making, crisis management . . . that's what this was all about. Clarissa studied her friends' faces. They honestly seemed not to want her to do it. But maybe that meant . . . they did. Maybe in some twisted Demi-Moore-homeless-shelter setup way . . . yes! This was their way of guiding her without deciding for her. Yes! That must be it. They probably really wanted her to film them. Brilliant stuff. And this time, she felt like she could really deliver.

"Dull side out, do you think?" Kate asked, gesturing with the scissors to the plastic sheeting on her lap.

"Whatever you think works best," Delilah said.

Clarissa turned her attention to Kate's craft project. "What is that you're doing?"

"I'm trying to construct some sort of protective suit out of this shower curtain for Delilah so she doesn't actually have to come into contact with any toxic waste," Kate explained.

"Toxic waste," Clarissa said, just to be sure.

"Toxic waste," Delilah confirmed, plucking at her left eyebrow with a tweezers. "It appears that, um, it's possible I will come into contact with . . . unpleasantries, if you will, on the job."

"That's a shower curtain Kate's got," Clarissa said quietly, feeling a dull roar rise up in her brain. "From what I remember from chemistry class, toxic waste is not afraid of plastic."

"I realize that. But we're roughing it," Kate said. "This is a harsh continent. We have to make do. You see, if we have a problem, we need to get creative and solve it ourselves."

"Uh-huh. Yeah, I know." *Since you two suddenly seem so reluctant to help me!* "Well, you have the right attitude. It's the power of positive thinking, isn't it?" Clarissa put her arms around the two of them. "And I say that Kate's going to be a four-star chef after this!" she said enthusiastically. "And Delilah's going to find cosmetic inspiration and create another company that Loralline will fall all over themselves to buy."

It didn't escape Clarissa's notice that the best she got out of Kate and Delilah at that comment was an odd shared look between the two and a couple of weak smiles.

"Um, yeah," Kate said, a little too brightly. Delilah just beamed like a lunatic.

Clarissa narrowed her eyes. "Is something going on?"

"What do you mean?" Delilah asked.

"I mean, is something going *on?*"

"Going *on?*" Kate asked Delilah.

"Going *on?*" Delilah repeated. "There's nothing going on at all."

They stood there in silence for a few moments. Finally Clarissa threw up her hands, feeling rather preoccupied anyway, what with coming up with some great pitch ideas. "Okay. Never mind. If there's something I should know, I know you'll tell me."

Chapter Sixteen

"There you are, Clarissa."

Clarissa looked up from her notes to find Lenny and Squiggy poking their heads through the doorway to her office. "Been looking for you. We have a situation."

"A situation." Not exactly the first words one wants to hear first thing in the morning.

"Yeah, you know. A situation."

She took a bracing gulp of expired soda, clasped her hands on her desk, and said as authoritatively as possible, "Okay, let me have it. What's the problem?"

"The segment we'd set up for tomorrow's shoot fell through."

"The greenhouse?"

"Yup. Apparently they've discovered some sort of microscopic parasite floating on the surface of the water in there and they're destroying all the plants and starting over."

"But that sounds very dramatic," Clarissa said. "Why not film that?"

"We thought of that, obviously," Lenny said.

Clarissa flushed. "Oh, of course."

"But it was a great idea," Squiggy said quickly. "Great minds think alike, right?"

She looked at him gratefully and had the oddest little flash of pity for poor Squigg, who always seemed to be getting railroaded—in the nicest possible way, of course—by Lenn. Sometimes she almost felt like Lenny was Squiggy's Kieran.

"But it's totally off-limits," Lenny was saying. "Quarantine or whatnot. I mean, for god's sake. People are so goddamn uptight about bugs out here."

"Well, it's kind of understandable. There aren't really supposed to be bugs in Antarctica," Squiggy began to explain. "If they come in on the planes it might change the ecosystem or something. You know, lead to the destruction of the planet and all that sort of thing. Which would be a problem. It's—"

"Unbelievable," Lenny ranted. "I found an aphid in some of that lettuce they flew in from New Zealand last week, and before I could say boo, some weird chick at the next table had saved it in a water glass as a pet. An aphid. As a pet. These people are insane."

"Yes, well, we'll simply have to find something else to film today," Clarissa said.

"I would love to do another animal segment," Squiggy said sadly. "I mean, microscopic bacteria can be a little inaccessible to the average viewer in Wisconsin, but we could have found an angle."

Lenny shook his head. "Yeah, quarantine and burning all the plants and everything? That would have been brilliant. We could have had an entire hour-long special out of just that material."

Clarissa cleared her throat. "I have an idea. I mean, it's probably really . . ." Stupid. She'd been about to say "stupid."

"Yeah? Really what?" Lenny asked.

"Really . . . different. It's probably really different."

Lenny and Squiggy looked at each other and shrugged. "Different's good," Squiggy said.

Clarissa rifled through her notebook for her ideas list. "Well, I think we can get access to one of the old seal camps. I haven't seen it or anything, but there are supposedly a few seals still popping up now and then. If nothing else, it would be great montage stuff, I'm thinking." She swallowed and said, "What do *you* think?"

Lenny put his hands out in the air, literally framing the idea in the air. "Oh, this is good. This is really good. This is really, really good. Clarissa, you're pure genius."

Clarissa felt an unaccustomed thrill, a sort of adrenaline shot. "Well, I think 'genius' is overstating the fact. It's just a seal or two."

"Yes, it is," Lenny said. "Genuis. Because we're going to take what you've just suggested, and *expand*. This is going to be *huge*."

"Expand? Huge?" So much for the thrill; Clarissa began to get a peculiar—and oh, too familiar—sinking feeling. Maybe there was something wrong with her hormones. Maybe she was PMSing. No, that wasn't possible. After all, Kate was the alpha female; Clarissa and Delilah just followed biological suit, and she hadn't said a word about it being that time of the month for her.

In contrast to her sinking sensation, Lenny seemed to be becoming more and more buoyant. "Squigg, are you thinking what I'm thinking?"

Squiggy scratched his head. "Um . . ."

Lenny put his arm around Clarissa's shoulder, bending just slightly at the knees. "Okay, look over there, over there." He pointed to the wall, which Clarissa interpreted to mean a far-off place of undesignated location.

"So, imagine you're outside." He extended his arm and made some sort of slicing motion. "You get what I'm saying? Outside."

Clarissa nodded, trying not to get distracted by all the limbs waving about in the air that were meant to clarify and explain.

"And what we're seeing isn't the seal, per se. Because we've got this special camera, a small camera that Squiggy can jigger up, right, Squigg? So we can play with point of view a little bit, and that's the bit that's going to be new. Special. Probably never done before . . . you still with me?"

Clarissa smiled for lack of a better answer.

Squiggy looked like he'd been struck by something heavy. "Oh! I get it. I so get it. That's very good, Lenny."

The guys paused. Clarissa could actually feel the dramatic tension build up in the room.

The two men bent down at the knees and yelled out, "Seal Cam!" This, followed by a hideous display of jazz hands, in sync no less.

Clarissa found herself becoming nauseous. And that was even before things got completely out of hand. She stared at the two men in silence, unsure where to go from here.

Squiggy leaned forward just a little too close for Clarissa's taste and said, "Oh, dear. You're not seeing it, are you?"

"I don't think I quite understand what you mean by Seal Cam," she said, very much afraid that she did understand.

"Like this." Lenny knelt down on his hands and knees and mimicked the presence of a camera on his forehead, then made some odd, flapping movements that were apparently supposed to approximate the physical behavior of Antarctic seals.

He stood up and folded his arms across his chest and looked at Squiggy. Together, they chimed in harmony, "Seal Cam."

Suddenly, the full weight of it all dawned on her. Clarissa nearly choked. "Wait a minute. You're not actually thinking you're going to go out there and strap a camera on a seal's head. That's not what I meant. I mean, that could easily be filed under 'harassment of wildlife.'"

Squiggy pshawed. "Oh, I'm sure it's fine. But if it makes you feel better, I'll put a call in to the Science Board and clear it."

She just gaped at them. It was all she could do. Wrong response.

Lenny frowned at her, then at Squiggy. "She doesn't understand her own genius."

"This wasn't quite my idea," Clarissa began.

"Okay, we need you with us." Lenny fished around in his messenger bag and pulled out a small digital camera. "Here we go . . ." He looked around wildly and then pounced on the tape dispenser at the corner of Clarissa's desk. "Squigg, could ya . . . yeah, that's right."

Clarissa shrieked as Squiggy leaped at her and grabbed her head.

Suddenly, Lenny was wrapping what seemed like at least six yards of masking tape around her head and face.

Clarissa panicked and flailed out wildly, making strange guttural noises, since they'd stuck some tape across her mouth. They mistook her distress for wildlife simulation, imagining there was serendipitous agreement over the project when really there was nothing of the sort.

When they finally let go, Clarissa immediately ripped the camera off her head, spluttering her distress in meaningless syllables.

"You totally get it! You were the seal!" Squiggy flapped her arms around wildly for her.

Clarissa wrenched away from him and threw down the mass of tape, taking an unfortunate amount of hair along with it.

She opened her mouth, unsure whether to sob or scream or what . . . and then she remembered. This was one of those moments when you just had to hang tough. She closed her mouth and breathed. She needed them; she needed this project. This documentary was everything now. It had become a symbol of a better, non-Kieran future.

And basically what this meant was that if they wanted to strap her up with masking tape in the name of science, it would be in her own best interest to let them. So rather then burst into tears, rather than tell them they were certifiable and storm out of there and pay another visit to the resident narcoleptic, perhaps taking her banjo as a hostage, Clarissa needed to pull herself together and make this thing happen.

Squiggy scratched his left sideburn thoughtfully and waited for somebody to say something.

"It's a great idea," Clarissa said forcefully. "I'll make sure Mitchell is available as a safety escort and we'll get this thing done."

Really, she should have been wild with excitement over having an excuse to see Mitchell, to test her hypothesis further. But under the circumstances in which she'd left Mitchell at Snow Survival School, the idea of going without a safety escort and, say, falling into an ice crevasse wasn't such a bad one at that.

But she was beyond issues of humiliation and bad self-esteem. She was taking the ball and running with it. "There was something else at one point, wasn't there? Another idea. Something that had to do with more variety." Clarissa looked Lenny straight in the eye. "Variety and bikinis, I think it was."

"That's right. We said we needed some . . . we needed some . . ." Lenny actually looked embarrassed.

Clarissa quirked her eyebrow and waited for him to finish.

Squiggy huffed. "Ass. He said we needed some ass."

Clarissa did her best not to smile. "That's what it was. Ass. How about instead of the seal, we follow up on that idea?" Look at her! She was already a sellout, without ever having set foot in show business.

"Later. The seal is too good," Squiggy said. "I think it's going to end up being very important. I mean, the seal segment could go a long way to solidifying the scientific legitimacy of the documentary. It was a great idea, Clarissa. We'll give all the credit to you."

"We'll share it," Lenny said quickly. "I'm okay with sharing. We'll share the credit."

"That's really not necessary," Clarissa said dryly. "I'm just thrilled to be involved."

Lenny shrugged. "You were instrumental. In any case, after we do the seals, you're absolutely right. We should get back to the . . . ass. Get those fabulous friends of yours for a couple of segments."

Clarissa was instantly sorry she'd brought it up. She made a lousy sellout. Relegating her dearest friends to "ass" was really not ideal, though she was quite certain Delilah and Kate would answer the call to action if she really needed the segments.

Lenny looked at his watch in the way people do when they have something on their mind, but they aren't really seeing what time it is. "Say, we've got tons of footage to comb through. You have a think about all those logistics. Just leave us a message as to the when and the where, and we'll meet you out on the shoot tomorrow."

Chapter Seventeen

*C*larissa hadn't seen Mitchell more than in passing since bursting into tears at snow school earlier in the week. Appearing competent in front of him was high up on her list of "to dos."

She needn't have worried, because Mitchell not only offered to pick her up and drive her out to the seal camp, but he seemed more than pleased to see her again.

In fact, it was sweetly thrilling the way her leg kept jostling together with Mitchell's, and so very touching the way he kept swinging his arm out at her chest level like some sort of amusement park ride safety bar whenever they hit a particularly bad rut.

On the surface of it, Mitchell was as different from Kieran as a man could be. Which, in a way, sort of meant that he was absolutely not the sort of fellow she was supposed to be interested in. He probably didn't have a five-year plan. He probably wasn't particularly ambitious. Most likely he spent money after he earned it and wasn't squirreling it away in various mutual funds and retirement accounts ... good god, what if he thought E*Trade was some sort of union?!

Stop it, Clarissa. That's ridiculous.

Mitchell was obviously smart, if unconventional. It was simply that he wasn't concerned with the future in the same way that Clarissa was used to. In Clarissa's normal circles, all you ever did was worry about, work for, and think about stabilization, warm fuzzy normalcy, all wrapped up in a giant-anxiety-inducing concept guaranteed to keep people like herself up at night called "The Future."

And what did obsessing about the future really get you, anyway? Well, perhaps a prescription for Prozac. And definitely bragging rights (e.g. "I've got *so* many different bank accounts. It's such a *pain*. I *really* need to consolidate my finances.") And, unfortunately, the sort of boring jobs that paid a lot of money from which you could never take a vacation to spend it without feeling guilty or somehow vulnerable.

But that aside, he was least as qualified, baseline, as Kieran had been. Intelligent, attractive, attentive, safe . . . he was definitely safe.

Interesting. Maybe he was aty least more like Kieran than it appeared at first glance—except that Kieran had more boring ideas about how to spend one's time at work.

Mitchell was an excellent choice as an anchor. The girls were right on about that, and there was no need to laugh or scoff at herself for thinking about him that way. For with that thought came a level of comfort that she hadn't really felt since she'd arrived.

And by the time they reached their destination, Clarissa was beginning to think her post-Kieran dating trauma was over before it had even begun.

"Hey, guys," Mitchell called out to Lenny and Squiggy as he bounded enthusiastically across the tundra like a golden retriever.

Clarissa struggled lamely behind him in the knee-high snow,

just about to overanalyze that the tendencies in him she'd seen surface at snow school were full-blown personality flaws, when he turned around very suddenly.

He plowed his way back to her and said, "Nearly lost you." With that, Mitchell lifted her in his arms à la over the marriage threshold and literally carried her over to the waiting Hollywood producers.

Clarissa squealed with delight and flailed around in his arms screaming for him to put her down without the least bit of desire that he should actually do so.

She was really rather sorry that they weren't just out for a romp in the snow and that they actually had to get down to work. And in fact, a few strides later, Mitchell set her down in the snow, and the two of them surveyed the scene at Seal Camp in mutual silence.

Seal Camp One looked like it was, for all intents and purposes, a ghost town. If science had ever been conducted there, it hadn't been recently. Because all Clarissa could see were a few flag markers left behind and, well, Lenny, Squiggy, their setup, and a large seal lying on the ice.

She glanced at Mitchell to see his reaction, even as that old sinking feeling begin to settle into her stomach. He seemed totally unconcerned.

It's fine, Clarissa. You can make something out of this. If it's possible to find an angle in microscopic surface-floating water bugs at the greenhouse, then it's certainly possible to find something useful here.

After all, it was an actual seal. Maybe they couldn't get a lot of action footage out of it, but a close-up on the seal's face, now who wouldn't find that adorable?

Squiggy and Lenny seemed to think the situation worth setting up for.

Squiggy had set up a folding chair upon which he'd taped a

piece of paper labeled "Craft Service." Four sandwiches, the ubiquitous juice boxes, a six-pack of Coors Light decorated with a Christmas theme from the Miller Brewing Company's 1998 holiday promotion, and a pile of mini-Hershey bars were piled up on the seat. The boys sat hunched over on a pair of director's chairs scripted on the backs with their names.

Their van was running and a ridiculously long orange extension cord snaked out from the crack in the door, out over the ice, and plugged into a satellite that at first glance appeared to have been constructed out of cardboard and tinfoil. Various wires and plugs ran haywire over the snow leading up to the small television set over which the boys were hunched.

It was like *Monday Night Football* in Green Bay.

But that wasn't all that was a mite peculiar. Mitchell was acting odd. Whenever Lenny or Squiggy would move, Mitchell would move such that his left side was always facing them. This made it a bit difficult to try and watch him converse. Frankly, it was distracting. Clarissa had to turn completely away from him to concentrate.

"I'm terribly sorry, gentlemen, but I'm going to have to ask you to disconnect your satellite dish," Clarissa said in a voice she wished sounded more authoritative.

"Oh." Squiggy looked at Lenny in confusion.

"You see, it disturbs the signals used in some of the delicate equipment for the various scientific experiments at all of the bases."

Squiggy leaped out of his chair. "Jesus, Lenn, I knew we should have asked. I mean, we could have just derailed the search for a cure for cancer."

"Whoa, whoa, whoa!" Lenny dove for the cord. "It's the Lakers, man, the Lakers!"

Clarissa cleared her throat. "Shall we get started?" Of course, she really hadn't the faintest idea what that entailed.

Lenny was still glued to the television set with Squiggy apparently too meek to interrupt him.

Finally, Mitchell reached over and pulled the plug on the TV. "You're disrupting science," he said, giving Clarissa a smile as if to say, "Don't worry, I've got it covered."

"Right, okay." Lenny stood up and pointed to the seal lying out on the ice. "There's our boy."

The three others stared out at the gray blob, which showed absolutely no signs of movement.

"Well, shall we?" Clarissa asked pleasantly, and started off toward the blob. The men followed her and they gathered around the seal.

"Where are the rest of them?" she asked.

"It's likely their migration paths have changed," Mitchell said rather authoritatively.

"Right, right," Lenny said. "But we can start here, and if he embarks on some epic journey to find his kin, we'll just turn his segment into a miniseries."

The seal managed to open one eye and blink.

Clarissa didn't vocalize her thoughts at that point, but it occurred to her that perhaps less motivated seals might not be the best subject matter. And given that a seal's daily activity consisted mostly of breaking through ice with their heads and faces, crawling onto the ice surface, and then lying for hours on top of the ice, it was a little disturbing to contemplate what a seal with less energy might be prepared to accomplish. But hell, it was definitely variety, so she kept her mouth shut and just nodded.

Lenny and Squiggy stared blankly over at Clarissa. She stared blankly back at them.

The seal leaned its head to one side and blew a spray of snot out of its nose.

Squiggy folded his arms across his chest. "Maybe this one's too old. Maybe we need a younger, more energetic seal."

It occurred to Clarissa that there really must be a reason there was only one seal out here. Something must be wrong with it, even though it looked perfectly content. This was just more than she wanted to deal with.

The seal looked rather elderly in Clarissa's opinion, not that she was particularly qualified to judge. The seal in question was a very large seal, a very languorous seal, and it had areas of distinctly gray fur. This was no alpha seal. This was clearly a seal much closer to the omega side of the life-and-death spectrum. And if there was going to be any epic journey, it was more likely to be one that would take a while.

Lenny bent down in front of the seal and cocked his head. The seal opened one eye, blinked, and closed it again. "Nah, he's just sleepy. He'll be fine."

Everyone looked at one another.

"Okay, so I'm going back to the van and make sure the equipment is working and film the setup. You take the supplies and go out there and do the installation."

"Do you guys need any help with the setup?" Mitchell asked.

Lenny pulled a small portable camera out from inside his parka and handed it to Squiggy. "Yeah, that would probably be good."

After everything that had happened, all the challenges that she felt she'd been unable to gracefully rise to, Clarissa felt oddly as if this time she need to prove to someone she could take care of things herself. "There's no problem, Mitchell. I can help them with whatever they need. You can just do your . . . safety thing."

"No, I'm good," Mitchell said pleasantly. "And I can stay out here as long as you need. I've cleared my desk for the day. Clarissa, would you like me to handle this?"

"Too many people might upset the seal," Squiggy said, nodding.

Clarissa was beginning to feel crestfallen. She was about to simply smile brightly and gracefully excuse herself, but she couldn't. This was her project, not Mitchell's, god bless him for trying to help her this way, and she was going to stay right here and take care of business. "I'm fine," she chirped. "I'm in."

Mitchell looked the tiniest bit surprised, but to his credit, he recovered quickly and said in a most supportive manner, "I'll just be here if you need me. I'll just be standing right here, 'on call,' if you will." He took a few steps back, and settled in by crossing his arms over his chest.

Clarissa smiled and he smiled back.

"Great, Clarissa, so your next choice is whether you want to go back to the van and work from there with me or work on the seal with Squigg," Lenny said.

Aside from wanting to make some sort of point about her abilities, Clarissa decided that she'd better be directly on-site if they were planning to actually touch the seal in some way. She nodded toward Squiggy. "I'll work on the seal with Squiggy."

Lenny nodded. "Okay, here's the glue, and here's the camera . . . oh, well, you might as well just take the whole bag. Here."

Squiggy slung the supply bag over his shoulder.

"What now?" Clarissa asked.

"Select, sedate, shave, and secure," Lenny explained as he consulted his yellow pad.

Clarissa must have looked as puzzled as she felt.

"Okay, number one, select a seal subject. Number two, sedate the subject. Number three . . . shave the head and a small patch on the back of the subject. Number four, secure camera module and backpack to the subject."

"What?"

"Select, sedate, shave, and secure. Seems pretty clear. Here." He handed the pad to Clarissa. "All set?"

"We've got it," Squiggy said, and saluted his friend.

"Great. I've got my walkie-talkie and I'm headed back to the van." Lenny turned and headed back.

"So, let's see. Lenn got a special sedative . . ." He searched the bottom of the bag and pulled out a pink pill. "This must be it." Mitchell squinted. "Interesting."

"There's no way we're going to get that seal to take this pill," Clarissa said, looking suspiciously at the pill.

Squiggy grinned triumphantly. "Oh, ye of little faith." He pulled out the rest of the equipment and laid it out on the ground next to the seal.

An electric razor, an extension cord that traveled all the way from the power generator, what looked to Clarissa like a black back supporter with a jumble of wires, what looked like a tiny digital camera, a squeeze bottle of some sort of special cold-weather glue adhesive, a huge horse pill, and . . . a fish filet in a Ziploc bag.

Clarissa reared back but Squiggy didn't seem to notice.

"We just need to disguise the pill so the seal doesn't recognize it. I'm going to wrap the pill in this cod . . . like . . . so." He took out an enormous hunting knife, ran it down the seam of his fish, then inserted the sedative and rolled the whole thing up. Then he gingerly placed the cod next to the seal's face.

The seal seemed unimpressed. Clarissa made a mental note to look up the Antarctic Treaty and refresh her memory as to what constituted 'harassment of wildlife' since paparazzi behavior and medicating were apparently A-OK.

"He's not hungry," Squiggy said, stamping his feet and flapping his arms against the cold.

"Maybe he ate before he came," Mitchell joked, checking his watch with a shrug.

Suddenly, the seal twitched. He'd smelled the fish. He finally lumbered up on his flippers, poked at the cod with his nose, and ate the whole thing in one bite.

The three of them silently cheered with raised fists. And then they waited. And waited. And waited some more. Clarissa and Mitchell kept looking at Squiggy, who was standing there with his arms crossed patiently over his chest. And then looking at each other as it was occurring to both of them, though they wouldn't say so aloud, that they were waiting for a seal who already seemed as lackluster and comatose as it was possible for a seal to be, to become sedated.

"I think he's comfortable now." Squiggy pulled out his walkie-talkie. "Lenn? You there?" A pause, and then the sleepy sounds of Lenny saying "Wha?"

"It ate the sedative."

"Great," Lenny said. "Go ahead and shave it." The walkie-talkie clicked off before Squiggy could respond.

"We need to shave it," Squiggy repeated rather unnecessarily. "Like I said, the seal is comfortable now."

Clarissa looked around nervously. "I'm not sure *I'm* comfortable. Did you really clear all this with the National Science Board?"

Squiggy slapped her on the back. "I put in a call this morning."

Not that anyone ever picked up on the other side. Clarissa suppressed a sigh and put on her most polite smile. "Um, would you mind walking me through the details of each step, just so I know what we've got coming?"

Squiggy adjusted his shades and hooked one thumb into his bib suspenders. "We shave the seal's back and head. Then we glue the battery pack on its back and install the camera on its head. He won't feel a thing, I swear."

"How do you plan to, er, 'install' the camera?"

"We've got this special epoxy." Squiggy rummaged around

in the bag. "Damn. Where is it?" He huffed, then looked up at them. "I've gotta go back to the van for a minute. You guys keep an eye on things."

As soon as Squiggy headed off for the van, Mitchell turned to Clarissa. "Are you cold?"

Clarissa thought about it for a moment. "Only a bit."

Mitchell smiled and unwrapped the scarf from his neck, walking up close to Clarissa and slowly wrapping it around hers. "We can't have that, now can we?"

His hands reeled her in on the end of the scarf until she was standing right up against him, his giant puffy parka against her giant puffy parka, which in reality meant that they were still a good three feet away from each other as far as naked body parts were concerned. Not that such a thought was relevant to the work at hand.

He put his arms around her puffiness. "Good?" he murmured.

Clarissa smiled into his puffy parka shoulder. "Good," she said.

He pulled her in a little tighter. "Better?"

"Better," she said, noting the butterflies in her stomach.

Mitchell pulled away a bit and sort of shuffled her around slightly, which was a little odd, but maybe he was doing it to keep her warm. Then he tucked each little pompom from her hat behind each ear and looked at her mouth and she knew he wanted to kiss her.

Instead, he frowned. "I owe you a huge apology."

She looked at him in surprise. "For what?"

"For snow school."

She shook her head. "Mitchell, I think you've got it mixed up. I'm the one who made it all such a muddle!"

"Nah. It was hard on you. I wasn't trying to set you up for any of that. I thought I was helping you . . . expand your horizons. Do things you might not have otherwise done. But if I hurt your feelings in some way, I'm really, really sorry."

Clarissa smiled to the bottom of her heart. He was rugged *and* sensitive. How perfect. Manly yet in touch with his emotions. Had she found "the one" after all, when she was least expecting it, when she wasn't really even looking?

Quite certain Mitchell was going to kiss her now, she looked back at Lenny and Squiggy to assure their privacy.

They waved. Clarissa took a step toward the van; Mitchell took a step toward her and closed the space back up.

"Do you need something?" Clarissa called out to the boys.

Mitchell grabbed her arm and held her back. "They're fine."

"We're fine!" Squiggy called. "Just keep doing whatever you're doing."

Clarissa stared back at them uncertainly, then for a split second focused on the white and blue icy mountains looming in the distance.

Wow. Whatever it was she'd wanted or needed from Kieran, she didn't want or need it anymore. She was so over him.

Mitchell's arm snaked around her again, and he shuffled her around in a circle once more. Then he positioned her again, face-to-face, raked one hand through his hair in dramatic fashion, grabbed her by the shoulders, and planted a kiss on her mouth.

This was no rebound-guy kiss. This was chemistry. This was cool air, hot mouth, arms holding her safe and sound. This was head spinning with the snowy mountains encircling her, this was just Clarissa and Mitchell alone in the middle of a place that held the promise of something clean and new.

When he finally released her, they both took a deep breath. Clarissa touched her mouth as if she might make her fingertips tingle just by association. Mitchell grinned like he felt the same way.

And then they heard a sound. Looking back, they could see Lenny and Squiggy just standing there in the snow watching them. They waved cheerily.

Clarissa rolled her eyes. "How is it that there is less privacy at the bottom of the earth than in the middle of it?" She started to head toward them.

Lenny and Squiggy started waving their arms in the air now, in what seemed like an attempt to communicate that they wanted her to stay over there.

She held up her arms in a "why?" gesture. The boys just nodded cryptically in the negative.

"Come here, you." Mitchell took her in his arms, squeezing her in a bear hug. It felt so good to be held like that again. Like she belonged to someone. She felt so, so safe and warm.

And then he shuffled her around in a half circle again.

"What is that you're doing?" Clarissa asked into Mitchell's shoulder. "I'm really not that cold."

"What's what?"

Squiggy chose this moment to bound up to them with the epoxy, and Clarissa bashfully detached herself from Mitchell, remembering that she was supposed to be on the job.

Mitchell took the epoxy out of Squiggy's hand and tried to read the faded ingredients label.

"Is that stuff flammable?" Clarissa asked.

"I thought you were here to assist us," Squiggy scolded. "But I see that you have other interests," he teased. "So if you're not interested in participating in the project, just say so."

"She's just covering all the bases," Mitchell said in her defense.

Clarissa gave him a grateful smile and they exchanged dopey, longing glances.

The seal yawned.

Squiggy clapped his hands loudly. "Great. I guess we'll get on with it. So, we're going to glue the battery pack on and then buckle the straps underneath, against his stomach."

Squiggy took the cap off the tube of epoxy glue and, holding it out at arm's length, slowly approached the seal, who was now smiling in what appeared to be a drug-induced haze. "How much do you think I should use?"

"Whatever you think," Clarissa said absently, battling shivers that went up her spine every time she replayed the kiss in her head.

Squiggy squeezed some glue on the seal and spread it around a bit. The seal seemed to like that and made a seal sort of purring sound. Next, he gently pressed the battery pack on the glue and worked at the straps. Then he stood up and backed away. The seal got a little more active at this point, turning its sights on Squiggy and seal-flopping its way toward him.

"It seems to be becoming a little . . . randy," Mitchell said, his head cocked to one side.

The seal latched on to Squiggy at this point. "Oh, Jesus, Clarissa, the seal is humping my leg."

"Don't panic," Clarissa said, starting to panic.

The walkie-talkie beeped. "Everything okay over there?" Lenny asked in a tinny voice. "I'm seeing some pretty strange activity from back here."

"It's fine, Lenn. We're fine," Clarissa said hastily.

"Get him off me!" Squiggy yelped as the seal clung fast, oddly enamored with the guy.

"Are you sure the seal's a 'he'?" Mitchell asked.

Squiggy ignored the question, busy keeping himself from losing his balance with the seal attached to one leg and the camera remote in his hands. "Okay, I'm flipping the switch. Here goes!"

Nothing. No red camera light.

"It's not turning on . . . I think it's broken," Clarissa said.

"Do something, Clarissa! Do something!" Squiggy reared back and fell into the snow, the seal clambering on top of him.

"You're kidding me," Clarissa muttered, definitely feeling like she'd completely lost control of the situation—not that she'd ever had it. She didn't even want to look at the expression on Mitchell's face.

"Just knock it a bit, jostle it," Lenny suggested over the walkie-talkie.

"You want me to hit the seal?" Squiggy asked uncertainly.

"No!" Clarissa yelped.

"Just—oh wait, I think it's just a short," Mitchell said from behind her. "A couple of the wires on the unit look a little worn. One seems to have . . . disconnected . . . one sec . . ."

Suddenly the camera light clicked on.

From the walkie-talkie, Lenny weighed in. "It's on! We have contact! This is it, folks, the show begins!"

"Does anybody know if the epoxy is flammable?" Clarissa asked again.

"It's fine. Everything's fine. This is great," said Lenny's voice.

Squiggy finally scrambled out from under the seal and proceeded to flail through the snow back to the van.

Mitchell and Clarissa looked at each other. Then they looked at the seal.

The seal grunted.

"Well, you ready to head back in?" Mitchell asked. And then he took her hand and they headed back to the van.

Chaos was what they found: Lenny screaming bloody murder as he shook the contents of the knapsack into the snow.

Squiggy stood next to him, insisting that "it" wasn't his fault.

"Dude. Dude!" was pretty much all Lenny could say as he scrabbled futilely about in the bottom of his bag.

"What's the matter?" Clarissa asked.

"Where's my X? I had a tab in my bag." Lenny pulled out a tan pill from the bottom of the bag. "Duuude. If this is the sedative, where's my X?"

Clarissa, Lenny, Mitchell, and Squiggy slowly turned their heads and looked at the seal.

"Great segment, Clarissa," Squiggy said into her ear. She looked at him and they both had to turn away to hide their smiles.

Chapter Eighteen

I t happened only rarely. And when it did happen, one of them usually left quite soon thereafter. But, as it happened this time, it was just Clarissa walking in on one of the Death Squad Girls—Emily in braids, actually. The two opposing sides would have to meet.

As she stepped into the room, Clarissa saw immediately that Emily was alone. And with her newfound powers of leadership and competence, she decided to engineer a détente.

Clarissa walked full into the room and cleared her throat.

Emily, buried in one of Delilah's *Cosmopolitan*s, literally jumped from the couch in surprise and flung the magazine to the other side of the room in obvious embarrassment over being caught with something other than *The Field Guide to Glaciers*.

She stared in sheer horror at Clarissa, a red spot burning on each cheek.

Clarissa simply walked over and sat down on the couch and said, "Emily, I was hoping to get an opinion on something."

Emily looked at her suspiciously and slowly sat down. "On what?"

"Do you think giving an elderly Antarctic seal a tab of Ecstasy constitutes harassment of wildlife?"

The Death Squad Girl relaxed. "Is this hypothetical?"

"Let's say it's hypothetical."

"Darn," Emily said with a teasing smile. "Well . . . did the seal seem upset? Put out? In pain?"

"No, I would describe the seal as amorous."

"Just amorous?"

"Amorous and elderly," Clarissa said. "Toward the end of its life span, if you ask me."

"Then, no," Emily decided. "I would say you did it a service. Hypothetically, of course. Just think of it as seal Viagra."

"Good. I had my doubts, and I just wanted to get your take on it, since I'd be in serious trouble if it was a harassment issue."

"I think you're in the clear."

"And you don't feel this is somehow . . . unpleasant for the seal?"

"Lucky seal, if you ask me. And he'll be a reality TV star. Seal Viagra. Sounds like win-win to me."

"I don't know about that. It's not as if there was a girl seal around to court," Clarissa said. "What's the penalty again for harassment of wildlife?"

"Something like a ten-thousand-dollar fine and a stint in prison," Emily said.

"That doesn't seem like very much money."

"Ten thousand dollars for annoying a seal? If I had ten thousand dollars for every time someone annoyed me . . ." Emily shook her head in mock disgust.

"You'd probably have already made a million dollars today," Clarissa said.

Emily giggled. And it occurred to Clarissa that maybe Emily's three weren't so very different from . . . her three.

"Clarissa, can I get *your* opinion on something?"

"Sure."

"Do these work pants make my butt look fat?"

Clarissa grinned, but her answer was lost in the sound of familiar footsteps pounding down the hall.

A familiar high-pitched squeal preceded Delilah and Kate barreling into the room, with Kate throwing down, "We heard you kissed Mitchell Kipling!"

They saw Emily and stopped in their tracks. "Oh. Sorry. Didn't mean to interrupt."

Delilah stared at Emily nervously. "Hi."

Emily stared nervously back at her. "Hi."

"We were just going to ask Clarissa something, but it's just . . . silly stuff. It can wait," Kate said, hyperpolite in the sort of way one gets when one's good friend is acting friendly with someone you weren't entirely convinced they should be acting friendly with.

"Well, I wouldn't mind hearing about Clarissa kissing Mitchell Kipling," Emily said.

"Oh," Delilah said. "Great!"

If her privacy had to be the sacrifice to make this tentative truce possible, so be it. Clarissa sighed.

Delilah and Kate joined Emily on the couch and they all settled in. "Go," Kate ordered.

"Well, as you know I was feeling a little weird about seeing Mitchell again after that really embarrassing meltdown at snow school. But when we went out to this seal camp to film a segment, he was just wonderful. He apologized to me. I mean, at first, he pretended nothing weird even happened," Clarissa explained. "And as we were making our way out on the tundra, he scoops me up in his arms, whirls me around and carries me across the snow."

"Oooh," Kate said. "Nice."

"Oooh," Delilah gushed. "That's just so red cheeks, cuddly sweaters, and . . . and . . ."

"Hot chocolate delightful?" Emily supplied helpfully.

Delilah looked at her as if she'd found a long-lost sister. "Exactly! Hot chocolate delightful."

The détente was blossoming before her very eyes. Even Kate seemed to be impressed with Emily. "I know! And then it gets better," Clarissa said. "I could tell he wanted to kiss me, but the guys were there, you know. So he bided his time, giving me little signals, touching my shoulder, putting his hand on my back, staring at my mouth, that stuff. You know what I mean."

"We know!" all three girls chorused.

"And then he did it. He kissed me."

"So, whad'ya think?" Kate asked. "He's the first guy you've kissed since Kieran."

"There was serious chemistry. Serious chemistry."

Kate looked at Delilah. "This is a very good sign. I think she's in a healing place."

Clarissa wrinkled her brow, suddenly a little perturbed. "In fact, I keep forgetting to remember that I'm supposed to be upset about Kieran. That *is* a very healing place to be. But it almost bothers me. I mean, how could I have thought I wanted to be with a person for the rest of my life that I haven't thought more than fleetingly of in weeks? That's more of a negative comment on me than it is on him, don't you think?"

"What's the comment?" Emily asked.

"Well, just that . . . maybe that . . ." She looked up at them in alarm. "Maybe I don't love deeply enough."

Kate shook her head. "That's ridiculous. You simply stopped loving deeply when he stopped being worthy. I think the comment—and I don't consider it a negative one—is simply that he wasn't the one for you. If he'd been the one, you'd still feel sick over him. Thusly, you've managed to come up with proof that your separation from Kieran and subsequent moving on to Mitchell, or anyone else for that matter, is what you are really meant to do."

Delilah nodded her head in agreement. "Kieran wasn't the one for you."

"Clearly not," Emily said matter-of-factly.

"But you've never met him," Clarissa said. She chewed her lower lip and tried to figure the damn logic out. She simply couldn't make sense of it all. Once again, when told Kieran wasn't right, she began to panic that perhaps she hadn't given it a proper shot. When reminded of him, reminded that she'd forgotten him, she actually started to miss him. "I've just remembered I remember him," Clarissa said glumly. "And when I remember him, I almost think I miss him."

"Don't be ridiculous. It's merely the power of suggestion. I mean, honestly," Kate said, "if Kieran called you up on the phone and screamed 'Clarissa, marry me. I cannot live without you!' would you go back to him? I think not."

Clarissa didn't answer the question. Though it was a moot point, the idea of Kieran proposing in any manner had consumed her for so long, it was hard to imagine rejecting the offer under any circumstances. "Let's not talk about Kieran."

"Fine with us," Kate said. But the three girls sat forward expectantly and all Clarissa could do was shake her head and say, "Let me guess. This means we have to talk more about the kissing."

Chapter Nineteen

One would have thought that an entire evening spent dissecting one kiss would have been sufficient for any budding relationship. But there was more. In fact, Clarissa might have saved them all a lot of time and gray matter if they'd all just held off for another day. Things were about to become very clear. Or at least, clearly muddled.

When she got to her office the next morning, Lenny was already there, huddled around the TV-VCR, rewinding the tape for the dailies.

"Hey, beautiful," Lenny said. He reached over to the side table and poured Clarissa a mug of bad coffee.

"Good morning, Lenn. I've set it up with Delilah's and Kate's supervisors to go film in the afternoon. That gives us the whole morning for dailies." She settled into her desk chair and, cradling her mug like a precious substance, leaned back to watch.

"Perfect," Lenny said. "Squigg's double-checking all the batteries for today's big shoot."

"Great." Clarissa focused in on the first material she'd seen shot from the Seal Cam. Much of it was completely black, as when the seal appeared to fall asleep on the camera lens, or completely white, as when the seal walked straight toward a glacier for twenty minutes.

In a backdrop of VCR buzz punctuated by Lenny's snorts, Clarissa watched the tape with somewhat incomplete focus. She'd stayed up way too late the prior night talking about kissing boys, for god's sake, and now she was paying the price. She was getting way too old for this.

But as she dozed off slightly, it occurred to her that she was actually becoming rather comfortable with the reality of her life here on The Ice. This was all very pleasant. The pace of life, the emphasis on things different from home, there was something to be learned in all this.

All very pleasant . . . much to learn . . . zzzzzzzzzzzzzz . . .

It was only when she heard the sound of her own voice that she snapped back to reality. Her eyes flew open and it became immediately apparent that the screen was neither black nor white anymore.

"Are you cold?" she heard Mitchell ask.

She heard herself respond, "Only a bit."

Both Clarissa and Lenny were fully alert at this point, staring at the TV screen. There she was, with Mitchell, in all her glory. There was some flirty business with a scarf, subsequent flirty and inane comments on both parts, and then Clarissa watched the Mitchell on the television screen put his arm around her shoulder, shuffle her around a bit in a way that looked even odder on-screen than it had in real life, and . . .

Clarissa's mouth dropped in horror as she found herself sitting with Lenny watching Mitchell rotate her to put his best angle on camera and plant his discussed-to-death kiss on her, clearly in a manner best suited to position Mitchell's face to his advantage.

In short, Mitchell wasn't as "in the moment" as he'd pretended to be. "Pretend" being the operative word in this case.

Clarissa stood up, knocking her chair backwards, spilling coffee over the rim of her mug, and glared at Lenny, overcome by disgust. "That was private! All of that was totally personal, not for public viewing."

"It wasn't exactly private . . . we were right there, Clarissa. Besides, I dunno why you're getting so upset. It's not like you showed your tits."

Clarissa gasped.

Lenny shrugged. "Look, that's the thing with reality TV. You don't know what the edit is going to make you look like. I swear, we get that all the time, reality TV stars complaining we made them look unsympathetic," he said, as if he knew anything about what he was talking about.

"Lenny," Clarissa said, working hard to control her voice. "I never agreed to be on your show. You guys set me up."

Lenny shrugged casually, although he looked the slightest bit guilty. "We can't help it if the seal looks," he finally said lamely. "If the seal looks, the seal looks."

She crossed her arms over her chest. "That footage is *not* from Seal Cam."

"Of course it is." He sounded as unconvinced as Clarissa felt.

"No, it isn't!"

"Oh. Well . . . okay, right. I remember now. We added a second camera. We thought it would add some drama. Think of it this way, you're gonna be a star! You wanted to go Hollywood, right?"

"*Behind* the scenes. I'm interested in being *behind* the scenes." Clarissa slapped her hand to her forehead in despair. "This is outrageous."

"We'll be sure to give you a good reference," Lenny said sincerely. "You've been great."

On-screen, Mitchell appeared to be playing just slightly to the camera.

"Oh, gross. What a cad. He so knew what he was doing." Clarissa whirled around. "Tell me the truth. Did you know he was going to kiss me?"

Lenny shifted uncomfortably in his chair.

"Tell me!"

He sighed heavily and pulled a piece of photo card stock from his briefcase. "Mitchell just happened to have one of these and gave it to us and we thought he would be useful."

"Mitchell just happened to have a black-and-white head shot handy?"

"Well, you know how we needed to up the drama quotient. We just told him that since he liked you anyway, if we could add a little romantic subplot to the show, the ratings would be a lot higher and he'd be sure to get more screen time."

She stared down at the rather attractive photo and shook her head. Lenny flipped it over and she could see that the back was squared off into four quadrants. One showed Mitchell, tuxedoed, in a full body shot, one showed his exquisite profile, one showed him in "funny" mode dressed as a ventriloquist with a matching puppet, and one showed him with a sort of 1950s sensibility wearing an old-fashioned ice cream uniform.

Clarissa looked up at Lenny, furious now. She was also done catering to every whim of the dynamic duo. He sat slumped at the desk looking appropriately downcast.

Suddenly, he brightened up. "Okay, okay, here's something that should cheer you up."

She just glared at him.

"No, seriously. This is cool. Vostok called. They picked up our signal yesterday. They must be bored out of their skulls."

"What's Vostok?" Clarissa asked.

"The Russian Antarctic station. They called to thank us. Turns out they misjudged the supplies they would need and have had to use their porn as toilet paper. They were grateful for the fresh entertainment."

"You're not going to do that again, are you, Lenn? Broadcast footage of me without my consent?"

"Are you sure you don't want to? We've had some e-mails already which are very favorable. Basically, the audience wants to see more of you." Lenny pulled a file out from behind his back and shuffled through the contents. " 'We want to see her boobs,' says this one. 'I'd watch if they had sex,' said this one."

Clarissa sucked in a gasp of horror. "You've made me the T, you jerk! I'm the T!"

Squiggy chose this moment to pop his head in. "Trouble?"

"I'm the T and Mitchell's the A!" Clarissa screeched.

"Huh?" Squiggy repeated, clearly still not understanding.

Lenny huffed impatiently. "T & A, Squigg. Get it now?"

A huge smile came over Squiggy's face. "Oh, yeah, the dailies from Seal Cam. Yeah, you're the tits, Clarissa."

Lenny winced.

Sweet, clueless Squiggy. He'd said it as if it were somehow an honor. Well, quite a few people considered landing the front cover of *Playboy* an honor. Squiggy was nothing if not sincere; it was hard to be mad at him. Especially with Lenny calling almost all of the shots.

Clarissa just groaned. "How am I ever going to be respected in entertainment media if I . . . Oh, my god, he might not even have kissed me if it wouldn't have gotten him on television." She made a face. "Yuck."

"Nah, the guy really likes you," Squiggy said. "I think our suggestion really just sped up the whole process. I mean, you could look at it as something that brought you two closer together . . . sooner."

Clarissa groaned again and put her head in her hands.

"You've heard of total global domination? This is total global humiliation."

What was I thinking? Have I been blind? Did I just jump for the first guy who came along? Well, anchors were all well and good, but Mitchell was turning out to be the kind of anchor that just weighed you down. Maybe he'd meant part of the kiss; it certainly felt like he'd meant part of it, but maybe that just wasn't good enough.

After all, she didn't have to have a man in her life at all times. She had Delilah and Kate, friends forever, and totally dependable.

"I'll tell you one thing," Clarissa said, her hands on her hips. "If you think after this that I'm going to let you exploit my friends today—"

"We promise you'll have complete artistic control over the Kate and Delilah segments," Lenny said in a oversoothing tone that made Clarissa even more furious. "Consider it your directorial and production debut. We'd be able to upgrade your credit line."

"Oooh, Lenny, you make me so mad!"

He smiled boyishly, an overdramatized, aw-shucks shrug nailing the performance. Clarissa started to laugh. He'd gone and used the magic words. Clarissa was to have control over the segments. She'd be able to protect her friends and come up with the perfect segment.

But if she said yes, *would* that be selling out? Or making major strides in her leadership abilities? Awfully hard to tell. The question was, what would the girls tell her to do? They'd tell her to do it. After all, she was doing what it took to "make things happen." That's what she was supposed to do, right?

Lenny looked at Squiggy as if she'd already announced her answer. "We'll see you this afternoon, then?"

Clarissa leaned back in her chair and took a fortifying swig of coffee. "I guess you will."

"Kate, you look adorable! What on earth are you doing in here?"

When Kate turned around in the pot room she looked about as deer-in-the-headlights as Clarissa had ever seen her. She was staring over Clarissa's shoulder at Lenny and Squiggy and probably also at the blinking red light of the camera. "In here? I'm, ah, I'm . . . doing some pots."

"That's so very democratic of you." Clarissa was really impressed. Kate normally was of the frame of mind that "there were people for that sort of thing." "Why don't you take a break and come let us interview you."

Kate looked around nervously. "I don't think that would be such a good idea."

Clarissa frowned. "But you love being the center of attention."

"I don't want to be on film looking like this," Kate hissed. She put her soapy palm in front of the camera lens, causing Lenny and Squiggy to squawk simultaneously.

"What's the matter with you?" Clarissa scolded her friend. "You're in here doing a gracious service, donating your time to the dreaded pot room of your own free will . . . ."

The look on Kate's face indicated one of two things: that free will was not involved, the most logical conclusion being that she'd been kidnapped and forced into subservient labor; or that—dear god, could it be???—this was actually her job.

Clarissa smiled pleasantly at Lenny and Squiggy. "Could I have just one moment, please? Just one moment with my friend here . . . great, thanks."

As the boys retreated to the other end of the room, Clarissa put her arm around Kate's shoulder and pulled her to the side. "What's wrong with you?"

Kate's pinched mouth didn't reveal anything, but two crimson spots burning in the center of each cheek did. Something very wrong was happening here.

"You can tell me, Kate. You know you can."

Kate suddenly looked around wildly. The other pot room denizens gave her puzzled looks but dutifully attended only to their tasks at hand.

And without another word, Kate flung herself into Clarissa's arms and burst into tears.

Clarissa stared at her in shock and tried to comfort her friend as the tears flowed. Kate wasn't really a crier. Sure, she'd seemed a little moist around the eyes a few days ago, but Clarissa didn't really think she'd break. Kate had the thickest skin of all three of them.

Finally, Kate hiccupped and said, "I didn't want anyone else to know."

Clarissa held her by the shoulders and forced her to make eye contact. "It's just me. Go ahead and say it."

"I'm not a sous-chef! It's like a huge, sick joke being played on me by the universe. You would THINK that the universe would have better things to do with its time than play around with me. We have ongoing problems with world hunger, diseases, and white pumps after Labor Day. I'm small potatoes."

Tears streamed down her face once more. Her chest heaved and she only managed staccato breaths forced out between gulping pauses.

This was serious business.

Kate swiped at her tears but still couldn't quite overcome the sobbing thing. "Can I just say, this is a nightmare," she hissed, throwing her arms wide open at the "this," nearly whacking

Clarissa in the chest. Moaning and dragging the back of one hand across her forehead, she added, "Apparently it says in the contract that they can move you to another job at will if they find you're of more value in some other position. The job descriptions are a little loose."

"Loose?" Clarissa asked. "Well, you said you had less responsibility, but—"

"Well, I was fudging. Demoted is more like it. 'A little loose,'" Kate repeated in an extremely hostile tone. "That's what my boss told me. Can you believe it? I mean, *loose* is Brie instead of Camembert. *Loose* is . . . is . . . arugula instead of endive."

Kate leaped off into the center of the pot room, her fists clenched in a sort of Scarlett O'Hara I'll-never-go-hungry-again moment. "*Loose* is most certainly NOT kitchen wench instead of sous-chef!"

Clarissa backed herself to the wall to where the other pot room specialists had already retreated. Kate tended to need a lot of space when she was in this sort of state. "When you say 'kitchen wench,' I'm not exactly sure I understand what you mean," she said. "Could you be more specific? It's the, um, the 'wench' part that needs a bit more description."

"I'm a . . . I'm a . . ." Kate started to turn really red at this point. She placed the back of one hand over her mouth, pressed the other hand to her chest, clutching at her hideous polo shirt, and finally uttered, "Adrishcrapple."

"What? You're a what?"

She dropped her hands. "Okay, okay. A *dish scraper.*"

"I beg your pardon?"

"That's what I said. A rinser of food, a cleaner of plates, a SCRAPER of DISHES." Kate began to hyperventilate. "And I've been trying to be strong for your sake, because that's what Delilah and I decided."

"Okay, Kate, let's just calm down and we'll think of something."

Telling Kate to calm down seemed to have the opposite effect. Fresh tears burst forth and all Clarissa could think to do was to give poor Kate a big hug and let her cry on her shoulder.

And as Kate sobbed there on the left, Clarissa stared off to the right and desperately tried to think of something to fix matters.

Knowing that things had gone really wrong for Kate, that she'd been suffering a terrible wound to her pride, that she'd been too embarrassed to say anything, and had been willing to stick it out for Clarissa's sake . . . well, Clarissa felt touched and sorry all at once. She knew it wasn't pleasant to suffer in silence and after all, what were friends for?

But it reminded her of something she'd sort of forgotten. That while she was busy wallowing in her own poor self-esteem and feeling inadequate and pathetic and all that, thinking that somehow everyone else had their shit together and were wallowing in happiness and basking in success, the truth was that nobody really had everything totally together.

Nobody had their shit together. Nobody wallowed in happiness and basked in success as much as everyone else thought everyone else did. And the whole human race was probably comprised of a bunch of people hiding their problems while they assumed that nobody else actually had any.

It was clear Kate was really in some sort of internal agony over this. Her embarrassment, the humiliation, especially coming on the heels of being downsized . . . it was a lot for anyone.

Lenny cleared his throat loudly. Clarissa patted Kate's head and leaned her friend back against the wall while she headed to the side for a powwow. "Maybe I could go get your other friend," he said. "The makeup artist or whatever, and bring her over and get Kate straightened out, and then we can shoot the interview portion with . . . with . . ."

"Delilah."

"Right, with her. And then we'll go back with Delilah and get the in-action stuff and then we can call it a day. How about that?"

"I don't want to leave Kate. Let's take Kate with us."

"I don't think you should go there at all," Kate said from her slumped position. "Leave poor Delilah alone."

Lenny, Squiggy, and Clarissa swung around and looked at her.

"Poor Delilah?" Clarissa asked, particularly suspicious now, in the face of Kate's total breakdown.

"Thrusting the paparazzi on her like this." Kate clucked, much dismayed.

Impatient noises were beginning to come out of the mouths of the two men, and though Kate's mental welfare obviously was most important right now, Clarissa was really beginning to feel very nervous about Delilah for some reason, not to mention about the welfare and outcome of this seemingly doomed documentary.

Besides, she was beginning to feel quite useless in the face of Kate's tears, and Delilah would probably know what to do.

So she took Kate by the shoulders, hyperaware of Lenny and Squiggy watching, and said, "Kate, we're going in. I don't want to leave you here, so please come with us. But even if you don't, we're going to see Delilah now." With that she turned, swung on her parka, beckoned expertly over her shoulder for the men to follow and, noting with great satisfaction that Kate had chosen to join them, headed straight for the door.

Chapter Twenty

Five minutes later, Clarissa hopped out of the van, the two men and Kate trailing after her. She frowned at the shack up ahead and took a crumpled sticky note from her pocket to have another look at the information. "That's odd. I expected something . . . different."

She led the way through the front door with an odd sense of foreboding.

Inside the building were three people hacking away at some discolored ice that smelled, well, really bad.

One of those people was Delilah.

Clarissa's jaw dropped.

Lenny and Squiggy both grimaced at the smell. Squiggy mumbled something about "What we do for great cinema" and readied the video camera. He pointed it at Delilah's ass and smiled. "Maybe this isn't so bad."

All three ice hackers looked up; there was no disguising the look of horror on Delilah's face as she saw Clarissa staring back at her.

"It *is* you," Clarissa said, taking a surprised step backward. "What in god's name are you doing?"

Delilah looked up at the four spectators plus camera and turned a pale shade of green. "Oh. Oh, my god. I am so not ready for my close-up, right now." Her hand hightailed up to tug at her hair, which was strapped down with a turquoise bandanna. And then she just fixated on the camera lens and seemed to freeze up.

Clarissa grabbed Delilah by the sleeve and hustled her outside, Kate trailing behind. "We're just going to freshen up a second, guys," she called out over her shoulder.

As the door closed behind them and they stepped out into the cold air, Clarissa took a deep breath and in her kindest, most gentle manner said, "You've been lying to me, Delilah."

"Concealing," Delilah said, rather morosely. "Big difference. We just didn't want to tell you for your own good. We thought it might demoralize you. We realized you were on the edge, and well, you know . . ."

"Just . . . what's . . ." Clarissa threw up her arms and flailed them about. "What is all this? What's going on?"

"I'll tell you what." Delilah looked over her shoulder at Kate as if to get confirmation that the jig was really up. She pressed her fingers to the bridge of her nose and uttered, *"Disastré!"*

"Oh dear," Clarissa said. This couldn't be a joke. Whenever Kate cried and Delilah pretended she could speak French, things were really, truly bad.

"She knows about me," Kate said, her voice cracking.

"Are we packing yet?" Delilah asked.

"No, we are not packing." Clarissa moved to try and block this intramural conversation business between the two girls. "You said you had less responsibility," she said. "Is that what this is about?"

"Less responsibility is what we agreed we would say. Because we wanted to stay for your sake. Because this was your big opportunity. The truth is, I've . . . I've . . . I've been demoted."

Clarissa stumbled backward, stunned. "Demoted?"

"In the real world, nobody, and I mean *nobody*, demotes Delilah Aranahi. So you can only imagine what it's been like." She looked at Clarissa and the façade cracked, her face crumpled, and in a much smaller voice, she said, "It's been very, very trying."

Clarissa took her by the shoulders and sat her down on a wooden crate next to where Kate was standing, swaying a little dazedly, looking like she'd just taken meds. Then she put her hands on Kate's shoulders and pressed her friend down on the crate next to Delilah.

The two of them blinked up at her and Clarissa had the oddest sensation of being in charge, being the responsible one. They were looking at her for some sort of answer, for some sort of fix.

Kate and Delilah were rarely vulnerable, and when one was, the other called the shots. Until now, they'd never actually managed to be weak and vulnerable at the same time. Clarissa was now the go-to girl. It was a foreign concept, and Clarissa felt like she was wearing shoes—or bunny boots—a size too small.

Suddenly, Clarissa herself was the anchor. "I feel like the third-string quarterback who's been unexpectedly called into Super Bowl action," she said.

"What?" Delilah asked.

"The third-string . . ." Clarissa made a mental note to purge herself of the sports-related metaphors she'd learned in order to facilitate communications with Kieran. "Like when you can't find your mascara and the backup mascara is in the car or something, and you have to use that sort of dried-out tester mascara that you kept meaning to throw away and never in a million years thought you'd ever use again because they say old mascara breeds bacteria?"

"Oh! Totally."

They continued to look at her expectantly, and Clarissa could feel herself already begin to freeze up. "Oh. Right. So . . ."

Kate started to make hyperventilating sounds to convey that she was still upset, and not to be outdone, Delilah began snorting and clicking again.

Finally, Kate and Delilah looked at each other. Kate sighed egregiously and said, "Come on, Clarissa, take the reins, here. Do something."

"Oh! Well, I . . . I . . ."

"Come *on*, Clarissa. We NEED you."

"I know you do," she whispered. "I'm trying." *This is your moment, Clarissa. This is where you show what you're made of. You are strong. You are capable. You can be a leader.* "Well . . . Delilah, if you're not happy, we should—"

"*If* I'm not happy?" Delilah repeated. "Do you realize what they've reassigned me to?" She took a deep breath, and after a shaky exhale, dramatically uttered, "Waste management."

"At least you're still in management," Clarissa said, trying to lighten up the mood a bit. "Kate's been demoted to kitchen wench."

"Are you making fun?" Kate asked. She turned to Delilah. "My god, she's making fun. We saw her through the Kieran Debacle and she's making fun of us. She's kicking us now that we're down."

"I'm not making fun, and there's no kicking. I'm merely trying to put the best face on the situation."

"The best face? There's no best face!" Kate said, her face screwed up to project her utter disgust.

"Waste management. Me. Can you believe it? I haven't smelled bad or been around anything that's smelled bad in . . . well, *ever*. Waste management. I never! I mean, we're talking about garbage. Refuse. Bad Stuff." Delilah wrung her hands together vigorously. "Merde . . . *merde!* It doesn't get any merde-er."

"Well, look at what I'm dealing with. I show up at seven in the morning and start rinsing off disgusting, half-eaten food from the plates and trays. It's like working at the junior high school cafeteria. And the food's about the same. I mean, I just don't think I have anymore of this left in me."

Clarissa flip-flopped between the two of them, then honed in on Kate. "Okay, okay, let's break this down. It is, of course, just food. Food that hasn't spoiled or anything."

"It's not 'just food,'" Kate said in outrage. "First of all, you just try and tell me that everything we're being served is actually an edible substance according to the FDA. I mean did you see what they had out there at lunch today? Mongolian Surprise. There was about zero percent Mongolian and a hundred percent Surprise. Not to mention, once it's been removed from the serving warmers, it has CROSSED the THRESHOLD." Kate flung her arms out wide for dramatic effect.

"Once your ladle goes in, up, out, and splat . . ."—here she illustrated the process, pantomiming the motions involved in serving oneself slop—". . . you cannot touch it. It's contaminated." Her face was becoming very, very red and her eyes were beginning to water again. "You know all this. Why are you trying to convince me otherwise?"

"Have you ever been to Mongolia?" Delilah said. "You were quick to judge the Amazon Death Squad, and Clarissa says they turned out to be nice. Maybe you're being a bit hasty in your conclusions about the Mongolians."

"Excuse me?"

"I'm just concerned about the Mongolian peoples."

"The Mongolian peoples? I wasn't judging the Mongolians. My point was that it in no way resembled Mongolian cuisine.

This has nothing to do with the Mongolians. I don't even know any Mongolians."

Delilah put her hands on her hips. "Then you couldn't possibly know enough about Mongolian cuisine to judge them."

Kate turned to Clarissa. "Why do I feel like I'm having a conversation with Jessica Simpson?"

"Oh!" Delilah turned away, very much offended.

"I can tell you with great security, that I know enough about Mongolians and their cuisine to know that whatever they served just now in the dining hall wasn't it!" Kate continued. "My original point was that this stuff I'm expected to touch has crossed the food-garbage threshold. Food once disturbed is no longer food. It's waste. *This* is my point. I'm touching other people's waste matter."

Delilah's eyes flew wide open. "No, *I'm* touching other people's waste matter!"

"Nobody's actually touching anybody's waste," Clarissa said quickly. "That's why they have latex gloves."

Kate reared back. "I'll get a rash if I keep this up; I shouldn't be wearing latex."

"I shouldn't be wearing latex, either," Delilah said, working herself toward full-blown hysteria. "I'm sure I've already got thrombosis."

"What?" Clarissa asked. "Delilah, you do not have thrombosis."

"I wasn't finished," Kate said loudly, clearly concerned that Delilah's trauma would overshadow her own.

Delilah muttered that she felt she'd heard quite enough.

Kate apparently disagreed. "Clarissa, this is serious. Now that you know what we've been dealing with here, I think we should seriously consider going home. I mean, I've been demoted to the bottom of the food chain, so to speak. All those hopes, those brilliant ideas about revolutionizing the world of institutional cooking? Now it doesn't matter that they used processed cheese and expired canned goods that look like they're about to explode, showering rancid acid everywhere, in something called a Mongolian Surprise . . . because I'm not involved. It has nothing to do with me. I'm not any sort of chef, and I haven't cooked a goddamn thing since I got here. Mongolian Surprise is not my concern."

"I'm so sorry," Clarissa said weakly, silently vowing not to eat anything invoking Mongolians as a source of cuisine or using the descriptors "Surprise," "Medley," or "Jumble" during the remainder of her stay.

Delilah sniffed. "Well, I should think processed cheese and rancid acid *would* concern you since you're the one scraping it off everybody's plates."

Kate gasped. "That was low."

Delilah picked up the thread and kept running. "Food can't be food one second and then magically convert to waste in the next second simply by virtue of its location."

"What do you know about it?" Kate snapped.

"What do I *know* about it?" Delilah said, now clearly miffed. "I'm in waste management, for god's sake, you'd think I'd know a little bit about what constitutes waste and what does not."

"You chip urine out of MILVANS!" Kate yelled. "Besides, that's not the point. All I said was that I thought we should go home. It's not like you've had any great artistic epiphanies about a fabulous new lipstick color whilst standing in a smelly MILVAN. What's more, you complained about coming here in the first place. You said you'd rather go home. So let's go home."

"You've misquoted me again. You're always misquoting me."

"Okay, what did you say?"

"I said 'I want to go home.' Not, 'I'd rather go home.'"

"Are you kidding me?"

"Enough!" Clarissa bellowed out.

The girls fell silent.

"We are not playing 'My Life Sucks More' anymore."

Kate put her hands on her hips. "Fine. So, what should we do?"

"Kate's right." Delilah brushed a stray lock of hair out of her eyes in a most weary fashion. "Let's go home. We should all just go home. We just don't belong here."

Kate tucked Delilah's unruly hair back under the turquoise bandanna. "I'm with you one hundred percent. And you know what else, we didn't fight at home. I think this place is bad for us."

"But isn't this what we came for?" Clarissa asked softly. "For the challenge. What else did we expect to find when we decided we needed to start over? Look how hard we worked for our lives back home in the first place." She paused dramatically, hoping it would give some heft to her next statement. "Change isn't easy. And that is why we're not leaving."

Kate and Delilah stared at her as if she'd just announced her candidacy for U.S. president. "But you want to leave. Don't you want to leave?" Kate asked rather desperately.

Clarissa folded her arms across her chest and took a wide stance. "I do not want to leave. We're not leaving. End of story."

Kate scratched the side of her head. "You were the one least inclined to come here in the first place."

"Well, now I'm the least inclined to leave." Clarissa dusted imaginary dust off her hands. "You'll just have to make the best of it. I mean, I didn't get what I expected to get, either, what with the entire documentary project dropped in my lap and Lenny and Squiggy, the B-list Wonders—god bless 'em—as my only reference when this is all over. But you don't see me having a nervous breakdown, do you?"

"You're right. How strange," Delilah said.

Kate nudged her. "That's probably because she's already had one."

Delilah looked at her suspiciously, then looked at Kate. "You know, it is odd that Clarissa really doesn't want to leave. Don't you think that's odd? I think it's extremely odd."

Kate narrowed her eyes. "Hmmm . . . are you thinking what I'm thinking?"

"The boy," Delilah said.

"You have no idea how wrong you are," Clarissa said.

Kate waved her protest away. "I think we've just hit on it. We're stuck here because Clarissa wants to be with Mitchell. We've been derailed by a boy."

"Why didn't you just say so, Clarissa?" Delilah said. "Clearly, Kate and I will stick our arms in waste above our elbows just so you can be with a boy. And as a sidebar, I just want to point out that I freely admit I am not drawing any creative inspiration for a new cosmetics line by chipping frozen urine out of a MILVAN. I would like to officially register that as supporting argument for leaving."

"I hardly think that sort of tone is necessary," Clarissa said, quite miffed, not to mention surprised at the unusual amount of venom in Delilah's voice.

"Oh, Delilah," Kate said, equally sarcastic. "Isn't that lovely? Clarissa goes and finds her anchor and now we can't leave."

"Yes, we can," Delilah said. "We'll just leave Clarissa on her own."

"You can't do that," Clarissa said, stepping forward.

"Why not?" the two girls demanded, in unison.

"Because . . . well, for one thing, it's extremely rude to drag me across the world and then abandon me. Grossly inappropriate. It could very well ruin our friendship forever. For another,

I've decided not to pursue a relationship with Mitchell, and thus I do not have an anchor. I have only me."

She was sort of making it up as she talked. But once it came out of her mouth, it really seemed to make sense. Mitchell was just another Kieran. Well, he wasn't really, of course . . . but he sort of was. *I have only me.* Clarissa began to sweat at that thought. She was doing good. No, she was doing great. But if Kate and Delilah abandoned her now . . . she couldn't let them go. Like she'd just said. She'd have "only me."

"Look," Kate said wearily. "We're highly educated, we've already worked for years in the corporate world, we've achieved—and become accustomed to—a certain level of prestige and salary. We've tried to keep all this quiet and stick it out for your sake, because we thought this place was really doing something for you, but let's face it. Out here, we're nothing. And being nothing does not feel good to me."

"Or me," Delilah added. "I feel like a loser."

"But that's what we're here for," Clarissa said. "To learn about ourselves. In some way, to start over. To avoid defaulting to the boundaries, the expectations of our social circle."

"Frankly, I miss the boundaries, I miss the expectations," Kate said. "At least they're familiar and we know how to navigate them."

"Well, I'm not leaving," Clarissa said, digging in.

The three girls stood there in silence.

"We have a problem. Two of us want to go home and the other wants to stay," Delilah said. "We should have thought about this before. Sort of like one of those partnership dissolution agreements."

Clarissa leaned against the wall. They were serious. They were completely serious. And if they wanted to go, she didn't want to stop them. But it wasn't quite over yet. She still had a couple of trump cards up her sleeve. "If you really want to go, Delilah, by all means, go. But I think it's bad form to quit."

"Quit? I didn't say anything about quitting. I'm talking about leaving." Delilah frowned. "I don't quit things. I adjust my direction."

"It's quitting," Clarissa said firmly. "And really, Kate, it's okay to be weak. I understand. I'm not here to judge."

Kate reared back, a look of horror on her face. "Weak? I am NOT weak."

Clarissa managed to suppress a smile. Finesse.

Delilah looked at Kate. "I don't quit."

"And I'm not weak," Kate said, looking at Delilah.

The two girls swiveled around and stared at Clarissa. "We're not going home, are we?" Kate asked with a sigh.

Clarissa smiled, feeling surer about this than she had about anything in a long time. "No, we're not. We're going to finish the season just like everybody else," she said definitively. "You guys are fantastic. You can do anything. You always could. So you just need to find that extreme something inside you that's going to get you to the end of this experience. You'll be the better for it. We all will."

"Wow," Kate said.

"Indeed," Delilah added. "Well. In that case, I guess I'm just going to have to become one with my inner sanitation engineer. And to think before this, I'd never even cleaned a toilet in my entire life."

"There's still time for you to have a major creative resurgence, Delilah. Inspiration can be found in the most unlikely places. And in spite of my rather . . ."

Here Clarissa looked over her shoulder where Lenny and Squiggy had set up the camera and were shooting. "In spite of my rather 'difficult' project, I still have the potential to have my name attached to a high-quality documentary before this season is through. And as for Kate," Clarissa continued, "Kate will . . . Kate will . . . Kate will develop such empathy for the workers in her condition that when she eventually opens her own restaurant, employee-employer conflict will be practically nonexistent."

Kate didn't look too impressed. "Whatever."

"What do you say?" Clarissa asked. "Are you with me? Are you in? I know we can make it through all this and when it's over, we're going to be glad we stayed. So, what do you say, girls?"

"I say . . . that if we're here to stay, I'm going to need a nice cold expired beer as soon as we get done with this shoot."

"Me too," Delilah said. "Huddle?"

Delilah and Kate got off the crate and closed the circle with Clarissa.

"Thanks for the pep talk, Clarissa. You're the best," Kate said.

"Yeah, the best," Delilah said. "But I've really got to redo my mascara."

"And I think I have a poppy seed in my teeth. I hope to god I don't have a poppy seed in my teeth," Kate said. "Delilah, show me where the bathroom is. Clarissa, we'll be right back. Don't go away."

She wasn't going anywhere. She was happy just where she was. And as Clarissa watched her best friends head off to freshen up, she realized that she hadn't felt this good about herself in a long, long time.

"They're walking, they're walking . . . fade to black . . . and that's a wrap!" Lenny called out from somewhere behind yonder. "Great segment, Clarissa."

With her back to the camera, Clarissa allowed herself to indulge in a big, wide smile. "Yeah, great segment."

Chapter Twenty-one

Things were really rolling along now as the three girls headed toward the end of the season. It could actually be said that Clarissa, Delilah, and Kate were adjusting to life on The Ice.

Except for one thing. With the documentary going so well, Clarissa had too much time to contemplate her love life, which was still totally on the fritz. Days continued to pass without her tying up the loose ends with Mitchell. Part of it was that he'd been instructing at another snow school. And part of it was that she was starting to waffle about whether throwing him over simply because he'd gotten a little self-involved in front of the camera was the right response.

Anyone could easily be seduced by the notion of getting a lucky break in the Hollywood scene, though she did question Mitchell's judgment as far as thinking that Lenny and Squiggy's documentary might be the ideal vehicle for possible success.

With Kate's furry friend returning to town after one of his far-flung diving trips and Delilah engaged in "field exercises" with her firefighting sleep-buddy, Clarissa was feeling a little lonely. She had too much time to wonder where she'd gone wrong with Kieran, and too much time to wonder when, if, and how she'd go wrong with Mitchell.

So she went with Kate and Delilah and the Garanimal and the firefighter to Open Mike at the bar and tried not to get totally mixed up by the slew of excuses she was formulating for Mitchell in her head as she made herself comfortable with a couple of margaritas.

Kate nudged Clarissa. "Isn't that Mitchell huddling back there on the stage?"

"Oh, it couldn't be." But Clarissa couldn't really see in the dim light. "I can't imagine he's the sort. I'm not even sure he's back from snow school yet, though he was scheduled to come in this morning."

Delilah and Kate gave her sympathetic looks; she smiled and quickly looked away, to the stage.

A bald drummer with a soul patch large enough to qualify as a small animal began tapping a rhythm with the cymbals.

Cha-ch-ch-cha-ch-ch-cha . . .

The figure cloaked in darkness came forward into the light. It *was* Mitchell. Clarissa gripped the sides of her chair. "Oh, my *god.*"

"Apparently, there *is* something less appealing in a boyfriend prospect than footie pajamas," Delilah whispered.

Kate hadn't yet picked her jaw off the floor. She did so now, then turned to Clarissa and said, "I'm so glad you never slept with him."

Clarissa by this time had sunk lower in her chair, muttering, "It doesn't make him a bad person or anything. It's not like it changes his personality. Didn't I mention that he's an actor?"

"No, you didn't. And by the way, that . . ."—Kate gestured gingerly toward the stage—". . . *that* changes everything. As in final nail in the coffin. You were already going wishy-washy on him. Just admit it."

Clarissa chewed her lower lip.

"No, don't analyze." Kate shook her head. "There's nothing to think about. Extracurricular activities must be included when considering the person."

Delilah leaned over and pointed at the stage. "Does that turn you on? Be honest. Are you feeling butterflies in your stomach over that? I mean, I'll support you if you are, but I'm just asking."

Clarissa looked up at the stage and winced.

"Exactly," Kate said. "It's not a comment on how nice he is, how much money he makes, or if he's using you to gain an en-trée into Hollywood." Clarissa rolled her eyes at that as Kate continued and said, "It just is what it is. Are you telling me that you feel even a modicum of sexual interest staring up at that stage?"

"I'm not telling you anything."

"It's so over," Kate said to Delilah. "Clarissa can do so much better."

Clarissa downed her margarita and sighed heavily as Mitchell launched into his routine. He was dressed in a sort of a barbershop quartet outfit and his doll wore a matching suit. In all fairness, Mitchell's visual did make Bill's Garanimal business look downright sexy. Kate was right. It didn't make her a bad person to admit it, but for god's sake, sleeping with a ventrilo-quist was just totally out of the question.

She'd probably wake up in the middle of the night to find that horrible grinning doll with the movable mouth standing over her with a cleaver. Not to mention the sort of bizarre mut-terings one might find projecting from the toaster or one's eggcup during breakfast. Clarissa wasn't a morning person, and the last thing she needed was a boyfriend throwing multiple voices from inanimate objects at eight in the morning.

"There goes my best anchor possibility. I make the worst choices," Clarissa said despondently. "What's wrong with me? I mean, it must be me. They just are who they are. I'm the one picking them out and going with it. What is *wrong* with me?"

"Oh, Clarissa. Don't be so dramatic," Delilah said, patting her hand. "You're just fine."

"I'm not. I can see clearly now. There's something wrong with me. No wonder Kieran left me. I'm flawed. I have major psychological problems . . . and my arms are disproportionately short for the rest of my body."

"Your arms are not too—"

"I'm way too much trouble," Clarissa interrupted, cutting Delilah off. "Troublesome, that's me."

"You're fine," Kate said. "How many drinks is that, anyway?"

"Why do people keep saying that to me? I'm not fine."

Delilah raised an eyebrow.

"Am I desperate? Couldn't I just find some hobbies, or something? Why do I spend time thinking about and searching for a man when the problem is in my selection criteria. It's a doomed enterprise. Why do I do this?"

"Well, it's not as if your job is particularly taxing," Kate said. "It takes up a mere fraction of brain space and then you're left with all that free brain power just aching for something to do."

"Good point. You know, I find this all a bit alarming."

"What's alarming?" Delilah asked.

"That I'm where I'm at and yet my behavior is only changing for the worse. I'm in Antarctica. I should be experiencing a sense of Zen and finding meditation as a life force, or becoming gobsmacked by the beauty of the nature that surrounds me after which I take up cross-country skiing or insist on running around in the snow for my physical edification, or turning into a vegetarian recycling activist."

"You're fine, Clarissa," Kate said.

"No, what's actually happening is that I'm becoming shallower and more ridiculous. Once I could string more than a few deep thoughts together at a time. Now I drool and stutter. This is not the personal growth experience I was hoping for."

"Yesterday you seemed all empowered and happy. I think you should visit that place again." Delilah moved one of the drinks in danger of being upended in Clarissa's distress. "And for goodness' sake, don't be so hard on yourself."

Clarissa looked at her two friends and considered that. "Wait a minute, I'm not being hard on myself. Now that I really think about it, the root of all my problems has nothing to do with me." She paused dramatically and focused on not slurring. "I'm not my fault."

Delilah lifted an eyebrow. "Whose fault are you?"

"My parents, of course," Clarissa said. "It's become disturbingly clear to me that good parenting and an exemplary childhood have ruined my life. I'm not flawed because I had a horrible childhood, I'm flawed because I had it too good. The experience has left me scarred. I can't make a move—I mean, I'm literally incapable of functioning properly without a set of worried, concerned, involved parent-like figures directing my every move."

She looked at Delilah. She looked at Kate.

Clarissa stood up and confronted the girls. "How dare they ruin me in this manner . . . Oh, my god. You're my mom and dad."

"What?" Delilah looked confused.

"Oh, stop it. Your parents are very proud of you," Kate said.

"Would this be an inappropriate time to mention that I just had a flash of something?" Delilah asked. "It's possible a break-through is imminent."

Clarissa and Kate looked at her expectantly.

Delilah suddenly raised her palms. "Something's coming . . . this is it, folks!" She stared excitedly into blank air. "Uh-huh . . . uh-huh . . . I'm seeing something . . . I'm seeing . . ." The smile disappeared. "No, no, that's not possible. That's not going to work. I would never do black lipstick. Well, it's a step forward, I guess . . . oh, never mind." She sighed heavily and folded her hands in her lap.

Silence. Kate turned to Clarissa. "Um, so were we done with you?"

Clarissa threw up her hands. "*I'm* done with me."

"Good, because—"

Kate's Garanimal leaned down between them and handed Kate the phone which he'd strung over from the bar. "Phone call for you."

Kate looked at Clarissa, made a funny face, then took the phone. "Hello? Yeah, this is me. *Who's* this again? Oh!"

Delilah and Clarissa looked at each other.

"Uh-huh . . . wow . . . I see . . . oh, my god . . ." Kate's eyes had gotten very wide. And she was clearly getting some pretty serious news. News, in fact, which seemed like it might be good news.

"I can do that," Kate said. She looked at the other two and gave them a thumbs-up. "Right . . . not a problem . . . this is right up my alley. Have I done this before? Oh, of course!" She waved her hand in the air as if to say "No problem," and Clarissa and Delilah looked at each other again, this time with that sinking sort of concern they'd learned to have whenever Kate insisted that she absolutely knew what she was doing when she very clearly had no idea.

Kate hung up the phone and looked at them in silence, so excited that she couldn't even put it into words.

"Well," Clarissa asked, "is it good news?"

"It's great news!"

"What is it?" Delilah asked.

"I don't think I've ever been so happy in my life," she said in a reverent whisper.

"What happened?"

"The entire cooking staff has come down with food poisoning!"

Delilah and Clarissa looked at each other. Delilah swallowed nervously. "What did they eat?"

"Well, the cooking staff clique is always having these sort of exclusive get-togethers. Apparently, they had a twenty-fifth anniversary party for some canned yams somebody found in the back of a food storage locker. Might I just point out that they did NOT invite the dish-rinsing staff to said celebration."

"That's certainly lucky," Clarissa said.

Kate was just euphoric. "In fact, now that I think about it, when they held that private party for the gnat the chef found in that crate of spaghetti sauce last week, I said to the rest of the rinsing staff that management's exclusionary policies would come back to haunt them."

"This is great," Delilah said. "So, do you get a promotion?"

"The upshot, the moral of the story, if you will, is that there's no one left to cook the Thanksgiving banquet except the dishwashers and kitchen cleaners and the rinsers! But that's not the point. They've put me in charge! I'm the cook! I have the most relevant experience."

Clarissa was tempted to ask how it was possible to have less than zero actual restaurant experience, but instead, she managed an enthusiastic, supportive, "Wow. You're responsible for the Thanksgiving banquet?"

"I've been promoted to interim head chef. That makes me Thanksgiving Banquet Coordinator. Can you believe it?"

Clarissa looked down at the dregs of her margharita and swallowed nervously. "Indeed, I can. But Thanksgiving for a thousand. I mean, I support you one hundred percent, but . . ."

"But what?"

Clarissa didn't want to say it. She didn't want to be unsupportive. Delilah apparently had no such compunction.

"I think what Clarissa is getting at," Delilah said, "is that you don't want to be forever known as the girl in Antarctica who screwed up Thanksgiving for a thousand people."

"It is a big, stressful job, Kate. People can become very irrational about their holiday food," Clarissa said.

"Well, I've cooked for ten and it's really a simple multiple."

Delilah and Clarissa looked at each other.

"What? What's the problem? It's a little math, a little adjustment. And I'm just going to do what I got to do. This is my big break." Kate breathed in deeply, then exhaled, as if she actually had finally found Zen. "I just knew that if we stuck with it, we'd get something out of this. There are, indeed, lessons to be learned, and I am off to learn them!"

She pushed away from the table. "Well, gotta run. Oh, and Clarissa?"

Clarissa looked up hopefully. Kate was pointing to the opposite side of the table and when she turned to follow her gaze, there was Mitchell in his barbershop ventriloquist suit. Her heart sank. He looked so cute in his outdoors' clothes. How was she to know this lurked beneath it all?

"Hi, Clarissa."

"Hi, Mitchell."

"Do you mind if I sit down?"

Clarissa smiled. "Feel free."

"I heard from Lenny and Squiggy that you saw the dailies and weren't too happy about it." He looked down at his ventriloquist doll, fiddling with the little bow tie.

"Well, to be honest, I wasn't. It really seemed like you were more into the camera than into the kiss," she said.

He put the doll aside and reached across the table for her hand. And in spite of his ridiculous outfit and that icky doll, it was really very nice to have him holding her hand.

"I want you to know that I'm very sorry that I got carried away by the whole filming business, but it in no way lessens the fact that I'm totally into you, Clarissa."

Wow.

"And if I could have that moment back, I would shut off the cameras and kiss you endlessly."

Wow.

"I'm back, now, and I'm going to make sure that you don't have to lift a pinkie for the rest of the season, what do you think about that?" He moved in close, poised to kiss her. And even in her margarita haze, Clarissa realized that all she'd really managed to do was to replace one Kieran with another.

She smiled at Mitchell and, enunciating carefully, said, "Mitchell, thank you so much for the lovely words, but I'm just not interested right now."

He jolted back in surprise. "Is it the ventriloquism thing?"

She smiled. "No. It was before that."

He took a deep breath and exhaled, then held out his hand. "Friends?"

Clarissa gave him her hand. "Friends."

He kissed the back of it and smiled.

She smiled back and pulled back her hand. And just like that, she pulled the anchor up and floated away on a tequila haze back to her room.

* * *

A very hungover Clarissa sat at her computer the following morning writing up short blurbs for each of the documentary segments. The walkie-talkie sitting on her desk crackled a bit; the video monitor behind her played without sound.

Glancing over her shoulder at the screen, Clarissa watched the proceedings back at Seal Camp. The boys had returned to film a few more bits for the Seal Cam segment. They'd mounted a videocamera on the van itself for big-picture stuff, and Squiggy was apparently handling close-ups.

They were using Mitchell as a sort of spokesmodel (AKA "Ass") for flavor since the seal still wasn't doing a whole hell of a lot and there was no longer any conflict of interest for Mitchell to worry about. As usual, he looked really fantastic in his outdoor gear, no sign of the ventriloquist at all.

Clarissa sighed. "What evil lies beneath," she muttered, and returned to her computer.

Suddenly, Squiggy's voice squawked through on the walkie-talkie. Clearly a bit befuddled by the technology, the panicked lilt of his voice still came through loud and clear "You there? Clarissa? Clarissa? It's Squiggy! Clarissa?"

"This is Clarissa, Squiggy," she said into the walkie-talkie. "What is it?"

"Are you watching the screen? I think we've got a . . ."

Clarissa tried to swallow but her mouth had gone dry. "A what?"

"A situation."

Doom. Utter doom.

"What kind of situation?"

"Turn up the sound on the video."

Clarissa fiddled with the knob. "Squigg, the lens is pointing—" Suddenly the view changed to a long, zoomed shot, taking in two people on their knees, huddled over the seal. Lenny and Mitchell.

Lenny looked at Mitchell. "Could you just help me disconnect this bit right here . . ."

Mitchell nodded, and tried to disassemble some of the more antagonistic Cam parts.

The seal started to twitch and a few sparks shot out of the backpack.

Mitchell froze, his hands hovering over the Seal Cam pack. He looked back over his shoulder toward Squiggy's camera lens and in a higher-than-normal voice said, "I think it's going to blow. I really think it's going to blow." And with that, he started to back away from the seal.

In the office, Clarissa rubbed her temples and stared hopelessly at the screen.

"It's okay, it's okay," Lenny was saying as he pushed Mitchell back toward the seal. "It's conflict, drama. The audience is going to love it."

On the monitor, Clarissa could see sweat soaking through Mitchell's balaclava as he leaned over the animal. The Cam pack was smoking now. "I'm looking for a little assistance, here. Anytime, now!" Mitchell looked into the camera lens and said, "Can somebody else come out here and assist?"

Clarissa sat glued to her seat, her head aching, her mouth like sand . . . and totally, completely useless as far as being of any help whatsoever in this impending crisis. But there was nothing she could do. By the time she drove out there, whatever was to be . . . would have already been. There was nothing to be done. When the real crisis came to call, she wasn't the one to handle it.

She picked up the phone and dialed.

"Lord High Demon Priest of Vengeance speaking."

"It's Clarissa. Sorry to bother you at home. We've got a situation, and I just thought you ought to know about it." She described what was transpiring and without further discussion, her boss hung up the phone.

Back on the screen, Mitchell wiped at the sweat on his face. "We've got three loose wires, here."

"Maybe we should look at the instructions," Squiggy said.

"There are no instructions," Lenny said.

"Well, there must be something. I think we should shut the thing off," Mitchell said, strain evident in his voice.

Clarissa grabbed a walkie-talkie, set the channel, and turned it on. "Okay . . . Mitchell, can you hear me? This is Clarissa."

On-screen, Mitchell's hand went to his radio. He clipped the microphone extension to his parka collar. "Clarissa? I can hear you fine. What do you think?"

Clarissa flipped through the paperwork on her desk. None of it, of course, had anything to do with seals or cameras or deactivating bombs. "Um . . . I really don't know."

"Well, somebody think of something," Squiggy's voice said from behind the camera.

Clarissa stared at her monitor. "Maybe try disconnecting the yellow wire?" she said weakly. Of course, she had no clue whether disconnecting the yellow wire was any better than disconnecting the blue one first, or the red or green ones for that matter, but it was as good an idea as any.

"Okay, I'm gonna squat here and work on the wires . . . am I in the shot?" Mitchell said. "Um, as long as I'm doing this . . . are you getting my profile, Squigg? I'm talking about the left side. The left side's my better side, if you can."

"I gotcha," Squiggy said.

Mitchell fiddled around with the Cam pack and frowned. "I can't seem to get my fingers . . . my fingers are too damn small." He stood up and looked into the camera lens. "Can we get somebody to come out here and assist?"

Lenny took Mitchell by the lapels. "Look, man. We're counting on you. Somebody's just got to defuse that seal. It may be the most boring, useless seal we've ever seen, but, by god, it's still somebody's . . . seal. You have it in you to do this. Now get in there, and do what you need to do."

"Jesus Christ," Squiggy muttered. But Mitchell really seemed moved by the pep talk. With renewed vigor, he bent down and started working again. Clarissa stood there in the middle of the office with the radio in her hand, just staring at the monitor with a sick sense of inevitability.

Mitchell managed to detach the pack and an audible sigh of relief came from all four of them. And then it happened. The detached Cam pack started to smoke and spark. Mitchell yelped and threw it at Lenny, who bobbled the equipment and threw it back at him.

Squiggy literally dropped his camera in the snow, and Clarissa switched to the wide-angle lens mounted on the van for a brilliant view of all three men panicking and passing the smoking Seal Cam from person to person.

"Throw it away!" Clarissa screeched into the radio. "Just throw it far away!"

Squiggy broke from the threesome, grabbed his camera, and tossed the equipment in the van just as Lenny was passing him the Seal Cam bomb.

It seemed like slow motion as the Seal Cam bomb went sailing through the air . . .

. . . through the open door of the van . . .

. . . swapping places with a squealing Squiggy who dove headfirst into the snow . . .

. . . as in perfect California-earthquake-preparedness style,

Mitchell and Lenny performed a duck-and-cover maneuver even the state governor would be proud of.

And suddenly Clarissa just knew. The thing was going to blow.

And it did. The van exploded.

"The van just exploded," Clarissa said matter-of-factly to no one in particular, seeing as how she was alone in the office, doing absolutely nothing as chaos erupted and the documentary film, still in the van, went up in smoke before her very eyes.

Chapter Twenty-two

"Kate! Kaaaaaate!"

They'd said they'd be backups, and it was backup time. Clarissa could do a reshoot using Kate and Delilah as subject matter, get their help on filming other segments, maybe by splitting up and fanning out . . . one of them could head down and catch the emperor penguin hanging out by the transition; Clarissa could maybe see if the greenhouse had any luck with something other than a microscopic fungus or whatever the hell that was; maybe she could convince a couple guys to pick a fight in the bar, yeah, that would be high drama; and . . . and . . . oh, god, she'd just have to take it as it would come.

She was wired. Nearly out of her head. Completely unwilling to give up on this project. The existing material was all completely destroyed, no question. But if they just kept working, maybe they could salvage the project by coming up with new stuff.

Clarissa made her way to the kitchen where full-throttle insanity was taking place.

"Kate?" She had to yell over the noise of the clank and the

spray and the steam and the slipperiness and the people running to and fro with those little paper hats on looking like crazed elves.

Clarissa looked at her watch and tried not to panic. "Kate!"

Kate was standing next to a giant worktable stacked high with approximately one hundred raw turkeys. A cluster of kitchen staff looked on. "Not now, Clarissa. This is not a good time."

She turned back to the assembly. "Did you understand what I just said? You've got to take the rémoulade . . ."

The men shuffled their feet uncertainly and looked at each other.

"Okay, okay." Kate wiped at her forehead with the sleeve of her chef's jacket. "Um . . . okay. Let's try this. Huddle up." She waved her hand. "That's right, you heard me. Form a huddle."

The guys formed a semicircle.

"Heads down, get your heads in the huddle. We've got to get these babies in the oven. So what we've got to do is, uh, right . . . so we're going to form two, er, 'Turkey Teams' and it's going to be a contest. You guys . . . against you guys. And here's how it works. Take some rémoulade and insert into the cavity—" The boys started to fade again and Kate quickly rallied. "Take some stuffing . . . shove it up the ass, slap some butter on top, rosemary sprinkles, and bring it home, baby. Touchdown! Whoever scores the most . . . Turkey Touchdowns wins. Got it? Good."

The men nodded and dispersed to their Turkey Teams. Kate turned back to Clarissa. "Sorry, but unless this is an emergency, I don't have time to talk. I've got to go explain to a bunch of volunteers from the fire department what crudités are. Can't you get Mitchell . . . oh, right. Sorry."

"Kate, this is *serious,*" Clarissa said. "I need your help. I have one week to re-create a couple months' worth of work."

"What are you talking about?"

"The documentary! The documentary!" Clarissa could hear herself and she sounded totally hysterical.

"What about the documentary?" Kate asked, her attention really not on Clarissa's problem with the documentary at all.

"The film, all my work, it's all been destroyed. You know how important this project is to me. You know what that documentary means to my future. I've got to re-create it somehow. I've got to deliver something tangible . . . I must have something to show for myself! Do. You. Understand!?"

"So the documentary got destroyed? My god, that's a huge nightmare." Kate's attention turned to the mashed potato station. "Remember, ladies, we need some with lumps, some with no lumps . . . and who volunteered to do signs? Did we have a food card volunteer?"

"Kate, Kate, focus on me here. It's me, Clarissa. And I need your help. I need you to help me film this stuff, and I need you to be my subject matter, and I need—"

Kate took Clarissa by the shoulders. "Clarissa. Stop it. I can't help you with this. I'm really, really sorry. But I think you need to take a moment to realize that you're not going to be able to re-create that documentary in the time we have left."

Clarissa just stared at Kate like she was drowning, but all Kate could do was shrug. "Try being responsible for a Thanksgiving dinner to feed one thousand people. *That's* serious." She walked past Clarissa and went over to the stove top where a tiny girl was stirring a huge pot of gravy. "Watch the bottom. Everything might look okay on the surface, but all hell could be breaking loose underneath."

"I thought I could depend on you! I can't do this alone."

"You don't need me for this! And you won't be alone; you've got Delilah." She turned up her nose as if sniffing the wind. "Look, I've got to run. I'm sensing a stall in the pie assembly line . . . let's make sure to hook up later for the big dinner."

"But you're my default anchor!" Clarissa screamed at the top of her lungs as two industrial-sized Mixmasters went into whipping cream overdrive.

"It's pumpkin time!" Kate answered with her fist raised valiantly in the air as she steered course for the pie station.

Clarissa glanced at her watch and began to sweat. She still had time to run over to the Waste Barn and catch Delilah. And hopefully, with the holidays here, her bosses might be a little more laid-back about hours and would let Delilah disappear for a little while.

But once she'd reached the Waste Barn it became obvious that nobody was cleaning, recycling, or chipping anything. In fact, the usual hubbub was reduced and all the noise seemed to be confined to one of the large warehouse spaces off to the left. Still breathing heavily from the sprint over, Clarissa followed the noise and was passed by a couple of girls who looked like regular trashies from the neck down except that . . . except that . . .

Clarissa distinctly recognized Delilah's imprint on the incredibly perfect makeup job from the neck up. Something was a little different about it, but she couldn't quite put her finger on it.

A line of women snaked out of the door and when Clarissa pushed through, she found Delilah at a makeshift makeup station, deliriously applying makeup from a case and then making notes of some kind on a pad of paper next to it.

Men were plucking each other's eyebrows and applying moisturizer and face masks made from a base of that box of dried guacamole mix Delilah had found in the kitchen supplies.

Delilah looked at Clarissa in the reflection of the mirror, her own makeup smeared, her hair damp with sweat and pulled back. "I've been trying to call your office. You are so not going to believe this. I've found the muse," she whispered hoarsely.

"I'm literally channeling it, right now . . . my god, Clarissa, I'm *back!*"

To her surprise the Death Squad Girls, made over within an inch of their lives, were taking instruction from Delilah and applying makeup to others in turn.

Clarissa carefully approached. This was a delicate situation. "Delilah, that's wonderful . . . the thing is, I really need your help right now."

"No can do, Clary. I'm really sorry, but when the muse shows up, you do not ask her to take five, know what I mean?" She grabbed her next subject by the ears and studied the left profile, then the right profile. "This is it. I'm not washed up. I'm not obsolete. I've really done it." She looked at the girl. "And to finish, red or clear on you . . . red . . . or clear . . . definitely clear." She shellacked some clear lipgloss on the girl's lips and sent her packing. "Next!"

"Delilah," Clarissa began desperately. "Help me. *Please.* I need to refilm at least six segments for the documentary."

"Why?"

"Everything's gone, the film's gone, the documentary . . . gone. I've got to do something."

"Let me tell you something, Clary. You don't need that documentary. The point isn't the finished product, it's—"

"But that's just it!" Clarissa wailed. "The documentary *is* the point. It's the only proof I have that I've really done something. That I've accomplished something."

"You've got to hear this. Tell me what you think." Delilah lifted her arms out, her gaze starry-eyed. "Trashed: the Compacter Collection. It's hip, it's now, it's portable, it's Tomb Raider meets Heroin Addict . . . and it doesn't violate the conditions of my no-competition clause. I'm back in business, Clary, and it's all coming together. Right. Now. Good luck with your situation, sweetie. *Next!*" A dreadlocked girl who looked like she probably thought cosmetics had something to do with Russian space travel sat down in the chair and Delilah went into the artist's zone.

Delilah was gone in muse-land; she didn't even notice as Clarissa slunk out of the building and made her way back to the office. It was empty when she got there, the only evidence of the day's debacle a note signed by Lenny and Squiggy informing Clarissa that they were taking the day off.

They didn't understand either. It was their damn documentary and they didn't understand.

Chapter Twenty-three

Something vaguely resembling a tailgate party was mobilizing on the white tundra below as Mitchell drove Clarissa, Lenny, and Squiggy out to film the penguin at the transition.

In spite of the fact that it could only really provide one segment, which was hardly a replacement for the numerous lost ones, Lenny and Squiggy were delighted with the prospect of a penguin-centric segment and acted like she was brilliant for having thought of it. Needless to say, Clarissa was beginning to feel the slightest bit better.

Squiggy, practicing with some borrowed equipment, began to record in the intoned hush of a pedigree-dog-show announcer, "Segment number one: The emperor penguin stands alone . . ."

Mitchell snorted in disdain.

"Tall and proud. He is big. He is black. He is also white. And he is also yellow. He has—"

"Squigg," Lenn said impatiently. "This is why we have cameras. You know, *cameras*. Pictures speak a thousand words, eh?"

Squiggy cowered sheepishly back into the seat and Clarissa shot him a sympathetic look just as Mitchell set the parking brake and they all lurched forward.

Collecting themselves and their gear, the foursome clambered out of the car to join a huge ring of people who had gathered around a single, impossibly cute, rather nonplussed penguin.

The emperor was, indeed, big, black, white, and also yellow. He seemed like a sturdy, substantial fellow. And every time he took a step forward, a murmur of delight would pass through the crowd.

There were pictures, laughter, hijinks of all kinds, including people getting down on their knees and mimicking penguin-like mannerisms involving bad Charlie Chaplin imitations and sliding on the snow on their stomachs.

As far as Clarissa was concerned, the penguin definitely noticed, and her smile drooped just a little at that.

After all, she was the sort of person who frowned upon tourism in the Galapagos in the sense that one false step by a careless Bermuda-shorts-wearing tourist from Kansas and an entire species could be wiped out. "Oops, there goes a bird's egg. Guess we won't be seeing any White-Tongued Whip-poor-will-Red-Breasted Loon again. Ever."

But maybe if Lenny and Squiggy captured the mix of sentiments in the moment, maybe if they were somehow able to convey the bizarre hypocrisy of it all . . . well, it could very well be the most compelling material they would find. Hopefully it wouldn't be the only material they would find.

Of course, that's when Lenny walked up to the penguin and stuck a light meter in its face. Squiggy was manning the camera and called out, "Do you think we should get him to sign a release?" and laughed.

Clarissa looked at Mitchell. "Isn't this harassment of wildlife?" she asked a little timidly.

Mitchell shrugged. "People get a little excited. It's the only penguin we're likely to see anywhere near town, so it's the only penguin we're likely to see this season."

"Oh." Clarissa looked around. Flat white to the left. Flat white to the right. Sure, beautiful, flat, white, but . . . "Where are its friends?"

"It got separated from its community. Went out to look for food and got separated, mixed up. They really don't like to be on their own. They don't do so good alone." He crossed his hands over his chest and looked at the penguin in a rather academic manner, his head cocked to the side, at a very you've-seen-one-penguin-you've-seen-them-all slant.

Clarissa stared hard at the ground, wishing he hadn't said that, wishing that penguins were naturally solitary creatures. She concentrated on inventing in her mind a new penguin reality for the species, on creating a fake happiness subtext, a new epic about overcoming the odds of nature, for why this penguin would be strolling toward town on his own. Like shopping. Yes! The penguin was coming into town to shop. His name was . . . Petey. And he was a very happy penguin, because he—

Lenny walked up to dish around in his duffel bag. "This is terrific. This is great montage stuff."

"Hey, Mary," Mitchell said not very enthusiastically from behind her.

Clarissa looked behind her at a woman so short and so wide all you could really see was the giant bell of her oversized parka bearing down on them.

The woman stopped directly in front of Clarissa and Mitchell. "Hey, Mitchell." She looked at Clarissa's name tag, then checked her clipboard, then looked up at Clarissa and smiled. "He's a good one. He made the list."

Mitchell snorted.

"The list?" Lenny asked curiously, as if he smelled a possible segment opportunity.

"My name's Mary Gallo," she said, apparently not planning to answer the question. But she shook Lenny's hand vigorously, and then Clarissa's. "I'm with the NASA-CIA coalition working today for a happy tomorrow in space."

"A happy tomorrow . . . in space?" Lenny repeated eagerly. "As in outer space or earthbound architectural space?"

"Outer space. We're a covert detail—" She stopped abruptly, perhaps realizing that being part of a covert detail meant not really talking too much about how you were part of a covert detail. "I'm really a sort of cultural anthropologist here on station, and I was wondering if you new people would mind taking a few minutes of your time to answer a couple of questions."

Clarissa really just wanted to watch the penguin waddle about in the snow, but Mary seemed the persistent type and the CIA seemed like the sort of entertainment company with whom Clarissa was supposed to be networking. "Of course."

"Hey, wait, this could be good," Lenny said. "Don't you think this could make a good segment? A cultural anthropologist . . . and the CIA? I mean, that's good shit."

"Um . . ." Clarissa looked at Mary uncertainly. "It sounds confidential."

"It's really just a sort of test." Mary reached up and touched her hair lightly with the palm of her hand. "This is for a movie?" she asked.

"A documentary," Lenny said, and pointed to Squiggy still filming the emperor penguin, which had done absolutely nothing new since the last time it had blinked. "I think Squigg's got enough reel. He can always catch it again, after. Maybe when the fella starts to take bigger strides or something."

"Oh, a documentary," Mary said. "Well, if it's science, we can certainly accommodate."

"Great!" said Lenny, who immediately called Squiggy off the emperor penguin assignment and pointed vigorously in the direction from whence Mary had appeared.

"Clarissa," she said, "why don't you step into my tomato for a moment and we'll do this right now."

Clarissa would have assumed Mary Gallo *was* the tomato, but the woman marched off toward a red, freestanding oval rubber structure a few yards off the transition which did, indeed, vaguely resemble a large tomato. As Clarissa and Squiggy trailed after her, it occurred to Clarissa that it was possible Mary had actually planted the penguin out here as some sort of bait or ruse. After all, if she was involved with the CIA, it was just the sort of thing that they might do. And the theory actually buoyed her spirits because it provided a plausible explanation why the penguin was more likely a happy penguin and not a sad penguin destined for a miserable, lonely future.

"This way, please." Mary led her through the door of the tomato, which was crowded with all manner of equipment, some of it faintly alarming in a rusty, wires-sticking-out-everywhere sort of way.

"Go ahead and sit down."

Clarissa obeyed.

Mary looked up at Squiggy and said, "I need you to be absolutely silent. As if you aren't even here."

Squiggy grunted and readjusted the camera on his shoulder, and suddenly Mary grabbed Clarissa's arm, wrapped something around it, pulled it like a tourniquet and sat down calmly.

Clarissa looked down at her arm in alarm. Thin, slightly rusty bent wires threaded off the armband to a machine that looked like something out of the Frances Farmer auction catalog. If Mary so much as tried to attach anything to her head, she was so out of here. But apparently this experiment was limited to the forearm region.

"Don't worry, it's a little old, but it only rarely gives the tester a goose."

"A goose?" Clarissa squeaked.

"Electric shock." She waved her hand in the air dismissively. "Whatever. It's nothing to worry about. This shouldn't take long. Okay." She pointed at the machine. "It's a lie detector. Let's get started."

She held up a slightly squashed Tootsie Roll. "Does this strike you as funny?"

Clarissa looked longingly behind her at the door. Mary cleared her throat. Clarissa looked at the candy. "Umm . . . no?"

"Is that a no?"

"No. It's not funny, no."

Mary fairly leaped across the table and checked Clarissa's pupils with a penlight, ignoring Clarissa's yelp of surprise. She returned to her side of the table, rummaged somewhere underneath, and held up a white stuffed rabbit. "Is this funny?"

Clarissa reared back in horror and the lie detector squawked. Mary's eyebrow twitched. "*Is* this funny?" Now sweating profusely under her parka, Clarissa gripped the edge of the table and pursed her lips. "It depends on the context?" The machine made a disturbed grinding sound.

"Yes or no, please."

"Yes."

"Interesting." She shoved a thermometer in Clarissa's mouth and held up a picture of President Bush. "Is this funny?"

"Ympth," Clarissa said, nodding vigorously in the affirmative, actually somewhat relieved to find she really did feel strongly about something. No milquetoast, she.

Mary removed the thermometer, reviewed the result and popped it into a disinfecting machine. "Fascinating." Then she clasped her hands and leaned forward, a pleasant smile on her face. "So, how does it make you feel to know that penguin's going to die?"

Clarissa laughed. "Don't say that. He's so cute."

"Yes, he is cute, isn't he? Unfortunately, the rookery is like a . . . like a big family, a community . . . and when they get separated from it they just sort of fall apart. So, yeah, he's going to die." She glanced at her watch, impressing upon Clarissa that it just might happen any minute now.

Clarissa stared at her, struck. *Oh, my God. I'm the penguin.*

The woman looked at her closely. "So, how does that make you feel?"

Out of nowhere, Clarissa burst into tears.

Mary actually clapped her hands with delight a couple of times before she remembered her professionalism. She cleared her throat, but was completely unable to wipe the sheer joy off her face. "Oh, how wonderful. We don't have to worry about you suppressing your emotions to the point where your only outlet is to commit an act of violence against your peers. I guess that's about it. Congratulations, Clarissa, you've made the list!"

"What list?" Clarissa wailed.

"I'm responsible for surveying the yearly participants of the Antarctic program and determining who should be placed on the short list in the event that the government decides to staff a full-blown space station. You're a perfect candidate for the international space station."

"Congratulations!" Squiggy said from the corner of the tomato. "That's awesome. Maybe we can come film it."

Clarissa just looked straight into the camera, trying to blink and swallow back any further tears. It had been a long journey of battered self-esteem, second guessing, failed decision-making and interpersonal trauma. She felt a little dizzy, perhaps from the overly tight lie detector band still crushing her arm. She lurched forward in her chair, dragging the lie detector machine along the tabletop with her, and grabbed the collar of Mary's parka. She made a point to enunciate very clearly and said, "You can't put me on the list. I'm not what you're looking for. Space is all wrong for me—I'm all wrong for space. I'm not what you want. I can't make decisions. I think it's some sort of chemical imbalance."

Mary looked down at Clarissa's hand. "This is an interesting response."

Clarissa blinked, removed her hand from below Mary's throat and gently patted down the puckered cloth. "I'm telling you, I'm not the leader type. You're making a mistake."

"We don't need leaders—we need people who truly know how to follow." Mary detached the lie detector band from Clarissa's arm and began to tidy the equipment on the table. "We need people who will follow instructions blindly and march about like lemmings. You can't have a bunch of know-it-alls in space. It's bad news."

For some reason, Clarissa realized that meant Kate and Delilah wouldn't be going to space with her and this upset her all the more. Her eyes watered again.

"You're perfect," Mary said as she stood up and helped Clarissa to her feet, pushing her to the door. She grabbed at her, pushed her, and still managed to pump Clarissa's senseless arm in a single continuous handshake until just the woman's head and her arm stuck through the crack and Clarissa had been deposited back outside of the tomato.

Mary kept her head poked out, looked to and fro as if reminded that she was part of a covert detail that needed to always be on the watch . . . and then suddenly the door closed. "We'll be in touch," she said from inside.

Clarissa turned around and lurched forward, her right arm still stuck out in front of her, fingers splayed. Mitchell was waiting for her, god bless the guy. He started forward, a frown on his face, as Clarissa tried—and obviously failed—to play off her tears as a dislodged contact lens.

"Hey, relax," Mitchell said as he took Clarissa's outstretched hand, gently curled the fingers back in and moved her arm back down to her side as if it were a lever. "What did Mary say to you?"

"The penguin's going to die," Clarissa shrieked at a decibel level clearly in violation of the Antarctic Treaty against harassment of wildlife. "The penguin's all alone! Nobody's helping the penguin!"

Everybody, including the penguin, looked over at her and frowned.

"Jesus Christ," Mitchell muttered under his breath. "Hey, it's okay," he said by way of explanation. "It's nature. It's the, uh, life cycle of nature. You know, the animal kingdom." He looked around a little desperately, probably concerned someone was watching and would think he was the one who made her cry.

Clarissa staggered forward in the snow and raised her fist, shaking it vigorously in the air. "Why are you doing this to me? Can't you see I'm delicate, right now?"

Neither the snowy mountains nor the flat sheets of ice and snow answered.

"This is a cruel, cruel place!" Clarissa cried out in anguish. More fist-shaking. And then the sudden realization that more people were staring at her than at the penguin.

Mitchell came up behind her, put his hands on her shoulders, and steered her back in the direction of the vehicle. "It's all right, Clarissa. Everything's going to be all right. I'll take care of you."

"I don't *want* you to take care of me, Kieran!" she yelled. "It's over!"

"I'm Mitchell," he said quietly in her ear.

Clarissa stopped in her tracks, closed her mouth, and blinked, taking in the significance of it all. "It doesn't matter who you are. Because it's over," she repeated in a perfectly calm voice. "It's all totally and completely over."

Chapter Twenty-four

Over. Totally and completely. The documentary project was dead, that much was clear. Lenny and Squiggy didn't seem to mind. The Lord High Priest Demon of Vengeance certainly didn't mind. So really the only one who could possibly have minded was Clarissa. And she was doing her best not to mind, since nothing could be done about it anyway.

The fact was, she did mind. She minded that she didn't have anything tangible to show after all her hard work. She minded looking like a loser and disappointing people. And she minded calling Mitchell "Kieran" even though she'd glossed over it the way people sometimes do when something really excruciatingly embarrassing has happened and they can either freak out or pretend it didn't matter. Maybe there wasn't any "or," given that Clarissa had both freaked out *and* pretended it didn't matter.

The thing was that even though her internal hardwiring told her all this mattered, she couldn't really come to terms with what it all *meant*.

So what, Clarissa? she asked herself. *So what?* And yet

to look at Delilah's progress and Kate's progress in spite of what they'd secretly been dealing with, well, it just seemed to bring the point home even more.

And the truth was that if someone came up to her and said, "C'mon, Clarissa, I have a great idea for a segment, we can fix this thing!"—well, she'd jump up from this chair and follow their lead, at least give it a try.

I don't know what to do now . . . I don't even know what this crazy experience means.

She looked around her gloomy office. And since no one was around, she said very softly under her breath so that it was barely more than a squeak, "Um . . . help?"

Help. It was the same thing she'd said, writhing around on the bed in agony after Kieran had unceremoniously dumped her on what had supposedly been the cusp of the rest of her life. How funny that it precipitated a detour that proved that the rest of one's life had absolutely no inherent bearing on the part that came before. There was a certain kind of freedom in that, actually.

"Help?" she tested out again, a slight hollow echo bouncing off the walls. This time, she wasn't sure she was actually asking, so much as feeling out the word.

She felt the corner of her mouth turn up in a kind of smile. More of a doubtful sound to it now, she gave it one more try: "Help?" It sounded the way "Do you need some help?" sounds just before someone answers, "Oh, thanks, but no thanks."

And then suddenly the phone rang.

Clarissa leaped back in shock and surprise, her heart pounding as the desk phone continued to ring. She put her hand out, letting it hover over the receiver, her fingertips just barely touching the grimy beige plastic.

She picked it up and put it to her mouth. "Help? Sorry, hello?"

"Is this Clarissa Schneckberg?"

"Yes."

"Great. I'm patching in a call from the United States."

Clarissa stared at her surprised reflection in the now-dark video screen. "Hello?" she repeated tentatively.

"Clary! Baby, it's Kier. Are you okay?"

Clarissa's jaw dropped. She gripped the armrest of her chair with her free hand. *My anchor. Just when I needed him most!*

Clarissa's heart was in her mouth. They always said absence made the heart grow fonder. This proved he was still thinking about her. And there for her.

Kieran would know what to do. He was an excellent puzzle-solver, and every time she didn't believe in herself he pumped her up.

"Clarissa? It's me, Kieran," he repeated.

"Hi, Kieran," she said, her voice trembling.

"First, I want to make sure you're okay. I heard you went to that crazy place, and I just knew you were probably getting yourself into something you didn't really understand. So, are you okay?"

Am I okay? "I'm okay."

"Good, because you know how you can be." He laughed.

She knew exactly how she could be. Clarissa remembered the penguin down at the transition and how much being alone frightened her and how much she needed to learn to stand on her own two feet.

She remembered how much Kieran liked being the knight, the rescuer; it was probably why they'd stayed together so long. She'd fall apart, lose confidence, he'd build her back up. He craved it. She depended on him for it. It was why she'd felt so lost when he'd dumped her.

Silence. "So I've been researching how we can get you home earlier. You must be going nuts out there."

"Oh, wow!" Clarissa said, for lack of a better answer. This was it. She could surrender.

"Clarissa? Don't you want to come home? Do you need my help?"

Help?

Do you need some help? Oh, thanks . . . but, no thanks. It was that simple. Clarissa took a deep breath, and with her heart in her throat, she exhaled and said, "You know what? I'm going to stay until the end of the season."

Silence. Then, "Oh. I see."

"Is there anything else?" Clarissa asked, sad and funny tears pricking at her eyes. She knew this was good-bye. It was definitely over.

"Oh. Well, um, you know, I wanted to say, about what happened. Well, Luna and I are done. It was stupid. A stupid mistake. Maybe when you come back to town, you and I could, uh—"

Clarissa suddenly wanted off the phone. "Well, I'm sorry to hear that it didn't work out. I know you had such high hopes for your future together. You must feel just dreadful."

Silence on the other end of the line.

"Right. I deserved that. Well, here's the thing. I'm sorry. And I was an idiot." He paused, seemingly to wait for her response. She didn't give one. "Clarissa, are you still there?"

"Yes."

"Well . . . if you had a webcam, you'd see that I was on one knee. Do you get my drift?"

Oh, my god. This was the moment she'd been waiting for, for so long. The words she'd once longed to hear. The proposal that never came.

The drift. His drift. Clarissa chewed on her lower lip and

tried to think rationally. People went back to their exes all the time because people made mistakes. On both sides. Sometimes it took more courage to go back to someone in the face of everyone else's eye-rolling and gossiping than it did to stay apart.

Sometimes you realize you've been given a gift, in that you know the value of what you had—what you could have again.

And sometimes you realize that the one thing you dreaded the most was the best thing that could have ever happened to you.

Clarissa could tell that Kieran was in the first camp and she . . . well, she was firmly in the second.

The temptation to give in to such an easy solution was extreme, almost palpable. Kieran would have all the answers, her life would be back on track, heading down that path to normalcy and safety she'd always imagined for herself. She'd be anchored again.

"Clarissa?"

She took a deep breath and forced herself to relax before she broke down entirely. "You know what, Kier," she said softly. "I've got to go."

"Oh. Right. I see."

"Do you?"

The silence on the other end of the line was a little heartbreaking.

"Good-bye, Kieran," she said softly.

"Jesus . . . wait!"

"I can't. I'm sorry. Good-bye."

"Good-bye, Clarissa," he blurted out.

She hung up the phone and just stared at it, expecting to burst into tears at any moment.

So Kieran hadn't quite broken her heart after all.

For if she hadn't loved him enough for that to have taken

242 • Liz Maverick

place, then she hadn't loved him enough to be really, truly
sorry it was all over.

It should have been a relief, really. Should have been.

The trouble was, she'd really, intentionally, once and for all
let all of her anchors go. And still had absolutely nothing tangible to show for any of it. Nothing at all.

Chapter Twenty-five

"Clary?"

Clarissa lifted her head off the desk and looked up to find Kate and Delilah standing in the doorway.

"Hey," Clarissa said wearily. "I was just, um, having a time-out."

Delilah and Kate looked at each other.

"No, really, I'm not upset. I'm just . . . tired. Come in, guys."

Delilah came and sat on the edge of Clarissa's desk. Kate leaned against the doorjamb.

"You did a great job on that," Clarissa said, gesturing to Kate's outfit. Along with the sudden promotion, she'd finally been issued a sous-chef jacket.

Under what Clarissa recognized as the principle that if you're going to do something, do it well, Kate and Delilah had gone for the retro '80s look with all of their heart and soul, apparently. They'd taken neon green and pink highlighters and color-blocked the fabric. The seams were repiped in hot pink marabou . . . and the crowning glory, the hated gauzy hair-guard thingum had been refashioned into a sort of beret á la

Debbie Gibson worn at a rakish angle with a huge plastic flower glued to one side.

Of course, the MC Hammer pants were left alone, but Kate's wrists were packed with little black rubber loops that probably came from Delilah's waste management supply closet. Whatever spare part it was, they'd better hope another shipment was coming or the staffers for the winter season wouldn't be able to flush for their entire stay.

Kate held up her hand as she saw the direction of Clarissa's gaze. "Don't they look just like the Madonna ones? Delilah's brilliant!"

Clarissa nodded. "They absolutely do."

For her part, Delilah seemed perfectly content dressed down in a pair of nondescript grease-stained coveralls and some heavy work boots. Her hair was pulled back in a ponytail and her bib front had makeup smudges all over it. "We heard about the penguin," she said. "I feel so bad about earlier. I was just in a zone, or something. The muse is a very selfish . . . entity."

Clarissa smiled. "It's really okay. I don't know what I was thinking. I mean, there was really nothing anyone could do at that point."

"We let you down," Kate said, wrinkling her brow.

"No, you didn't. Really. I think you guys are the best friends in the world," Clarissa said.

Kate threw up her arms. "I was worried about the pie! Isn't that stupid? You needed help, and I was worried about freakin' pie."

"Did it come out good?" Clarissa asked.

"Yeah."

"Am I going to get some at Thanksgiving dinner tonight?"

A slow grin crept back over Kate's face. "Yeah. The dinner came out really, really good."

Clarissa grinned right back at her. "Well then, as long as I get some pie."

"Absolutely. In fact, I've got to get back to the kitchen soon. There's an issue about some cans of mandarin oranges that don't look as orange as expected."

Delilah pushed back her scruffy sleeve and looked at her watch. "And I've got to go finish the makeovers. Everyone wants a holiday look, you know."

"But we wanted to come and make sure you were okay, first," Kate said.

"I'm okay," Clarissa said almost cheerfully. "But there's something you should know. Kieran called."

"What!?" Kate lurched backwards. "Good god."

"*I'll* say."

"What did he want?" Delilah asked.

"He wanted to marry me."

Kate and Delilah stared at her. Kate left the doorway and sat down in front of Clarissa's desk.

"You heard me right." Clarissa shrugged. "The grass is always greener, I guess."

"What did you *say?*" Kate asked.

"I said I had to go. I said good-bye. It's over." She shrugged.

Delilah and Kate looked at each other. They looked back at Clarissa.

"Well, I guess you're really 'clean slate' now," Kate said.

Delilah put her hand on Clarissa's shoulder and gave it a little squeeze. "Clean *break*, that's what I'd call it. Good for you, Clary."

"Yeah. Good for you. We'd support you either way, of course . . . but can I just say thank god it's really over," Kate said, a most sympathetic, concerned look on her face. "Now you can just do whatever it is that you're meant to do."

Silence.

246 • Liz Maverick

"What is it she's meant to do, again?" Delilah asked.

"Oy," Clarissa said. She sighed and rested her chin in her hand.

"But this is great!" Kate shrieked. "I mean, you're really in the clear to do absolutely anything you want. You're completely free!"

"Mmm. What do you think about film school? I could become a documentarian."

"What do *you* think about it?" Kate asked.

Clarissa stared up at the ceiling. "I rather like the idea." She lifted her arm above her head and snapped her fingers. "Presto change-o, then."

"Presto change-o?" Delilah echoed dubiously.

"Yeah." Clarissa cocked her head and looked at her friends. "That's the thing, you know? We can do absolutely anything we want to do, on a dime. We can make last minute decisions. We can be spontaneous. And we can—"

"Snap our fingers and say 'presto change-o'?" Kate said. "Well, as long as you don't do anything silly, like move to New York. That's way too far away. I couldn't possibly support something like that. L.A, I could live with. I'm used to the idea now since you've been talking about it for a while. But New York would be a shock."

Clarissa nodded. "I'll take that into consideration. What about you, Kate? What happens now for you?"

"I've decided to go to cooking school." Here, Kate very dramatically adjusted the angle of her beret and gave the bottom hem of her jacket a sharp tug. "I think food service suits me. And I think I have a real talent for making edible, gourmet cuisine out of the truly grotesque. It's so much more fulfilling than shuffling papers."

"That's a wonderful idea," Clarissa said. "And I don't mind if you want to use Kieran for networking at some point. Granted, he's really just on the salad-dressing career trajectory, but I think the company has some other products, like Cheez-Supreme-O and Choc-O-Like. In fact, I think they have an entire division focused on totally artificial, processed food-like substances involving the uppercase letter O. Might come in handy one of these days."

"That's awfully nice of you," Kate said. "I wouldn't blame you if you wanted us to pretend he didn't exist. Cheez-Supreme-O sounds right up my alley. Just today I learned that the margarine-like spread that I've been using on our sandwich grill is only one molecule away from actually being plastic."

Delilah choked on her own saliva.

"Isn't that an urban legend?" Clarissa asked.

"No, this is the spread upon which the urban legend that got attached to margarine was based."

"Oh."

"I know! Fascinating, isn't it?" Kate continued.

"I think somebody's been feeding you a load of crap," Clarissa said.

"Literally," Delilah murmured. "I support you one hundred percent, Kate, but just know this. Whenever we do potluck, you're responsible for bringing the wine."

"Fair enough," Kate said. She pointed to Delilah's makeup-smudged bib front and said, "Can we assume we know what you're going to do next?"

Delilah nodded happily. "Well, my exit contract with Loralline says I can't compete with, and I quote, 'Any cosmetic product that connotes a girlie, glitter-specific gestalt.' But I've figured out how to get around that. What I've learned from the ladies in waste management is that there's, like, this whole market niche of women who don't like to fuss with makeup. At all."

Kate gasped and Clarissa put her hand up to her mouth to stifle the same.

"I *know*," Delilah said. "Hard to believe, but it's true! They just want the basics. They want to achieve a look, yes, but with as few steps as possible and with as few tools as possible. They're looking to me to take the guesswork out of it. So, we're talking one mascara, one dark eyeliner pencil with smear sponge on the end of it, one pearly beige cream eye shadow, one clear lipgloss, one foundation/concealer, and one perfect, classic red lipstick."

"It sounds very useful," Clarissa said. "You realize, Delilah, that you've learned to embrace minimalism."

"I *know*. I'm as surprised as you are," Delilah said. "Everything I mentioned all in one tiny, lightweight travel compact. If that isn't makeup minimalism, I don't know what is! I mean, this is the sort of collection you could take backpacking with you through Borneo."

"Brilliant," Kate said. "I'll take three."

"That's what I love about you guys. You're so supportive," Clarissa said. She looked at Delilah, then she looked at Kate. "I mean, who else would work day in and day out with . . . well, 'crap' . . . just to support a pal? I really hope you know how much I appreciate—"

A ruckus coming from the hall interrupted the moment. Kate looked over her shoulder. "I think we're ready."

"For what?" Clarissa asked.

"We invited a few people to your office for a little holiday toast. Thought it might cheer you up, though under the circumstances you're doing swimmingly already."

Mitchell suddenly appeared carrying a large box marked only by a white, generic-looking label that just said CHAMPAGNE in large block letters. "Happy Thanksgiving, ladies! Clarissa, you look lovely as ever. You all do."

"Happy Thanksgiving, Mitchell," Clarissa said, backing up to make more space as more people entered the office behind him.

A few folks from the adjoining offices started crowding in. Then some of the kitchen folks. And some of the waste management folks. Folks from all over the station, really.

"Happy Thanksgiving, Clarissa!" someone else called out over the growing hubbub. She recognized Emily's voice and saw the Death Squad Girls crowding into one corner, waving at her over the scene.

Delilah must have gotten her hands on them just before coming over here, because the Death Squad Girls were totally made over. She looked from Emily, Bette, and Mindy in all of their cosmetic splendor to Delilah in her grubby jumpsuit, and laughed at the reversal, waving right back at them.

Someone handed her a plastic cup full of champagne and she took a swig just as Kate shrieked with laughter. The Garanimal was now sitting on Clarissa's desk balancing Kate on one furry knee and whispering something into her ear. He caught Clarissa's gaze and shouted, "Happy Thanksgiving, Clarissa! Great idea for a cocktail before dinner!"

Clarissa gave him a thumbs-up and turned just in time to catch Lenny and Squiggy barging in from the hall with a camera. She headed toward them, squeezing by the banjo-playing narcoleptic HR girl, who was trying unsuccessfully to rouse the partygoers in a sing-along by repeating the refrain, "Ebony and iiiiiivory, live together in perfect harrrrrrmony . . ." over and over.

"Hey, Clarissa," Squiggy said. "Happy holidays." He didn't put down the camera. He just pointed it at her. "Say something holiday-like."

She shook her head and chuckled. "I can't believe you're even filming this. The documentary is so over." Lenny stepped in front of the camera with her and put his arm around her shoulder, waving at the lens. "It's just for posterity, Clary. It's not for any show. Just smile, will ya?"

She couldn't help it. She was already smiling.

"This is my friend, Clarissa," Lenny said to the camera. "Lenny and Squiggy love Clarissa."

"We love you, Clarissa!" Squiggy echoed from behind the camera. He waved his hand above the equipment.

"Clarissa loves Lenny and Squiggy," she said, waving back into the camera.

"You gonna come back to L.A. with us?" Lenny asked. "We could hook you up. We've got connect—oh, hey, look. It's the Lord High Priest Demon of Vengeance. He's a nutcase. Squigg, you getting this?"

Clarissa's boss approached wearing what appeared to be friar's garb made out of old potato sacking and a rope. He held his hand out to Clarissa. "Nice job."

Clarissa shook the Hand of Doom. "Considering what happened, I'm not sure . . ."

His attention had already wandered as Happy-Tomorrow-In-Space Mary walked by with a plate of vaguely suspicious brownies. "Mama's cooking!" she belted out. She looked at Clarissa. "I'm so pleased you're feeling better. Happy Thanksgiving! Only eat these if you have no allergies whatsoever."

"Happy Thanksgiving, Mary," Clarissa said, watching with some amusement as the Demon of Vengeance snagged a brownie before Mary moved on through the crowd. "What I meant was," he said with his mouth full, "was that you did a nice job. You had a go. It's not easy out here, you know."

"I know," Clarissa said. "On the other hand, it turns out that it's also really not that hard." She looked around the room at her assorted friends and acquaintances. "Once you adapt."

"Hey, we've got to run," Kate said from over her shoulder.

Clarissa excused herself from her boss and turned to the girls. "This was a splendid idea."

"Splendid," Delilah agreed. "Unfortunately, we're off. You seem fine, though. Are you fine?"

"I'm fine, but . . ." Clarissa looked at the girls. "Nothing's the same, is it?"

Kate and Delilah looked at her, then looked at each other. "Nope," Kate said, a slow grin breaking out over her face. "Nothing's the same. And I couldn't be happier."

Delilah nodded. "Can you believe it? Who would have thought we had it in us?"

"Well . . ." Clarissa started to say, feeling the need to qualify the statement.

"No 'well,'" Delilah said. "There's no 'well.' I mean think about it. It's not about the documentary. You know it's not."

Kate downed her champagne and tossed the cup into the wastebasket. "Delilah's right. It's not really about the documentary . . . or the stupid turkey . . . or the makeup, for that matter."

Clarissa looked into the depths of her cheap champagne. She nodded, downed her own glass, and tossed it after Kate's with renewed vigor. "No, it's not. You're both right."

"Huddle!" Kate suddenly cried out.

Clarissa jumped up and put her arms around her two best friends. "You're the best. I love you guys."

"Me too," Kate said.

"Me three!" Delilah yelped.

Clarissa pulled away, feeling like the human equivalent of an after-school special, and this simply wasn't the time or place. "You'd better get going, guys. Turkeys and makeovers."

Delilah gave her a big smack on the cheek. "We'll see you in a couple hours. Kate's going to save us both seats."

Kate straightened her jacket. "It's all about the timing, now. This is going to be a Thanksgiving we'll never forget."

Clarissa watched her two best friends make their way through the crowd and out the door.

It already is.

Chapter Twenty-six

It took Clarissa a moment to realize that Emily and the other Death Squad Girls were waving madly at her from across the room.

Emily finally put her hands up to her mouth and shouted, "Clarissa, come here!"

Clarissa squeezed through the partygoers and peered into Emily's face. "Wow. Delilah did a really good job on you. I really think the Borneo Backpacker's Beauty Kit has potential. You guys all look terrific."

"The Borneo what?" Bette asked.

"Oh, nothing," Clarissa said with a smile.

Mindy pointed at Lenny and Squiggy making the rounds of the party. "You're not still filming segments, are you?"

Clarissa watched Lenny thrusting a microphone in people's faces and soliciting interviews. "No, that's just Lenny and Squiggy doing Lenny and Squiggy."

"We heard about the explosion . . . and the penguin incident," Emily said. "We're awfully sorry. I know how much that project meant to you."

"Yeah," Clarissa said matter-of-factly. "I pretty much failed, but I'm already coming to terms with it."

"You didn't fail," Emily insisted.

Clarissa raised her eyebrow. "I'm coming away from this experience with nothing to show for it."

"It wasn't even finished, was it?" Bette said. "I mean, all the film was there, but it wasn't edited or anything. So it could have been worse."

"It's just that it was something tangible, you know? Something . . . tangible," Clarissa said. "It wasn't vapor; it was a real product, a real accomplishment. I lost my proof."

"Your proof?" Bette asked.

Clarissa's cheeks burned with embarrassment. "It's really silly when you make me say it out loud. Tangible proof of my competence, of my leadership abilities, I guess."

Bette waved away Mitchell's offer of more champagne, and leaned heavily against the wall. "You are competent, Clarissa. It may not be on tape anymore, but we know it . . . and you know it, too."

Clarissa stared at her. "I am competent," she said, rather lamely, testing out the mantra. It didn't exactly trip off the tongue, but maybe it was just because in the past she'd been so used to people keeping her safe, she'd actually begun to think she was rather inept.

Emily turned and whispered something into Bette's ear; Bette turned and whispered something into Mindy's ear. There was clearly some discussion about whether they should or should not do something. The something, of course, being the most interesting part, which Clarissa couldn't hear.

And finally Emily turned to her and said, "Clarissa, we have this thing we're going to do. A very secret thing. But we think you should come with us. It will be terrific. You'll be glad you did. But you can't tell anyone the details. Not even Kate and Delilah, because if they aren't with us, that's the rule."

Clarissa couldn't possibly do something that had to be a secret from Kate and Delilah. Could she? And . . . oh, god, was this a setup? Was this like that Stephen King movie where poor innocent Carrie believes for one shining moment that the other kids really like her enough to make her prom queen?

"You know, we cried, too, our first season," Bette said gruffly.

"But we didn't harass wildlife," Mindy said. Bette elbowed her and said, "Why don't you come with us, Clarissa?"

"I don't understand where you're going. And Kate and Delilah—"

"Aren't here," Emily finished with a shrug. "I'll bet they'd be sorry they'd missed it, though. Come on. Let's get our gear on and go."

"Our extreme cold-weather gear? The official stuff?"

"Parkas, bunny boots, bibs. The whole nine yards," Bette said.

Clarissa looked at the three girls. They'd once seemed so foreign, so . . . opposite to what she was used to. They'd once been enemies, though in all fairness that was mostly Kate's doing. Now they were her friends. They were clearly not the sort of people that were going to let a bucket of goat's blood fall on her head while she was wearing her best dress.

"I'm in," she said. "Let's change."

The four of them went back up to the room, suited up, and were ready to go do . . . whatever it was they were going to do, in a flash.

Bette had somehow commandeered a truck and all four girls, a pile of blankets, a first aid kit, and an extra bottle of champagne crammed into the front cab. She sped off in the direction of the New Zealand station, and as they drove past the edge of Palmurdo, Clarissa began to feel a distinctly euphoric sensation in her gut.

"It looks cold out there," Emily said as Bette parked the truck at a stretch of no-man's-land just below the Kiwi base and the four of them stared through the windshield in silence.

"There it is," Mindy said reverently, and somewhat unnecessarily.

"It" was a worn six-person tent situated in the middle of stark, bright, flat, white . . . nothingness. What looked like a hastily carved ice-fishing hole in the middle of the nothingness appeared to be the object of desire. And suddenly, the euphoric feeling went on high alert.

"Have you ever heard of the polar plunge?"

Clarissa's mouth dropped open. "You're kidding."

"We're not," Emily said.

"You're kidding."

"We're not."

"You're not."

"No."

"A person could die," Clarissa pointed out. "I'm quite certain this would be an example of an unsanctioned, unofficial activity during which your internal body organs would shut down and you would die."

"Heart attack, maybe. From the shock. But not likely."

"You're kidding."

"We're not."

Pause. "There's no way," Clarissa said automatically.

"Isn't there?"

"How cold is it?" Mindy asked. "Did anyone check the screen before we left town?"

"Below forty," Emily said. "Not counting windchill."

Clarissa's euphoric sensation wavered. "Um, doesn't the polar plunge involve removing one's clothes?"

"Yep," Bette said. "All of 'em."

"Oh. I see. Maybe we should have a drink first?"

"After."

"But—but your makeup! You'll ruin it."

Emily looked at her. "It's just makeup, Clarissa. You'll help us do it over before dinner, won't you?"

"Well, of course I will, but . . ."

"But what?"

Bette looked at Clarissa, then gave Emily a sort of "told you so" look. "She doesn't want to. You don't have to, Clarissa. There's no peer pressure here."

Clarissa stared out at the tent. Of course she didn't *have* to. She didn't *have* to do anything anymore. But the point was also that she could do anything, if she wanted to. That's what she'd been talking about with Delilah and Kate. "Of course I'm doing it," she said firmly.

Emily squealed with delight and gave Clarissa's shoulders a squeeze.

"So, how does this work?" Clarissa asked.

Bette crossed her arms over her chest. "Drop trou. Put a blanket around you. Run to the hole. Drop blanket. Jump in the water. Get out. Get warm." She looked as though she were expecting Clarissa to back down.

And Clarissa realized, deep down inside, that there was no way in hell she was going to do that.

"Right. No problem." Clarissa took a deep breath and started to get out of the truck.

"Wait a sec! Wait a sec," Bette said, looking rather concerned. "You sure you're okay with this? Just so you know, we'll be next to the hole to spot you just in case."

Clarissa smiled. "Of a heart attack?"

"Yeah."

"Perfect. Shall we?"

The girls all looked at each other and nodded, then burst into giggles. With maximum drama, Clarissa pushed open the truck door and they all piled out onto the Antarctic shelf, grabbed their gear, and headed purposefully for the tent.

The tent, of course, was freezing. It was one of those grubby greenish grayish military types, that had clearly been invented before REI ever existed. The only thing inside was a large hinged wood trunk from which Bette pulled a large pot, some government surplus powdered hot chocolate packets, and a camping stove. Clarissa thought of the Snow Survival School fiasco and decided to leave the cooking business in Bette's care. She opened the flap and fetched some snow out the side of the tent and added it to the pot along with a little water from Mindy's water bottle.

Once Bette had the water boiling, Mindy handed out the blankets. "Well, I'm thinking we'll sort of pair off. Emily and Clarissa will be on deck. Me and Mindy will be on support with the camera and hot chocolate. That work for everybody?"

Emily and Clarissa looked at each other, started laughing hysterically, and began to strip down.

Clarissa pulled off all of her cold-weather gear until she was standing in her bare feet on top of her discarded clothing. The word "insane" kept popping into her head, but then, she considered, the word "insane" had popped into her head quite often during the season. If nothing else, she was consistent.

"I'm stark raving naked," she pointed out, shivering happily with her arms hugging her body. "In Antarctica. This is one for the scrapbook!"

"I'm nekkid, too!" Emily shrieked, and burst into giggles. "And I'm freezing my ass off!"

Bette threw a blanket at each of them and the girls swathed themselves in the fabric. "Oh, shit," she suddenly said. "Did someone bring the camera?"

"I've got it," Mindy said, fishing it out of her parka. "We're covered."

"Great," Bette said.

The four girls stood there and looked at each other, huge grins on their faces.

Clarissa was shivering more from excitement than from the cold. "Well, what now?"

Emily stuck her fist out of her blanket. "Let's ro-sham-boh to see who has to go first."

"I'll go first!" Clarissa yelped.

The girls looked at her in surprise. Then Bette just shrugged. "Fine," she said. "Clarissa's first, Emily's on deck. Mindy takes the picture. I stand by in case of emergency."

Emily nodded. "Clarissa, when you get back, you get dressed and then you're the camera person and we rotate until everyone's gone."

"Okay. This is insane," Clarissa said, a euphoric grin on her face.

"See you out there," Bette said, and slipped outside.

"Are you ready, Clarissa?" Emily asked.

Was she ready? Part of her was sorry that nobody who knew her from her old life could see her now. Nobody would believe it. Of course, that was the point of the picture. Proof. Bragging rights.

"You can do it!" Mindy yelped. "Go for it!"

Clarissa opened the flap and peeked out toward the hole in the ice. Bette had already walked out there with a rope, a first aid kit, and a walkie-talkie. How comforting.

"Are you ready?" Emily asked again.

"I'm ready." Clarissa took a deep breath, stepped outside, and started running across the ice toward the hole.

"AAAAAAAAIIIIIIIIGGGGGGGGGHHHHHHHHHHHHHHH!" she screamed joyously at the top of her lungs.

The blanket flapped around her, icy air swirled around her legs; the ground felt so cold it was almost as if it were burning the soles of her feet.

When she reached the edge of the hole, vaguely aware of Mindy snapping pictures and Bette cheering and pumping her fist in the air, without even a moment's hesitation . . .

Clarissa let the blanket drop and jumped. *Oh. My. Goodness!*

She had never really understood the concept of freezing until now, and to say the least, the shock was intense. It couldn't have been more than a matter of seconds that she was submerged, but it all seemed like slow motion.

The taste of ocean salt in her mouth triggered an image of her former life in her mind. A pink bikini. Trailing behind Kieran, holding on to his hand as he guided her into the water in Hawaii. She remembered squealing with dismay about the possibility of fish nipping at her toes.

Clarissa surfaced out of the inky black water, spluttering and shaking as two arms helped pull her up to the smooth, white surface surrounding the plunge hole. In spite of her chattering teeth, she couldn't stop smiling.

Mindy kept snapping pictures as Clarissa hightailed it toward the tent in a cloud of her own steam. She'd show the pictures to Delilah and Kate, of course, but only because it would give them a laugh.

They were already proud. They didn't care about proof. They knew she had it in her, if she wanted to use it. Most of all, Delilah and Kate just wanted her to be happy.

As Clarissa burst through the tent flap, soaking wet, chilled to the bone, totally naked, she raised her arms over her head with that same enormous grin on her face, and yelled at the top of her raspy, half-frozen lungs, "Footie pajamas!"

Anchors away!